Vinyl Cafe Turns the Page

ALSO BY STUART McLEAN

Fiction

Stories from the Vinyl Cafe

Home from the Vinyl Cafe

Vinyl Cafe Unplugged

Vinyl Cafe Diaries

Dave Cooks the Turkey

Secrets from the Vinyl Cafe

Extreme Vinyl Cafe

Revenge of the Vinyl Cafe

Non-Fiction

The Morningside World of Stuart McLean

Welcome Home: Travels in Smalltown Canada

Vinyl Cafe Notebooks

Time Now for the Vinyl Cafe Story Exchange

Edited by Stuart McLean

When We Were Young:
An Anthology of Canadian Stories

STUART McLEAN

Vinyl Cafe Turns the Page

VIKING

VIKING
an imprint of Penguin Canada Books Inc., a Penguin Random House Company

Published by the Penguin Group
Penguin Canada Books Inc., 320 Front Street West, Toronto, Ontario M5V 3B6, Canada

Penguin Group (USA) LLC, 375 Hudson Street, New York, New York 10014, U.S.A.
Penguin Books Ltd, 80 Strand, London WC2R 0RL, England
Penguin Ireland, 25 St Stephen's Green, Dublin 2, Ireland (a division of Penguin Books Ltd)
Penguin Group (Australia), 707 Collins Street, Melbourne, Victoria 3008, Australia
(a division of Pearson Australia Group Pty Ltd)
Penguin Books India Pvt Ltd, 11 Community Centre, Panchsheel Park, New Delhi – 110 017, India
Penguin Group (NZ), 67 Apollo Drive, Rosedale, Auckland 0632, New Zealand
(a division of Pearson New Zealand Ltd)
Penguin Books (South Africa) (Pty) Ltd, 24 Sturdee Avenue,
Rosebank, Johannesburg 2196, South Africa

Penguin Books Ltd, Registered Offices: 80 Strand, London WC2R 0RL, England

Published in Viking hardcover by Penguin Canada Books Inc., 2015

1 2 3 4 5 6 7 8 9 10 (RRD)

LIBRARY AND ARCHIVES CANADA CATALOGUING IN PUBLICATION

McLean, Stuart, 1948–, author
Vinyl Cafe turns the page / Stuart McLean.

Short stories.
ISBN 978-0-670-06943-9 (bound)

I. Title.

PS8575.L448V55 2015   C813'.54   C2015-902068-9

eBook ISBN 978-0-14-319429-3

Visit the *Vinyl Cafe* website at **www.vinylcafe.com**

Visit the Penguin Canada website at **www.penguin.ca**

Special and corporate bulk purchase rates available; please see
www.penguin.ca/corporatesales or call 1-800-810-3104.

For A

Art can move and alter people in subtle ways because,
like love, it speaks through and to the heart.

Martin Luther King, Jr.
in a letter to Sammy Davis Jr.
December 20, 1960

CONTENTS

SAM'S UNDERWEAR

Morley's birthday is several weeks past, but she's still smitten by the gift her son, Sam, made her. It's on the kitchen counter, by the toaster, and she's reminded of it every time she passes: a small green binder with the word *Recipes* on the cover, written in Sam's hand. All the pages in the binder are blank, except for the first. On it Sam wrote, "We will fill *every* page." It's the best thing *anyone* has ever given her. Her favourite present in years.

The binder was the culmination of a series of dubious events that began on a Saturday in early spring—a grey and windy day with bits of snow speckling the sky. The kind of day to stay put, to hunker down, to revel in laziness. Nothing was going to drag Morley from the comforts of central heating and cozy slippers that Saturday.

To be precise, it was two-thirty in the afternoon. Morley was still in her pyjamas, savouring this delicious and unusual turn of events, when it dawned on her that Sam was in his pyjamas too.

"Why are *you* still in your pyjamas?" she asked.

"Because I *can't* get dressed," said Sam.

He said this with a dramatic, faux anguish—which Morley was about to point out, until he added, "I have no underwear."

Instead of calling out his delivery, she rolled her eyes and, with less patience than might have been required, said, "You have a whole drawer stuffed full of underwear."

Sam rolled *his* eyes, picked up his comic, and said, "They're all too small."

Morley put down her coffee.

She stared at her son.

It was one of those moments when her parental ship—a ship that had been sailing along pleasantly enough, the decks clean and ordered, the sails full and trim, the sea a deep and pleasing blue—was suddenly, because of its inattentive and likely incompetent captain, bearing down on the rocks.

"All of it?" she said incredulously, sitting up. "All your underwear is too small?"

"Except the grey ones," said Sam. "And they're in the wash."

It took a moment for this to sink in.

Where had the rocks come from? She'd thought they were miles from shore.

She tried to remember if she'd seen any of his underwear go through the laundry lately. Had she folded any in the last few weeks? Had she carried any upstairs? Had she put any away? She was trying to remember—she was drawing a blank, and it was worrying her.

She said, "How have you been managing with one pair?"

Sam didn't look up.

"Improvising," he said.

And so ended the peace of that afternoon. Morley got up, brushed her hair, and got dressed. In her imagination, a concerned childcare worker was peering at her poor pyjama-clad son. "Exactly how many months did you go with only one pair of underwear, dear?"

Just as she was stepping out the door, Dave stepped in.

"Hey," he said. "Where you going?"

Morley looked at his boots—at the cold, damp, dripping snow. She didn't feel like going anywhere.

"Underwear shopping," she said morosely.

"Excellent," said Dave. "Could you buy me some too? But not the kind you got last time, the other ones."

She had no idea what he was talking about. She had no idea what kind of underwear she'd bought him last time.

She didn't ask.

She left, closing the door behind her a little hard, she thought.

She went to a department store—to the boys' department first.

She loaded up on underwear for Sam.

Then she headed for men's wear. She chose several packages—some cotton, some knit, and then, more out of spite than love, a pair made of clingy, synthetic fabric that looked more like bike shorts than underwear.

She wondered if she should visit the women's department to get something for her daughter, and then it occurred to her that that was probably the *last* thing Stephanie would want. It had been years since Stephanie had asked Morley to buy her anything. She was happy for Morley to *pay* for things, but not to *pick them out.* And that's when it struck her that Sam would soon stop needing her to shop for him, too. Soon, instead of asking for things, he would ask her to stop picking things out, and soon after that he would stop wanting her to do *anything* for him.

If all went well, he would need her less and less, he would slip further and further from her orbit and into one that was wholly his own, a trajectory she would glimpse, when she was permitted, from a distance.

Motherhood, she thought, as she stood there between the display racks of men's underwear, *was a poorly planned journey.* It wasn't a sailing trip. It was more like a race. And it started with a sprint. One moment you were standing still and the next you were running as fast as you could, the cries of your baby ringing in your ears like the bang of a starter's pistol. You were racing *to* the crib and *with* the stroller. You were darting from high chair to grocery store, from laundry to bath time. Then you were tearing off to kindergarten class, and swimming class, and music class. You were packing lunches and cooking dinners and taking temperatures and kissing scraped knees. You were baking birthday cakes and helping with homework and hosting play dates. You were running, running, running. Always with too little time and not enough sleep. Somewhere it had changed from a sprint to a marathon. And you realized that you were, surprisingly enough, in pretty good shape. And just as you were catching your breath, just as you were hitting your stride, just as you were getting in the zone, someone said, "Hey. What are you doing? I don't want a sandwich."

And you stop, a limp peanut butter and banana sandwich in your hand, and you stare at the someone in amazement, not sure who they are, and why they would be saying this to you, until you realize, to your dismay, that it's your child you're talking to, and that you've been benched. You're still a mother, but you are not in the race anymore. You're watching from the stands. You're a spectator.

This is what Morley was thinking as she stood in the underwear department staring at the Spandex briefs that a moment ago she thought were mildly, if a bit aggressively, funny.

Which is why, a few moments later, Katy Singh, seventeen years old and working her first shift at the department store, found Morley sobbing between the racks.

This was not something they had covered on training day.

Katy found her supervisor and told him about the weeping woman.

"Oh for heaven's sake," he said, putting down a handful of invoices. "Not again!"

A week passed. Another Saturday arrived. Morley was getting ready to head out again—to *return* the Spandex underwear. She hadn't even given them to Dave. Her little joke had not seemed so funny once she got home. It had occurred to her that Dave might like them. That he might *wear* them.

As she gathered her house keys and purse, she looked at her son, who was once again on the couch, once again reading a comic. She'd been trying all week to think of something fun that they could do together.

As she stood by the door with the keys in her hand, it occurred to her that she'd been thinking too hard. All she wanted was to spend some time with him.

"Sam," she said. "Why don't you come shopping with me? We'll get you some new jeans."

Sam said, "I dunno." It was dismissive. But was it displeasure? Or just disinterest?

"It'll be fun," said Morley. "We'll get lunch after. Hot chocolate."

And so he struggled up and the two of them headed downtown. They returned the underwear. Then they headed to the boys' department. Fifteen minutes later Morley was having second thoughts about shopping with her son. She had tried to find jeans he'd like, but each pair she held up was greeted with a shrug.

When she suggested he try some on, he threw his head back with such force that she thought he might have hurt himself.

What had she been thinking? She'd been married for over twenty years—and had been a mother for almost as long. How could she have imagined that a shopping trip with a boy would be anything other than a voyage of the doomed to the island of misery? Sam marched past the racks of suits and shirts toward the change rooms with the enthusiasm of a prisoner in a labour camp.

They passed an anxious-looking young man flipping hesitantly through a rack of dress pants. He looked as if he'd be happier having a root canal. The men's wear department was clearly not the place to look for a good time on a Saturday afternoon.

Katy Singh was at her post at the change-room doors. It was her third shift at her new job.

When she saw the weeping lady from the previous week, Katy blanched.

"I'm sorry, ma'am," she said nervously to Morley. "These are the men's change rooms. You can't go in."

Katy pointed at Sam. "He has to go in alone."

A few minutes later, Sam emerged from the change room in a pair of starchy new jeans. There was a pained expression on his face.

"These jeans," he said, "do *nothing* for me."

The next time, he came out, turned on his heel, and headed back before Morley could say a word.

"Not my style," he said over his shoulder.

Five minutes passed. And then two more. Morley poked her head down the change-room corridor.

"Sam," she called, "are you coming out?"

"No," called Sam sadly, "I don't want anyone to see me like this."

There were still several pairs to try. He said he'd come out if he liked any of them. Morley, who figured she might be waiting awhile, sighed and sat down on a chair outside the change-room doors.

As she did, the strap of her purse caught on the arm of the chair and its contents flew across the floor in front of her. She watched her favourite lipstick roll under a rack of housecoats.

"Figures," she muttered.

In the change room Sam was staring at the pile of jeans he had yet to try on. The pairs he'd already tried were ugly. What were the odds that any of these others would be better? Maybe he was more of a sweatpants guy. Or shorts. Maybe he should wait until summer, and move straight into shorts. That way he could avoid the jeans dilemma until fall.

Morley was on her hands and knees crabbing across the men's wear floor, gathering her hairbrush, her wallet, her car keys, her sunglasses. She'd just begun to squeeze herself under the rack, reaching about, patting the floor in the dark, looking for her lipstick, when Sam came out of the change room.

Sam paused near the chairs where he had expected to find her. She was nowhere in sight.

She'd always told him that if he got lost in a department store, he was to go to the nearest checkout and wait there.

He headed to the cashier. When he got to the counter, it was deserted. He sat down on the floor with his back against the counter to wait.

Morley's fingers curled around the familiar silver tube. She crawled out from under the rack and sat back down in the chair, her purse securely on her lap.

Five minutes passed.

Sam should have come out by now.

Another five minutes.

What was he doing? Was he reading in there? Had he fallen asleep?

Morley decided she had waited long enough.

She stood up.

And she stood at the precise moment that Williams Van Kirk began his little meltdown. Williams was standing in the far change-room stall. He was staring disconsolately at a pair of grey gabardine trousers that lay crumpled on the floor. Williams was looking for an outfit to wear that night. He was taking his girlfriend to dinner. He was planning to propose between the main course and dessert. He wanted to look his best. But now he was wondering what he'd been thinking, shopping by himself. He'd rarely shopped for clothes on his own. He'd always had help from the women in his life—his mother, his sister, and more recently, his girlfriend.

Amanda was into clothes. Or more particularly, *fashion*. She had a way of making the selection of an outfit sound like a job fraught with danger. There were, apparently, rules. Not just ideas, or theories, but hard and fast rules about what he could and could not wear. Williams found this terrifying. According to Amanda, there were things he could "get away with." When he was trying to decide on a tie before they went out, he'd often hold one up and she would step back and cock her head and say, "Yeah, I think you can get away with that." This made him nervous, especially if there was doubt in her voice. What would happen if she was wrong? What would happen if he couldn't "get away" with it?

One day, when he was in grade five, Williams wore to school a purple-striped T-shirt his aunt had given him. He'd been in the playground only five minutes when someone, he couldn't remember who, but someone *bigger*— he remembered that much—had made some "purple-pants" crack and then walloped him with his lunch bag. Williams had gone home with an eye that matched his shirt. So he understood that fashion mistakes could be painful. At some level he was worried that if he went out in a pair of gabardine trousers he couldn't get away with, a large man in an impeccably tailored suit would appear out of nowhere and wallop him with his briefcase. Or worse, Amanda wouldn't marry him.

"How could I marry someone who would wear *those* pants," she would say before she hit him with her purse and abandoned him in the restaurant.

Williams was standing there in his underwear, staring at himself in the mirror, thinking how ridiculous he looked with his shirt hanging limply over his hips, his socks bunched around his ankles—how unlike the men whose pictures he saw in fashion magazines. Williams, paralyzed with indecision, battered by doubt, and overcome with apprehension and anxiety, heard a noise outside his change-room door.

It sounded to him like someone with a briefcase.

It was, of course, Morley—with Katy Singh trotting close behind.

"Ma'am, ma'am," Katy was saying, "you can't go back there, ma'am."

But Morley wasn't listening. She was lurching past one door after another, calling her son at each one. "Sam? Sam?"

There was no response.

She came to the last in the row—the only closed door in there. She stopped in front of it. She didn't even hesitate.

There's nothing like a woman breaking through a change-room door and slamming into an anxious, half-dressed stranger to liven things up. Morley burst in, Williams made a desperate grab at the pants, and then he toppled onto the floor.

Sam heard the commotion and headed over. So did the department supervisor. He looked at the man on the floor and the frenzied woman scrambling down the corridor.

"For heaven's sake," he sighed. "Not again."

Ten minutes later, Morley and Sam were in the car, driving home.

Sam had cheered up considerably.

"Hey," said Sam. "We never got lunch."

Morley had forgotten all about eating.

Mortifying embarrassment tends to have that effect.

"Right," said Morley. She peered down the road, looking for some beacon of kid-friendly dining. "What do you feel like?" she asked. "Hamburgers? Pizza? …"

"I was thinking sushi might be nice," said Sam.

Morley glanced over at her son.

He seemed to be—serious.

"Sushi?" said Morley. "I didn't know you liked sushi."

"Yeah," Sam said.

"Yeah?" said Morley.

"Well, I'm developing a taste for it," said Sam.

"Really?" said Morley.

"Well, I'm *hoping* to develop a taste for it," said Sam, almost wistfully. He was quiet for a few seconds. Then he said, "Mr. Harmon said I would like it."

Morley looked over at her son. "Mr. Who?" she said, trying to quash the alarm in her voice.

"Mr. Harmon," said Sam. "Harmon's Fine Foods."

That Mr. Harmon. Morley had always found Mr. Harmon and his little specialty store intimidating.

"When were you talking to Mr. Harmon?" asked Morley.

"Last week," said Sam. "After school."

"You go into Harmon's?" said Morley. "After school?"

"Not always," said Sam. "Last week he had oysters from Malpeque."

She was parking. Looking over her shoulder. It was hard to concentrate on both things.

"He let me try one," said Sam. "One of the oysters."

There was a little Japanese place across the street.

They sat together at the counter and watched the chef mould the sushi rice in his hand; watched as he sliced a block of red tuna with his sharp blade. Sam was fascinated when the chef took a bamboo mat and sheet of seaweed and rolled the seaweed around a cylinder of rice and cucumber strips.

When their food was ready, Sam stared at the small green plate in front of him.

He picked up a piece of the salmon.

"My first sushi," he said, beaming.

He took a tentative bite and then turned to his mother.

"I don't think it's cooked enough for me."

Morley showed him how to pour soy sauce into his little side dish and stir a bit of the green wasabi paste into the soy.

"Try dipping it first," she said.

"Okay," said Sam.

He tried everything but the eel. And the octopus.

"What do you think?" said Morley.

"I liked the avocado fish the best," said Sam.

They were walking down the street, the spring sun warming their faces.

They were heading for Harmon's.

"Hello, Sam," said Mr. Harmon.

"Hello, Mr. Harmon," said Sam. "This is my mother. I want to show her the pasta."

Morley remembered the last time *she* was in Harmon's. It was a couple of years ago. She needed olive oil, and she thought maybe she would get a nice one. There was way too much choice. And she was overcome by Mr. Harmon. All his questions. Did she like grassy flavours? What about the bouquet? She had left empty-handed.

Sam said, "Come on."

She followed him past the bins of perfectly arranged vegetables, down a narrow aisle of cans, and then to the back. To a cooler filled with little packages of exotic pasta. Squid ink pasta with Gruyère. Acorn squash with garlic and chicken.

She didn't notice Mr. Harmon standing behind them.

Mr. Harmon didn't for a moment think there was anything unusual about a young boy browsing in a gourmet food store. In fact, Sam reminded Mr. Harmon of himself as a child.

"We have a pasta class on Saturday afternoons next month," said Mr. Harmon. "I've been telling him he should come."

They were back on the street. Back in the sun.

Morley said, "Do you want to take the class?"

"I couldn't," said Sam. "It's all adults."

"I could come with you," said Morley.

Sam looked at her. "Would you tell people that you made me go?"

"I could do that," said Morley.

Morley noticed they were holding hands. She hadn't noticed when they'd started. She did notice, however, when they began swinging their arms back and forth, the way they used to when Sam was younger.

Morley smiled softly. It was true: the race was almost over. Apparently, though, she still had a while left to run.

RIDING THE LIGHTNING

Summer came and summer went, sashaying through town like a girl in a cotton dress—languid, long of leg, and saucy enough to turn heads. Slow enough too that everyone who turned caught at least one last glimpse before she disappeared.

It was the summer that Kenny Wong's restaurant, Wong's Scottish Meat Pies, had a bad turn. Oh, the regulars still came, but the new burrito place down the street and the vegan café around the block were siphoning off some of the lunch traffic. Kenny had to lay off a chef and return to the kitchen himself for the first time in years.

It was the summer that Dave's neighbourhood nemesis, Mary Turlington, had her infamous meltdown at the Bistro Ouimet.

It's not clear what transpired in the little café. Mary was, safe to assume, wound up as tight as a seven-day clock. The incident happened, after all, during the hot spell at the end of July, and you surely remember how fragile everyone was *that* week. The conflagration, that's what the paper called it, had something to do with the PLEASE WAIT TO BE SEATED sign, and the fact that a lot of *waiting,* but not a lot of *seating,* was going on. What *exactly* happened no one knows for sure. There was a dust-up. That much is certain. Though I don't want to leave the impression that it got physical. As far as I understand, it didn't get physical. Though someone said that the owner was called at home—and the police. Or some sort of security.

And the restaurant hostess *did* go on sick leave. And Mary *did* end up at the family doctor. It was the doctor who delivered the ultimatum. Either psychotherapy or meditation. Choose one.

"You have to chill out" were his exact words.

"You have to be kidding," said Mary. "Surely there's a chemical option. If this was Hollywood there would be a chemical option."

The doctor didn't bat an eye.

"I will not chant," said Mary. "Or go to an ass-ram."

"Ash," said the doctor. "*Ash*ram."

He gave her the name of a private meditation instructor. She had her first class Labour Day weekend. She had to sit for half an hour a day, doing nothing. She found it *intolerable.* But she persevered.

Finally, and surely most unsettlingly, it was the summer that Jim Scoffield had his heart attack.

"Episode," Jim said. "It was an episode."

Except it was more than an episode. Jim went to the emergency room at three in the morning with all the classic symptoms: indigestion, pain that started in his chest and radiated down his arm, and a general sense of doom.

"But I always have a general sense of doom," Jim protested.

It wasn't a serious attack.

"I didn't lose any heart function," said Jim.

But it was serious enough.

"It was a warning shot," said Dave.

"I guess," said Jim.

Jim is fine. He had a bypass. And he went through rehab, stopped smoking, and started exercising. A walking program.

"Whatever works," said Dave.

It's not clear who thought of the defibrillator.

"You're joking," said Jim.

"Not for you," said Dave. "For everyone. For the neighbour-hood. This is a high-risk neighbourhood."

Lots of men, over fifty.

The idea was that they'd all chip in and then store it somewhere central. If they could get ten families to commit, it would cost less than $200 each.

"Listen," said Dave. "*You're* fine. It might be me who needs it."

In the end there were twelve families who chipped in, so there was money left over. They organized a barbecue. And hired a trainer. They ate burgers and fries and learned CPR.

So August came and August went, and September too, and the pretty girl in the summer dress disappeared down the street and into the crowd. Jim was fine, and Kenny was back in the kitchen, and Mary, who did not enjoy the meditation business one bit, not one little bit, worked away at it nevertheless. She lay there on her bed half an hour a day, counting her breaths: in and then out, smiling at her breath as it came in, and smiling at it as it went out, trying to ignore all the thoughts that bounced into her mind and the infernal racket of the world around her—the dogs barking, the doors slamming, the car alarms.

The best place for the defibrillator, everyone agreed, turned out to be Dave and Morley's garage, the most central and accessible place in the neighbourhood.

At the start everyone treated it with great earnestness. The trainer said they should practise, have drills. "You need to do it," he said, "so you can do it without *thinking,* if you ever have to do it for real."

And so they drew up a schedule, and they gathered in little groups, on Saturday afternoons, in Dave's garage.

Dave, Carl Lowbeer, and Bert Turlington were there one Saturday, hanging around the way guys do, until one of them said, "Okay. Let's do this."

Dave said, "I'll be victim."

He clutched his chest dramatically, moaned, staggered around, and then laid himself gingerly down on the garage floor.

Bert looked at Carl and said, "You go first. I'll time you."

Carl nodded. Bert pulled out his phone.

Now. For all intents and purposes, a defibrillator is foolproof. When you attach it to someone, the first thing it does is evaluate their heart rhythm. It has to recognize a life-threatening rhythm before it recommends administering a shock.

Once you turn it on, it gives you step-by-step voice instructions. "Remove the patient's shirt. Pull the sticker off the first pad. Place the pad on the chest below the left arm." All you do is follow the instructions.

So even if Carl *had* stuck the pads on Dave's chest, it wouldn't give him a shock if he was in a healthy rhythm.

And for times like this, when they were just practising, there was the safety mode.

"Go," said Bert.

Carl ran across the garage and popped the little lunchbox-sized machine out of the bracket on the wall. Then he ran back and knelt beside Dave. He flipped the case open and pressed the On button.

"Initiating device," said the machine soothingly. Then, "Remove the patient's shirt."

They all knew this was just a scenario. They all knew that the machine was in safety mode, and that Dave, lying there on the floor with his eyes closed, had *not* had a heart attack. But they also knew that Carl was kneeling beside a machine that was capable of delivering two hundred joules of electricity. So even though they began all casual and jocular, as the scenario progressed a certain seriousness settled on them.

Carl unbuttoned Dave's shirt.

"Okay," said Carl. "If this was real I would rip it open."

The machine said, "Remove the sticker from the first pad."

Carl said, "Okay. I am removing the sticker."

He wasn't really removing the sticker, he was just pretending. Those stickers are expensive.

The machine said, "Place the sticker on the patient's chest below the left armpit."

And so it went, for the first sticker, and the second sticker, and the testing of the heart rhythm—Carl's face screwed up in concentration. Carl biting his tongue.

"One minute," said Bert.

"One minute, thirty," said Bert.

And then the machine said, "Prepare to shock the patient."

Bert said, "Make sure that you're not touching him anywhere."

If you're touching the patient, *you* are going to get shocked too.

Carl said, "Clear."

The machine said, "Shock the patient."

These things can start to feel real.

Carl held his breath.

Dave scrunched up his eyes.

Carl checked one more time to be sure that he wasn't touching Dave anywhere.

"Here goes," said Carl.

He pressed the red "shock" button.

And that's when Bert, who was standing right behind Carl, leaned over so that the paper bag he'd blown up was no more than six inches from Carl's ear. He swung his hands open and clapped them together.

There was a terrific explosion.

Carl levitated.

There is no other way to describe it.

Carl lifted right off the ground—which is not an easy thing to do when you're kneeling. One moment Carl was on his knees beside Dave, his hand on the red button, the next he had lifted off. Howling.

It was as if *Carl* was the one who'd been shocked.

Dave and Bert whooped.

Dave and Bert staggered around the garage, hysterical, clutching onto the side of the car.

It took ten minutes for Carl to settle down.

Carl was still fluttery and crazy, standing up, sitting down, calling the two of them *unspeakable* things.

"I can't *believe* you did that. *I* could have had a heart attack."

"Well," said Bert. "We've got the defibrillator for that."

And that is when Ted Anderson arrived.

When he spotted Ted, Carl pulled himself together. He looked at Dave and Bert, and Bert nodded. Carl turned and smiled slyly at Ted. Then, all earnest and serious, Carl said, "Hey, Ted. I just finished. It's your turn."

Bert was in the corner, inflating a new paper bag.

And so went the autumn, bags popping and leaves bursting into orange and red, and then came the smoky afternoons, as the reds faded to yellow, the yellows to brown, and then everything to grey. Pretty soon the defibrillator in Dave's garage was just another summer memory. Not forgotten, but no longer the first thing anyone thought about on a Saturday morning. No longer a preoccupation.

Except for Dave, of course. After all, it was in *his* garage. He walked by it morning and night. Stare at something like that, day in and day out, and it's only natural that you're going to start obsessing about what it would be like to use it. In real life. It would be—Godlike. The power to give life.

In hospitals, the ER doctors call it *riding the lightning*.

"It has baby pads," said Dave to his pal Kenny one day at lunch.

Dave was sitting at the back counter, staring at a steaming plate of Kenny's pork dumplings.

"It still delivers a shock. But a kid-appropriate amount."

Even the adult pads wouldn't kill you. If you were shocked by accident, Dave explained, it would get your attention. It would knock you around. It would hurt like hell. But it wouldn't kill you. It would stop your heart—and then? Your heart would start again.

But those were the adult pads. What harm could the infant pads do?

"No way," said Kenny.

"Come on," said Dave. "Take off your shirt. For science."

He wanted to try them out so badly.

"How about your dog?" said Dave.

"There is just so much wrong with that," said Kenny. "To begin with, you would have to shave my dog. You're not shaving Szechuan."

They settled on a twelve-pound roast. A rump roast. Kenny had one in his cooler.

They took it over to Dave's, shut the garage door, and duct-taped the roast to the pads so that they wouldn't have to hold on to it.

What happened was a lot of nothing.

"Sort of disappointing," said Dave.

He'd been thinking of Carl. He'd been hoping it would bounce around or something.

Kenny called the next morning.

"Get over here," he said.

Dave couldn't get him to say any more.

"Just get over here."

So he got dressed and headed over.

The breakfast rush was done and the restaurant was mostly empty by the time Dave arrived. There were two moms with strollers in a back booth and a couple of construction types near the door. Dave slipped behind the counter, poured himself a mug of coffee, and settled onto his regular stool. A minute later Kenny came out of the kitchen carrying a plate of something to the women at the back. Then he disappeared again without a word. He was gone about five minutes.

When he returned, he set a plate of steaming beef in front of Dave. He stood back and crossed his arms.

Dave looked at the plate and then at Kenny.

"Go on," said Kenny.

It was quite possibly the tenderest beef Dave had ever tasted.

"It actually melts in your mouth," said Dave.

"I know," said Kenny.

"It isn't …" said Dave.

"It is," said Kenny.

"You didn't …" said Dave.

"I did," said Kenny.

Dave looked around and lowered his voice.

"Is that, like, to code?"

That afternoon they tried the adult pads on a different roast, but the adult pads seemed to toughen the meat. They tried other roasts on various settings. But it didn't have the same effect.

They had stumbled on the sweet spot on the first try.

"Dumb luck," said Kenny.

They spent hours in the garage perfecting the recipe.

"What you doing out there?" said Morley.

"Nothing," said Dave. "Nothing."

It's not that they were doing anything wrong. Dave had done the checklist. It wasn't immoral. Or unethical. Or dangerous.

It just *seemed*—wrong.

They kept at it, but they didn't tell anyone.

"Are you sure it's to code?" said Dave.

"Code?" said Kenny. "I'm selling twice as much beef and broccoli as last month."

And twice as much again the month after that.

Word was getting around. A columnist mentioned it in a review.

Business picked up. Kenny hired back his chef, though he continued to make all the beef dishes himself.

And then the bone-white moon of winter slipped into the sky, and the stars seemed to double and move farther away. The night deepened, and got longer and colder—until one morning, out of nowhere, someone said, "I woke early. For no reason."

And someone else said, "Me too."

The crows were back.

Pretty soon the robins were back, too.

That was April.

Then came May, May, the lusty month of May.

Kenny opened a backyard patio and stayed open for dinner for the first time ever. Jim, who'd been walking in malls since November, started outside again. And Mary Turlington moved her daily meditation from her bedroom to her back garden.

And the sorry problem with that is that when you're standing on Dave's back porch, on the stool in the far corner, hanging clothes on the clothesline or just, you know, hanging out, you can see clearly into the Turlingtons' yard. And the problem with *that* is that if you're there, on the stool, for *whatever* reason, and you see Mary splayed out on the ground, just lying there, not moving, not a muscle—well, you can understand that it might be easy to jump to the wrong conclusion.

Especially if there happens to be a defibrillator in your garage.

"Hello?" called Dave. Tentatively.

When disaster comes calling, no matter how prepared you might be, no matter how much you think you're courting it, it is never a welcome thing.

"Hey," called Dave again, climbing down off the stool, thinking, *Mary was probably asleep.*

But Mary didn't wake up. Mary didn't move. No matter how many times Dave called, Mary just lay there. So now Dave is running for the garage, and he is running as fast as he can.

Mary had been working hard at her meditation all winter. Just the week before, her instructor had told her she was doing well. It didn't feel like that to Mary. Okay, once or twice she'd lost track of time and entered some joyful state of—well—she wouldn't have used the word out loud, not to you, nor to me, but to herself, and to her teacher; it was the only word she could come up with that described it:

"A state of … bliss," she said.

But as soon as she'd noticed it, as soon as she'd become aware of it, the sensation went away, popped like a soap bubble.

She had tried to get it back. But she couldn't.

Her teacher said, "Do *not* try."

Her teacher said, "To hold on, we must let go. Just breathe. Just breathe in and breathe out. Just notice each breath. Just notice what is."

"I notice everything," said Mary. "That's the problem."

"It *is* the problem," said her teacher. "But it's also the solution. Just notice. And let go. Notice and let go."

And that is when Mary heard the latch of her garden door open and close. *Bert must be home early,* she thought.

Last fall Mary would have opened her eyes and said something. Probably would have snapped at Bert.

But Mary had progressed. She noticed the gate. And she let the gate go.

"Mary?" said Dave.

Mary didn't move.

Not a muscle.

Teacher said there would be a moment like this.

"Every moment is a learning moment," said teacher.

Breathe in and breathe out.

"Mary," said Dave.

She was not going to succumb.

There is no doubt a list of things that even the most experienced meditator might find difficult to notice and let go.

And one of the things at the top of that list would surely be your neighbour's hand landing on the top button of your blouse and tugging.

Mary opened her eyes.

"What is going on?" said Mary.

Dave, who was fiddling with the machine now, said, "Just relax. I'm here to help."

He turned and slapped the first pad in place.

Mary said, "I don't think so."

And she started to get up.

Dave reached over and pushed her down.

The air around Mary, Dave, and the defibrillator became a whirl of arms and legs and wires.

And the thing about those wires is, they're not meant to be jostled around like that. They're not meant to be attached to a person who is leaping about like a circus performer—folded like a pretzel one moment and airborne the next.

If they are, the defibrillator is going to pick up an erratic signal. And the little voice is going to say, "Shock the patient."

Any sudden crisis requiring action, any emergency, that is, requires a number of things to go *right* if things are not going to go—wrong. After all, an emergency is, by definition, a shifting landscape. Cool heads must prevail. Emergency workers must roll with the punches, accurately assess reversals, quickly change direction. Dave does not have a gift, or talent, for any of these things. What Dave has is perseverance. What Dave has is the ability to get a job done—even if it *doesn't* need doing.

"Shock the patient," said the machine.

"For God's sake," said Mary.

"Just relax," said Dave.

And they both watched, in that horrible slow-motion way, as his right hand, the one not holding her down, descended toward the big red button.

There was an odd pause, a moment of silence—the two of them staring deeply into each other's eyes.

Then there was a terrifying shriek.

Well, two shrieks, actually.

Bert came home about ten minutes later.

When he didn't find Mary inside, he went into the backyard.

He found the two of them lying on the grass beside each other.

Dave's hair and his wife's clothes both in disarray.

There was an odd smell in the air.

As if, perhaps, one of them had been smoking.

Mary never meditated again. She tried, but her eyes popped open with every sound, every voice, every footstep. Every distraction was just too distracting. Everything she heard was *him* coming *her* way.

She went back to the doctor, and he said, *okay, okay.* He referred her to a psychotherapist, who met her for five minutes and put her on meds.

There was a neighbourhood meeting. Everyone agreed it would be best if they moved the defibrillator from Dave's garage.

"For Mary's sake," said Carl. "Bert says she's having nightmares."

June turned to July. July to August.

Kenny's beef sales went back to normal—not right away, but slowly over the summer.

And August turned to September.

As the nights cooled, so did the memories. What once seemed unforgettable just seemed memorable. What had seemed so horrifying just seemed funny.

Before you knew it, it was summer again.

This summer was different from that one. You could ask anyone from the neighbourhood—probably none of them would have much to say. No dust-ups to report, no heart attacks. They would probably tell you it was dull, a dull summer. Which, as far as Dave—and Mary Turlington—were concerned, was perfectly fine.

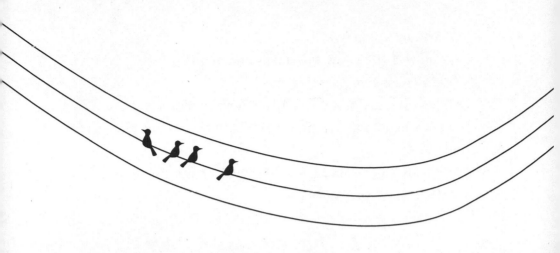

DANCELAND

On a soft summer evening, after dinner was done and before there were kids, sometimes even *after* there were kids, back in the summers when the kids were still young and the world was too, Dave and Morley would often go for a walk. Sometimes to the park, sometimes to the bookstore, sometimes on muggy nights for ice cream, or even just around and about the neighbourhood, into the church of the trees, through the cathedral of comfort. They would inevitably run into someone. And they would inevitably stop and chat.

"We don't do that anymore," said Morley. "Why don't we do that?"

"We lost the habit," said Dave. "Or maybe, Arthur."

It was such a lovely habit to have. To leave the dishes in the sink. Or better, to get them done. So when they came back from their walk there was nothing to do. Nothing pressing.

To put the dog on the leash—

"Arthur," said Dave.

Who was gone now, how many summers?

"I *still* miss him," said Dave.

They all did. But it didn't mean they shouldn't walk. And so, on a warm summer night, they did the dishes and they went for a walk.

"Which way?" said Dave as they walked out the door.

"That way," said Morley.

They came across the birthday party on their way home.

A squeal of little girls flying around a front yard with sparklers. Little fairies in gauzy tulle tutus, writing in the sky with fire.

They stopped and watched. Dave talked to one of the fathers. But they didn't watch long. They left before someone grabbed a hot sparkler end. They left before the tears.

And as they walked, the squealing girls still sparkling in their heads, Dave said, "You're thinking about dancing, aren't you?"

And Morley laughed. "That's *exactly* what I was thinking. How did you remember that?"

How could he not?

It was another summer. A summer long ago and far away. The summer Morley was seven.

An only child.

Her dad, Roy, was a policeman.

Her mother, Helen, stayed at home.

Under the watchful eye of the policeman and his wife, Morley grew up in a home of order.

The mornings belonged to Roy. Roy got up first. By the time Morley and Helen came downstairs, he had coffee in the pot and oatmeal on the stove. He would make the coffee and set the oatmeal simmering and then he would sit at the table and open the morning newspaper. Helen would serve what he'd made. Oatmeal with brown sugar, toast with jam. Roy read the sports, Morley read the comics, and Helen stood by the sink.

Dinner was at six: meat, potato, and veg. Except Saturdays, when Helen would let loose with a casserole or, if she was feeling wild, macaroni and cheese.

Mondays was laundry. Tuesdays ironing. Fridays Helen vacuumed and dusted.

They lived a life of routine that extended into civilities and leisure. Roy would compliment Helen's every meal. "You've outdone yourself again." Helen would ask Roy if he wanted dessert. He always wanted dessert.

Morley was unaware that things worked differently in other homes—until she went to school and began her independent life. She entered the knockabout world where children chase each other from room to room and hair is pulled and toys fought over, where beds are left unmade and clothing piles up on bedroom floors. The world where mothers shout at children and fathers bark at mothers.

Her first encounter was at Jenny Birrel's house. She was asked to stay for supper. It was so exciting, so grown up, so sophisticated to be sitting in their basement watching television, waiting to be called to the table. And then Jenny's brother Geoffrey came in. He wanted to watch something else, and he just changed the channel. There was a knock-down, full-on, hitting, screaming battle, with Morley standing on the sidelines, utterly bewildered.

Nothing like this ever happened in her life.

In Morley's house there were no siblings to squabble with, no enemy to divide and conquer. Arguing about the rules had never occurred to her. The rules in Morley's house were unassailable. Immutable. They weren't even *rules*. They were simply the way the world worked. They were—life.

Her world was peaceful and quiet. Her parents a united front.

Then came the election.

The four-term mayor was standing for his record-setting fifth term and the police union was lined up solidly behind him.

The son of Greek immigrants, the mayor was a salesman both by birth and occupation. His family owned a car dealership. His father had made a name for himself driving a 1928 Cadillac Town Sedan once owned by Al Capone. The mayor booted around in a gleaming Thunderbird he claimed had belonged to Marilyn Monroe.

He was a glad-hander. A booming, self-promoting, cigar-chomping cartoon character. And for the first time in his undistinguished career, he had a challenger. A university professor. A good-looking man. Like a young Jack Kennedy—toothy smile, thick hair. Helen knew his family. Without asking, she let them put a sign up on the front lawn. Without asking Roy, I mean.

That evening, Morley, draped over the back of the living room sofa, watched her father pull into the driveway, get out of the car, walk across the lawn, and stare at the sign with his mouth hanging open.

While he stared, the car began to roll slowly back down the driveway toward the street.

Morley knocked on the window and pointed. Roy waved back. Morley waved frantically. Roy glanced over his shoulder. He ran back to the car. A car, incidentally, that he'd bought from the mayor's dealership.

When Roy got to the car, he ran around to the back and leaned on the fender—as if he could stop its roll with his body. Then he hopped back to the driver's door and jumped in. The car shuddered and stopped.

Morley watched him get out of it a second time. He waved at her a second time, marched back to the sign, pulled it from the ground, and carried it toward the house.

He walked right into the kitchen. "What are you thinking?" he said to Helen, holding the sign up. "He's going to close down the department. You want me to lose my job? How are we going to survive if I lose my job?"

For Roy, being the breadwinner was a point of pride.

More than once he'd told Morley, "Your mother has never worked a day in her life."

He didn't mean it critically. He loved her dearly. What he was trying to say was that he looked after her, and that he always would.

It never occurred to Roy that Helen might *like* a job. But then, it hadn't occurred to Helen either.

Until recently.

Betty Friedan had just published *The Feminine Mystique*. Helen hadn't read it. In fact she hadn't even heard of it. But there are some books whose message is going to get through to you whether you read them or not.

Pat Mulligan had just quit the PTA and taken a job at a downtown lawyers' office. Everyone was talking about it.

Helen had wondered about getting a job herself. But working in an office held no appeal, and, if she were being perfectly honest with herself, she had no burning desire, at this point in her life, to start a career. But news of Pat's move had made her restless. It was the restlessness that had nudged her toward politics. She began listening to the election coverage on the radio, seeking out articles in the newspaper. She became convinced that young John Chazeralla would be a better mayor than the glad-handing, cigar-smoking, four-term car salesman.

"He won't close the police department," she said to Morley as she put her to bed. "That is just foolishness."

She called the Chazeralla campaign office the next morning and told them to put up another sign.

"Mine was vandalized," she said.

"We'll report it to the police," said the people from the campaign.

"Good idea," said Helen.

"You're being ridiculous," said Roy when he came home that night. "Do you want this city to fall apart? Do you want our taxes to go up? Do you want me to lose my job? Criminals running free in the street."

Helen didn't want any of those things. But she didn't want to take the sign down, either.

Morley saw the flush rise in her mother's cheeks. And then she watched in amazement as her mother heaved the watermelon she was carrying across the kitchen at her father.

"You cut this," said Helen when she tossed the watermelon. It was a friendly throw. *To* him, not *at* him. Underhand. He should have caught it. But he wasn't expecting it. Who would expect that? And anyway, the throw was short. Morley watched in disbelief as the watermelon exploded on the kitchen floor. The three of them stared at the pink juicy mess of it for a silent moment, and then Helen stormed off. In tears!

Morley, who was sitting at the kitchen table, looked at her father.

"Why is Mommy mad?" she said.

And so the sign stayed up. Roy knew when to give in. Sometimes the only way to win was to concede victory to the other side. But he wasn't happy about it.

The next day he came home from work with a bigger sign. For the other guy. The incumbent. Morley watched from the living room as he pounded it into the lawn.

A certain tension settled on the house.

Morley was seven years old. She had never seen her parents like this. She lay in bed at night and fretted.

She had no one to talk to. If she had had a brother or a sister they could have talked about it. But she was all alone.

It was clear to her that her mother and father were about to get a divorce. Just like Cathy Reddit's parents.

And just like Cathy, she'd be called into a courtroom where she'd have to swear to tell the truth, the whole truth, and nothing but the truth, and they'd make her declare with whom she wanted to live. Or worse, the police would find out about the watermelon, and take Morley away, and she'd have to live in a foster home. She would have to be careful not to mention the watermelon in court.

A week before the election, Roy went to Niagara Falls. It was the annual Police Association convention. Usually Morley's mom packed her father's suitcase.

"Pack your own suitcase," said Helen.

"I don't know what I wear," said Roy.

Morley sat on the end of her parents' bed while her father pulled clothes from his dresser.

"Do these go with brown pants?" asked Roy, holding up a pair of white socks.

Morley shrugged.

He left Friday morning. By Friday night a giddy, carnival-like atmosphere had settled upon the house.

Morley and Helen ate dinner in front of the television. They had never done that before. Not only that, they each had a frozen TV dinner—breaded chicken, mashed potatoes, and frozen peas in an aluminum tray—each dish with its own little compartment. Morley had dreamed of TV dinners. But she'd never imagined her dream coming true.

On election eve, the reality of the situation hit Roy like a flying watermelon.

The three of them were getting ready to leave for the school where Roy and Helen would cast their ballots when Roy, who was sitting on the hall stairs tying his shoes, had his revelation.

Helen was about to cancel his vote.

"Wait a minute. Wait a minute," he said.

Morley could see her father trying to stay calm. He led her mother into the kitchen and began to explain it to her.

"This is a democracy," he said. "If you don't vote for the mayor, my vote isn't going to count. You're going to cancel my vote."

Morley saw her mother shrug her shoulders. She was rummaging in her purse. She didn't even seem to be paying attention.

"Don't you know how important it is for each vote to count?" said her dad.

Helen didn't say a word.

Morley stood by door twisting her hair. Their house was beginning to feel like the Birrels'.

"Let's go," she said.

But when Roy stormed past her, he was by himself.

"Is he coming back?" asked Morley.

Morley and Helen walked up to the school and Helen voted. When they got home Roy was sitting at the kitchen table.

"Dinner's late," he said.

After they ate, Roy washed the dishes as he always did. When he was finished, they gathered in stony silence in front of the television to watch the election results.

"This could be the end of everything," said Roy when the special began.

It wasn't.

The cigar-smoking, car-selling incumbent won.

"See," said Roy. "I told you."

"But your vote didn't count," said Helen.

It took a few weeks, but things slowly returned to normal. Though not in Morley's mind.

As far as Morley was concerned, everything had changed. She could see things were better, but she knew it had been a near miss, and Morley didn't know that near misses were possible.

She didn't even know that shots could be fired.

She kept waiting for the end of the world. And then came Saturday, July the first. Firecracker Day.

Darkness comes slowly when you're seven years old and you're waiting on fireworks. In the morning Morley went over to Sarah Lochead's house. When she got there, Sarah took her into the kitchen and showed her the box of fireworks on top of the refrigerator. Then Sarah got out her pencil crayons and she and Morley started to draw, but the minutes ticked by so sluggishly that by ten a.m. Morley was ready to go home. She spent the afternoon reading in her room. When it was finally time for supper she was too excited to eat. When she was finally allowed up from the table, she ran outside and saw what she feared in her heart: that the sky was not yet dark. Once again, she was forced to pace in the lobby of the church of delayed pleasure.

Ever so slowly, neighbours began to appear—the older children first, followed by the mothers, holding the younger ones in their arms, and finally, the fathers. They stood in clusters in the Hampsons' driveway, everyone adding their fireworks to the pile in the wagon by the side door.

The big silver tub of sand. The dads like army captains, planning a campaign. The older kids hovering and being shooed away. The mothers and younger ones sitting on the lawn chairs.

Until Sarah's father caught Sarah's mother's raised eyebrow and said, "Okay, everyone. Stand back."

And it began.

The Cobalt Cannon. The Sky Storm. The Screaming Banshee.

Little explosions on the driveway. Some of them reaching as high as the Hampsons' second-floor windows.

They ended with sparklers. The kids dancing around like pixies, fountains of little stars following them, just as this night would follow them for the rest of their lives.

And then to bed.

And that was that.

Except it wasn't.

Helen tucked her in, but Morley was too excited to sleep. She lay in her bed staring at the ceiling. When she heard her parents' voices in the backyard she got out of bed and went to her window to spy on them.

The sky was black now. All she could see of the yard through the leaves of the maple were shadows. All she could hear was the murmur of her parents mixed with the murmur of the radio. The murmur of their voices and the music drifting through the branches. It was Bing Crosby. He was singing "I've Got a Pocketful of Dreams."

There was a sudden whoosh, and a flare that scared her, and she gasped and pulled back. Then she saw her mother in outline, sitting on the porch holding a sparkler. As she watched, a second one flared, and her mother got up and walked over to the tree where her father was standing. He took a sparkler in one hand and wrapped his other around her mother's waist. And they began to dance, right there on the lawn, by the sandbox, each of them holding a sparkler in their hands. Her mom was laughing, except it didn't sound like her mom. It sounded like someone younger.

Then she saw Helen put her head on Roy's shoulder. And the stars from the sparklers fell about them like little comets, as if her parents were floating in the sky.

It didn't make sense to Morley.

How could they dance like that? Didn't they realize how upset they were? Didn't they know about the divorce?

Morley fell asleep in the chair she was kneeling on. The chair by the window. Curled up with her little stuffed hippo. Her popo she called it.

She woke a few hours later to see her mother and father standing in the doorway staring at her. She pretended she was still asleep when her father picked her up and carried her to her bed. He laid her down and her mother tucked the blankets around her and kissed her on the forehead. She pretended she was asleep the whole time.

She always thinks of that night whenever she sees fireworks. The flares, the flashes, all the floating bits, Bing Crosby, and her mother and father dancing on the lawn.

"How could I forget *that*?" said Dave.

She never had. Forgotten it, I mean. Of all the things that her parents tried to teach her, all the little lectures, all the talkings to, all the summer trips and all the dinners, nothing had coloured her life like that moment.

It was the star-showered solidity of them. The rock-solid certainty. They were dancing before she came, and they would be dancing when she left. She was just passing through their lives. But they would always be in hers.

They were the beginning and the end of time.

They were home now.

She and Dave.

"I would never forget that," said Dave—meaning the story of her mom and dad dancing in the yard. He reached into his pocket and pulled out two sparklers.

"Where did you get those?" said Morley, laughing like a younger version of herself.

"Back there," said Dave, nodding up the street. "At the party. When I talked to the father."

And he said, "Wait here." And he ran inside and got a match. He lit one, and then he lit the second one with the tip of the first. When the second one flared, he gave it to Morley, and then he held out his arms. "May I have this dance?"

And so *they* danced, on *their* lawn, and while they danced he hummed "I've Got a Pocketful of Dreams," quietly and endearingly off-key.

BOY WANTED

It took a long time.

Three months in all.

A lot of people would have given up.

Most of them, probably.

Well, the fact is, most people wouldn't have started. Louis, for instance. *Louis* certainly wouldn't have started.

"It's crazy," said Louis. "Why don't you just *offer* him the job? If you want him to work here so much, why don't you make him an offer?"

"Because," said Mr. Harmon, "that's not how things are done. It's *important,* where work is involved, for a person to *apply* for a job. Better for him if it goes that way."

And so, every morning, just before the boy walked by the store on his way to school, Mr. Harmon slipped the sign into his grocery store window.

BOY WANTED.

As soon as the boy passed by, Mr. Harmon took the sign down.

He didn't want any other applicants.

"Why would you want such a *clueless* boy?" said Louis.

"He's not clueless," said Mr. Harmon. "He has seen the sign. He's *thinking* about it. He is building his courage. It's not an easy thing to do, to apply for a job."

Mr. Harmon, wise in the ways of boys, was wiser than most in the way of *this* boy.

But he couldn't be certain.

So when the boy finally did come in one day after school, wearing a white shirt, one of his father's ties, and a pair of dress shoes, and said, "Mr. Harmon? I saw the sign in the window. I'd like to apply for the job," Mr. Harmon almost hugged him.

But he didn't. Instead, he stood there beside the pomegranates, which he'd been stacking into a pyramid, and he said, "Do you have a résumé?"

Of course the boy had a résumé. Typed. It was five pages long.

It was Sam's first year in high school. And it was not going well. He'd headed off in September feeling like he was finally a big guy. He'd found out soon enough that he wasn't a big guy at all. He'd been a big guy in his *old* school. Now he'd returned to the underclass. A minor niner. He felt off balance, unsure and awkward.

And if *that* wasn't enough, something was wrong with his voice. At the most inopportune moments it would go crackly. And there were spots on his face, as if his body, which he'd never even *noticed* before, had suddenly turned against him.

One day at lunch a kid in grade ten knocked into him on purpose and his books went flying down the hall.

This wasn't the way he had imagined high school at all.

Mr. Harmon waited a week before he called him in for an interview.

"I will never understand you," said Louis. "Never. He applied. What are you waiting for? Give him the job already."

Eventually, he did. Four days a week, after school. All day Saturday.

Sam set off to work the same way he set off to school—with great hope. And just as at school, hope abandoned him almost from the start.

Let's begin with the uniform: beige pants, a white shirt, and a green apron.

"I look like a lime popsicle," he said to his best friend, Murphy—his gangly beige legs sticking out the bottom of the apron like little wooden sticks.

On the first day Mr. Harmon put him in charge of fruit. He had to sweep the section. He had to take the garbage outside. He had to restock, getting stuff from Estelle in the back. And he had to keep an ear open for Louis on cash, calling for a carry out. If he saw there was a lineup, he was supposed to help bag.

It sounded easy enough. But there was no training. And, truth be told, it wasn't *nearly* as easy as it sounded. It wasn't easy at all.

To make things worse, every time he turned around, there was Mr. Harmon—hovering, eager to point out his mistakes.

"No, no, no," said Mr. Harmon, nudging him aside as he bagged an order.

"You keep one hand *in* the bag so that you can set everything down carefully." Mr. Harmon was pulling things out of the bag that Sam had already carefully placed in there.

"These figs are going to get crushed," said Mr. Harmon. "Put delicate things in their own little bags. It stops them from falling to the bottom."

It wasn't only Mr. Harmon chipping away at his confidence. Customers kept asking him for things he'd never even *heard* of. Did they have pimentón? Where was the rambutan?

"I'll have to ask," he kept saying. "I'll have to ask."

He felt like an imposter. He kept thinking, *What am I doing here?*

The worst, however, was when Louis went on break, and Sam had to fill in on cash. Making change.

"Don't try to do the math in your head," said Mr. Harmon.

Mr. Harmon was standing beside him watching.

"How much was the bill?"

"Sixteen dollars and thirty-six cents, Mr. Harmon."

"And he gave you?"

"A twenty-dollar bill, Mr. Harmon."

"Don't subtract from the twenty. Count up," said Mr. Harmon. "You begin with the $16 and the 36 cents. Okay? $16.36 plus one-two-three-four pennies makes 37, 38, 39, 40. $16.40." Mr. Harmon smiled. "Then add a dime. $16.50." Mr. Harmon was pulling the coins out of the cash and handing them to Sam. "Now two quarters, $17. A loonie, $18. And a toonie, $20. See. You don't *have* to do any math."

Sam stared at him dumbly.

"You'll get it," said Mr. Harmon.

But he didn't. Not at all. Just like at school, he felt as if he was always a step behind. He felt clumsy. He felt he was always missing the point.

"I know what you're thinking," said Mr. Harmon.

He'd found Sam gazing dreamily across the store.

"Everything in here is alive."

Sam frowned.

Mr. Harmon leaned closer. "In a butcher store," whispered Mr. Harmon, "everything is dead!"

Mr. Harmon was holding a carrot.

Mr. Harmon said, "You could take the top of this carrot and put it in water and it will grow!"

Sam said, "Actually, Mr. Harmon, I was thinking about lunch."

Specifically, he was thinking about whether he should eat the ham sandwich his mother had packed him or go next door and get a burrito.

"Ah," said Mr. Harmon. "Lunch."

One afternoon, during his first week, Sam cashed out an older woman with an armful of fresh-cut flowers.

When she left, Mr. Harmon, who'd been standing by the cash watching, whispered, "You're thinking, *A waste of money,* right?"

Sam nodded. "That's exactly what I was thinking."

"And you are absolutely correct!" said Mr. Harmon. "A *total* waste of money." Then he turned and walked toward the back of the store. But he stopped halfway and came back and whispered, "Of course, that's the point."

Leaving Sam at the cash, scratching his head.

Even alone in his section he felt anxious.

Watering. Straightening. Fluffing.

"Make it beautiful," said Mr. Harmon on his first day.

To make it beautiful meant to stack the boxes of berries perfectly straight. To lay the bunches of grapes one beside the other. To wrap the apples, and the oranges, and the lemons in tissue and pile them in pyramids.

"Like in a picture book," said Mr. Harmon. "I want my store to look like a picture book."

On this day, he was working on pineapples when Mr. Harmon appeared beside him.

It was his third week. And he thought he was finally getting it.

"No. No. No," said Mr. Harmon. "Not like *that.* Rotate the pile as you build it. Move the ripe ones to the front, and put the hard ones on the bottom." Mr. Harmon nudged him aside and started fussing with the fruit. "No empty spaces. Every pyramid full, square, and straight."

Mr. Harmon stood back and smiled at the pineapples. He was proud of himself. But not only because of what he'd just done. Mr. Harmon was thinking that Sam was working out even better than he'd hoped.

Sam was thinking, *This is my third week and I can't even stack fruit.*

The next morning Sam was taking the garbage out when a group of his friends lurched past the store eating takeout. They didn't see him standing in the alley watching them bumping along. But Mr. Harmon did. And he saw the wistful look that crossed Sam's face.

At lunch Mr. Harmon wandered into his section and beckoned. Sam followed him to the little kitchen at the back of the store. Mr. Harmon nodded at a milk crate opposite the stove. Sam sat down. Sam was thinking, *I am about to get fired.*

But it wasn't *his* last supper. It was *their* first lunch. The beginning of their understanding. The beginning of their ritual.

Every day from that day on, Mr. Harmon took Sam into the kitchen at the back, and Sam would watch Mr. Harmon cook. Well … listen more than watch—because while he cooked, Mr. Harmon talked.

On this day, Mr. Harmon was holding a black knife over a ripe tomato.

"When you cut a tomato," he was saying, "you must always use a sharp knife. A dull knife will crush the flesh."

Then he said, "I used to be a barber." This is the way he talked, seasoning his conversation with a sequence of non sequiturs.

"I had my own barbershop," said Mr. Harmon. "Customers who came every week. Fancy businessmen. Big tippers."

He lay the blade of the knife against the skin of the tomato and looked at Sam. "I shaved them. Cleaned their necks."

He pushed the knife forward and then pulled it back toward him. The tomato fell into two perfect halves, seeds and juice leaking onto the wooden cutting board. Mr. Harmon brought one half of the tomato to his nose, inhaled deeply, and smiled.

He was easily distracted.

Sam said, "What happened to the barbershop, Mr. Harmon?"

Mr. Harmon was crinkling salt between his fingers.

"Flaked salt," said Mr. Harmon. "It's from the sea. See how soft the flakes are?"

Sam nodded. "But the *barbershop,* Mr. Harmon?"

Mr. Harmon said, "The Beatles came."

Sam said, "They came to your barbershop?"

Mr. Harmon shook his head.

Mr. Harmon said, "Just, they came. No one wanted haircuts anymore."

Mr. Harmon picked up a second tomato.

Sam said, "What did you do, Mr. Harmon?"

Mr. Harmon said, "I closed the barbershop and got a job in a factory."

He had four tomatoes cut in half now. He poured a little olive oil on each one. Some salt, some pepper. Then he put them on a stained baking sheet and into the spattered black oven.

"Three hundred degrees," said Mr. Harmon.

Sam looked at his watch.

Mr. Harmon was down on his knees, staring into the oven.

Mr. Harmon said, "After three hours they'll look like shrunken heads. And they'll taste like the *essence* of tomato."

But Sam didn't hear that part. It was break time. Sam had gone to relieve Louis.

Mr. Harmon didn't like the factory. He stayed for a year. He took a pay cut to work in his cousin's grocery store. After five years he bought the store.

It was a regular little store until the moment of the arugula.

"This was twenty years ago," said Mr. Harmon to Sam during one of their lunches.

A customer had come back from New York City, bursting with excitement.

"A salad," she said. "A salad with a spicy green leaf. A leaf that tastes like pepper. *Fresh* pepper."

"Arugula," said Mr. Harmon, as if this was something everyone knew. But no one did. You couldn't buy arugula back then.

"Italians knew it," said Mr. Harmon.

Mr. Harmon's Italian neighbour grew arugula in his backyard.

"So does *my* neighbour," said Sam. "Mr. Conte gives us arugula all the time."

"So I went to my neighbour," said Mr. Harmon, "and I said, 'Let me have some arugula.'"

Mr. Harmon sold everything he'd been given the next day, before lunch. Five bunches at ninety-nine cents a bunch.

That night he went back and cleaned out his neighbour's garden.

For two years he was the only grocer in the city who sold arugula. All the chefs used to come to his store.

"That's how I got my start," he said. "Arugula."

He was the first with arugula and the first with olive oil. He had olive oil back when everyone thought it was bad for you.

"They thought it would give them a heart attack," said Mr. Harmon. "Buying olive oil was like committing a sin."

There was one lady who bought it.

"I thought she was so smart," said Mr. Harmon.

"I asked her what she did with it."

She said, "Mr. Harmon, it makes my hair so shiny."

"I said, 'Try it on the arugula.' You know what she said? She said, 'Arugula? What's that?'"

Slowly the little store, like all little stores, became a reflection of its owner. Slowly, Mr. Harmon's love of food and his sense of order became apparent in the aisles.

Everything was prepped in the back by Estelle, so everything out front looked perfect. There were cauliflowers so pretty you could use them as centrepieces. There were regular beets, and golden beets, and striped beets and baby beets. There were heirloom carrots and twenty-eight varieties of tomatoes.

And pacing up and down the aisles in the middle of it all, like an orchestra conductor, was Mr. Harmon.

Under the old man's tutelage, Sam finally found something he was good at.

Facing the tomatoes.

It meant organizing the cans of tomatoes perfectly. The cans had to be lined up to the front of the shelf, labels facing out, no spaces. Sam loved the primary colours of the labels—the bright yellow and red cans beside the bright green ones. San Marzano tomatoes from Italy.

"The greatest tomato in the world," said Mr. Harmon. "You know why?"

"The water?" said Sam.

"Yes," said Mr. Harmon. "And ..."

"The climate," said Sam.

"That too," said Mr. Harmon.

"What else?" said Sam.

"The volcano," said Mr. Harmon. "The mountain of Vesuvius. The volcano has conferred fertility on the land. You are eating fire. There is a bit of ash in each one."

Tomatoes from Naples. Figs from Argentina. Grapes from Chile.

Sam was learning geography in the best way possible. With his stomach instead of his brain.

The first time Mr. Harmon cooked pasta at lunch was the first time Sam ate it without meat sauce. Mr. Harmon served it with olive oil and garlic and lemon.

"This is so good," said Sam, sopping up the olive oil with a crusty piece of baguette. Crusty baguette that tasted of fire, black on the bottom, brown on the top, soft and airy in the middle. The crust so hard it hurt his mouth.

"It tastes like burnt caramel," said Sam. "Except *sour*."

"Because it's made from sour*dough*," said Mr. Harmon, reaching for the salt.

Mr. Harmon showed Sam how you could tell by the bottom if the bread had been made by fire or by factory.

"If it has tiny circles on the bottom, it means it rode a conveyor through a factory oven."

He taught Sam how to dip the bread in olive oil instead of using butter. Sprinkling some of the flaky salt on the oil first.

Sam said, "You love salt, Mr. Harmon."

Mr. Harmon smiled.

Mr. Harmon said, "Flaked *sea* salt. From *England*."

After lunch Sam stood in front of the shelves of pasta and stared.

Pasta di semola di grano duro. Brown paper bags with cellophane windows: capellini, bucatini, spaghettini, linguine. And on a shelf of honour, all by itself, farfalle. Pastas shaped like bow ties, each one dyed with squid ink and beet water. Red-and-black-striped bow ties. So perfect you could wear them. They made him smile.

Now he had a favourite job *and* a favourite section.

One day Mr. Harmon said, "You've been here three months. You qualify for a professional discount. Twenty percent."

That night Sam took home a bag of pasta and a box of sea salt.

He finally felt like he belonged.

Not long after that, Mr. Harmon made Sam his first coffee.

A cappuccino.

Mr. Harmon made one for himself every morning. This morning he put one down beside Sam. He had sprinkled sugar on the surface of the foamy milk. Drinking the coffee through the sugar-foam made it taste like the bread. Burnt caramel.

"I like it, Mr. Harmon."

He felt grown up.

"You like this too," said Mr. Harmon. The two of them were sitting on their milk crates in the little kitchen at the back, a plate of greens covered with ribbons of salty Parmesan on their laps. Mr. Harmon was holding a bottle over the cheese.

"Balsamic," said Mr. Harmon. "From …?"

"Modena," said Sam. "Eighteen years old. Thick, like syrup."

Mr. Harmon smiled.

"And?" said Mr. Harmon.

"You can pour it on your vegetables," said Sam.

"Drizzle," said Mr. Harmon. "You can *drizzle* it on your vegetables."

Mr. Harmon held a wedge of the cheese in the air.

Sam said, "The whole milk from the morning is mixed with the skimmed milk from the night before."

"The *naturally* skimmed milk," said Mr. Harmon. "And aged?"

"For two years," said Sam.

"We want to educate people," said Mr. Harmon.

But it was Sam's education he was most concerned with.

"Fresh herbs," Mr. Harmon said, waving a sprig of thyme in the air.

"Fresh herbs breathe life into everything," said Sam. "Add them to cheese, you have a spread. Add them to stock, you have a soup. Add them to greens, and you have a salad. It's like magic."

"Fresh spinach." There was no stopping Mr. Harmon once he got going like this.

"Speak firmly and it wilts."

Mr. Harmon threw handfuls of fresh spinach into nearly everything he cooked: soups, omelettes, sandwiches. It didn't matter.

A piece of grilled fish on a bed of wilted spinach. Easy. Nutritious. Delicious.

"And no planning required," said Mr. Harmon.

Potatoes!

What can a potato *not* do? Fry it. Mash it. Roast it.

Shred it into soup and it tastes like cream.

"The chameleon of vegetables," said Mr. Harmon.

Sam's friends came and visited him at the store.

He was embarrassed that they saw him, in the too-large apron, looking like a popsicle.

But what they saw was that he had a job.

"How much do you make?" they asked.

"Minimum," he said. "Plus tips."

"My parents won't let me get a job," said Aiden. "How much is minimum, anyway?"

Jonathan bought a juice.

Louis said, "I'm going on break."

Sam had to cash them out. "$1.27," he said. "One, two, three cents makes thirty, two dimes to fifty, two quarters to a toonie."

They looked at him with awe.

"Did you do that in your head?" said Jonathan.

One day, when Sam and Mr. Harmon were eating their lunch, Sam said, "Mr. Harmon, working in your grocery store is like living in a cookbook."

"I like that," said Mr. Harmon. "Louis, did you hear what the boy said?"

He was sautéing rapini in olive oil.

"Someone bring me garlic," he called.

This was the moment he'd been waiting for.

The next day, Mr. Harmon said, "I'm going to the doctor tomorrow."

He was holding out a key.

"I want you to open," he said

There are moments in every life when things change ... forever.

When boy meets girl. Or girl meets boy. And there is a rustle somewhere far away. The sound of a page turning, of the cards being reshuffled, of a great flock of birds fluttering into the sky.

A coming together.

Or maybe it's a coming apart. Not a hello at all, but a goodbye. And the birds don't flutter, they wheel into the sky, twisting and turning so that you never see them again.

Or maybe you're working in a grocery store. Maybe you're a boy working in a grocery store and the owner gives you the key to the store and tells you he wants you to open in the morning.

Sam woke at six, an hour earlier than he had to. He tiptoed downstairs and sat at the kitchen table by himself, eating a bowl of Rice Krispies.

As he was leaving, his mother came down in her pyjamas.

"Good luck," she said.

He got to the store forty-five minutes early. He slipped the key in the door and ran to the alarm. He punched in the numbers that Mr. Harmon had written on the small piece of yellow paper.

He held his breath until the flashing red light turned to a steady green. And then he exhaled and went about his business. He turned on the lights. He uncovered the vegetables. He fetched the float from under the potatoes in the walk-in cooler. He put out the berries and other fruit. He set the sandwich board on the sidewalk.

And then, everything done, he made a coffee the way Mr. Harmon had taught him, frothing the milk in the stainless-steel steamer.

Finally, he opened the door and took the coffee over to the cash register and sat on the stool and waited.

He knew the day was going to be crazy until Mr. Harmon got there. He also knew he could handle it.

It was a lovely feeling—sitting in the quiet by himself.

It was a feeling he'd never had before. Like being onstage before a play. Or on a sailboat waiting for the wind.

A feeling of being grown up.

As it happened, the first customer was a young man. Older than Sam. But still, young. A university student.

The young man wandered around and then brought his basket to the counter, staring at his stuff tentatively.

"Cooking supper for a girl," he said.

Sam looked at the order and then up at the university boy.

"It's her birthday," said the boy.

Sam nodded. Then he pointed at the box of spaghetti and said, "May I ... make a recommendation?"

Sam walked around from the cash and over to the pasta section. He came back with a brown paper bag of the bow-tie farfalle and a little jar of homemade pesto.

He said, "I think this will make a bigger impression."

Then he said, "One more?"

The university boy nodded.

Sam picked up the iceberg lettuce and came back with a bunch of arugula and a small piece of Parmigiano-Reggiano.

He said, "Do you have a vegetable peeler?"

The university boy nodded.

Sam said, "Use it to peel the cheese. Let the pieces lie on top of the arugula like ribbons. Then drizzle it with some balsamic."

The university boy said, "Balsamic?"

"From Modena," said Sam, reaching for his coffee.

He was beaming.

If there'd been a thought bubble hanging over his head, it would have said, *This. Is. Awesome.*

Just as Sam was handing the young man the bottle of balsamic, Mr. Harmon arrived outside the store. He brought his hand up to shade his eyes, trying to identify the bottle through the window. He couldn't tell. Olive oil, maybe.

Balsamic? A slow smile lit his face as he watched Sam place one hand into a brown paper bag and lower the bottle in with the other.

Hiring is a tricky business. It's hard to get it right. But Mr. Harmon had known this one was going to work from the start. There was something special about the boy. He had an openness, a softness, an innocence. He wouldn't always work in a grocery store. Mr. Harmon had no illusions about that. But the things he was teaching him—to have pride, and to take care, especially with the small things—he would remember them all. And he would remember his first coffee, and how to slow-roast tomatoes, and the secrets of pasta. A boy could carry worse things with him as he began the long journey into manhood.

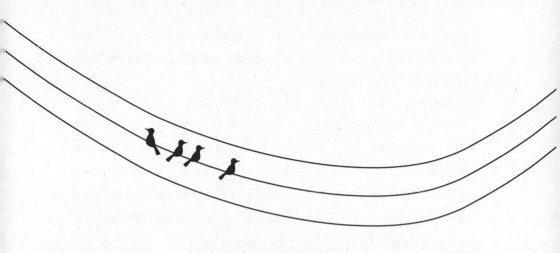

JIM AND MOLLY

On New Year's Day, Dave's neighbour, Jim Scoffield, called his mother in Nova Scotia. The conversation was brief—Jim's mother is anxious on long-distance calls. She grew up when long-distance was an extravagance. She still watches the clock when she's talking to someone from away.

So, as usual, when Jim called her, they talked just long enough for Irene to give him an update on her sciatica and to report on the price of bananas at the Lawrencetown grocery. Pretty soon after that, it was time to say goodbye, and Jim and Irene slipped into the same exchange they've had every New Year's since Jim was in his twenties.

"Well. Anyway. Happy New Year," said Jim.

"It will only be happy for me," said Jim's mother, "if you find yourself a wife and settle down."

Now, Jim is what people used to call "a confirmed bachelor." It's a designation, and a life, with which Jim is entirely comfortable. He's had various relationships over the years, but he's never met anyone who could convince him that he'd be any good at marriage.

Marriage, Jim suspects, is something that is not in his genes.

Jim grew up an only child. The only child of a single mom. He lived alone with Irene in the Annapolis Valley, South Mountain.

When Jim was small Irene told him that his father had died from a wound he received in the war. She said he died shortly after Jim was born.

Discretion was not a skill possessed by many of Jim's extended family. Jim learned the truth from his uncle during a Thanksgiving dinner. It was the Thanksgiving Jim turned nine.

One night, when Jim was only a few months old, his father had, apparently, sat up in bed and announced matter-of-factly that marriage wasn't at all what he'd imagined it to be. Before Irene could wipe the sleep from her eyes, he had packed a small bag and was out the door. He never returned.

Despite her insistence that Jim should be married, Irene never remarried herself. "I've had my kick at the can, thank you very much" was all she said when the topic came up.

But it wasn't his parents' failed marriage that convinced Jim to avoid one of his own. It was his grandparents' reputedly happy marriage that really put him off.

Married for over fifty years in the end, Lloyd and Edna Hickocks ran their marriage like an ongoing siege. The "happy" part of Lloyd and Edna's happy marriage came from the occasional victories they scored in the war of their lives; the happy part was the small acts of torture they inflicted on each other.

Every Sunday night, for example, Edna produced the only dessert of the week—a warm pineapple upside-down cake. She made pineapple upside-down cake because Lloyd had once said he hated it.

In the summer, after everyone else had eaten their dessert, Lloyd would take himself down to Miller's general store and buy an Oh Henry! bar as consolation. In the winter, he would remain indoors and wallow in self-pity.

But Lloyd never wallowed for long. Because at precisely eight p.m. each evening, just as Edna had finished the dishes, just as Edna was sitting down to relax for the night, Lloyd would produce his bagpipes and serenade her for half an hour.

"Serenade" was not a word that Edna would have used to describe it. Edna said the sound of Lloyd playing the bagpipes was like having an ice pick driven into her ears.

As Jim got older, he grew to admire his grandparents' combative creativity. But he knew that *he* didn't have the fortitude to engage in that kind of marital bliss. So Jim is content, quite happy in fact, to find himself on the far side of fifty and living alone. Well, that's not entirely true. Jim doesn't live alone. He lives with Molly. Molly is Jim's twenty-year-old cat.

Now most people who meet Jim wouldn't peg him as a cat man, and he isn't. In fact, Jim never had any intention of having pets. But one afternoon he went out to the garage to find his stepladder, and while he was rummaging around back there he heard a pathetic mew from the alley. He went out to investigate, and there was Molly, perched on top of a garbage can—tiny, dirty, thin, and sad. When she saw Jim, she began to mew with such intensity that Jim did something completely out of character: he picked her up.

He took her inside and gave her some canned tuna and a bowl of water. After a few phone calls and visits to the neighbours, Jim printed handbills and tacked them on telephone poles and at local businesses around the neighbourhood. He called the Humane Society.

No one came forward to claim Molly.

In the end, Jim felt this was for the best. During the short while they'd been together, Molly had made herself thoroughly at home. Despite her forwardness in the alley, she turned out to be more or less self-sufficient. She expected her food dish to be full and her litter box empty, but other than that she seemed to expect nothing from Jim. When she was feeling particularly friendly, she might sit next to him on the couch and allow herself to be petted. Sometimes, especially if the house was cold, she would sleep at the foot of Jim's bed. But most of the time she ignored him. Or at least gave the impression that she was *tolerating* his presence, in *her* house.

That was twenty years ago, so it shouldn't have been such a surprise at their last checkup, just before Christmas, when the vet announced that Molly was failing.

"Her thyroid," said the vet, "is underactive. She'll need medication. Every day."

And then he added, "Her kidney function is down, too."

Jim came home from the vet with a bottle of pills and a sense of foreboding. He set her little cage on the kitchen floor and opened the door. Molly stayed put.

Jim got down on his hands and knees and peered into the carrier. Molly was lying at the back of the dark box.

"Why didn't you tell me you were sick?" said Jim.

He stuck a little butter on the end of his finger and wiggled it in front of the door of the cage. Molly stood unsteadily and licked the butter. When she finished they both curled up on the sofa and took a nap.

Jim gave Molly her first pill that evening. It was a battle of heroic proportions. The only instructions the vet had given Jim were to put the pill at the back of the cat's tongue. He didn't mention how you were supposed to get yourself to the back of a cat's tongue, especially an angry cat. By the time Jim managed to get the pill into Molly, his hands were covered in tiny bite marks. He looked as if he'd been stapled to something.

At two pills a day, he'd be shredded by the weekend.

By the third day, however, Jim had figured out how to get the tiny pill, thoroughly engulfed in a glob of butter, down Molly's throat. "And I don't care what it does to your cholesterol levels," Jim told her.

By the fifth day, his shirtsleeves were stained with butter and his arms with scratches. And an unsettling thought had dawned on Jim. He had booked a flight home to visit his mother. He was leaving in less than a week.

Whenever he was away, Jim would get Dave's kids, Stephanie or Sam—or sometimes Kenny Wong—to take care of Molly. But he didn't feel right subjecting them to the new routine. He needed to find someone who could wrestle a sick cat.

He got Gwen's name from the vet. Gwen was a part-time veterinarian assistant who did cat-sitting on the side.

"She's great with all animals, but she's passionate about cats," said the receptionist.

Gwen arrived at his door a few evenings later. She came to meet Molly and receive her instructions. She didn't look to Jim like the sort of woman who was passionate about anything. She was wearing a tired wool toque and a dull blue parka with appliquéd penguins marching around the hem.

She appeared to be in her early forties, plump and earnest-looking with a broad forehead and a small mouth. The only remarkable thing about her was her shock of orange hair. As he took Gwen's coat and hat, Jim stared at her hair, wondering if it could possibly be her natural colour.

"So," said Gwen as she kicked off her boots, "what's Molly's routine?"

Jim stared at her blankly. "Routine?"

"Her day," said Gwen impatiently. "What does she like to do?"

"What does she like to do?" Jim realized that he was repeating everything Gwen said.

"She's a cat," said Jim.

As if that explained everything.

It didn't seem to explain everything to Gwen. Gwen was staring at him expectantly.

Jim tried again. "She's a *twenty*-year-old cat. She sleeps. She eats. If I'm lucky, she uses her litter box."

"What about exercise?" said Gwen, undaunted. "What do you do about exercise?"

"Well, I go to the gym," said Jim.

Gwen was glaring at him.

"Okay, fine. I used to," said Jim defensively.

"I was asking about Molly," said Gwen.

"Sometimes," said Jim apologetically, "she goes outside."

Gwen looked horrified. Gwen looked as if Jim had just said that he used the cat for scientific experiments.

"She goes *outside*?" said Gwen. "Don't you know that the average life expectancy of an outdoor cat is two years?"

"She's twenty," said Jim.

Gwen wasn't listening. She was waving her hands about as if she were swatting at flies. "There are predators," she said. "There is disease. Not to mention cars."

Jim took a step backward.

"But she's twenty."

It was all Jim could think of saying. Life expectancy seemed a moot point at this stage.

"She's been very lucky," said Gwen. "She could get hit by a bus tomorrow."

Twenty cat years are about the equivalent of ninety-five human years.

By the time anyone reaches ninety-five, thought Jim, *being run over by a bus might be better than the alternatives.* He glanced at Gwen and decided not to voice the thought. He offered her a chair instead.

"I'd rather meet Molly," said Gwen.

Molly must have sensed that she was wanted. It took Jim half an hour to find her. When he dragged her from under his bed and held her out to Gwen, Molly was covered in dust bunnies.

"Poor baby," cooed Gwen, taking Molly from Jim's arms.

Gwen spent half an hour with Molly that night. She made it abundantly clear that she felt Molly was being taken for granted.

"Understimulated," she said.

At the door, pulling her toque down low over her orange hair, her expression toward Jim softened slightly. "You know, Jim," she said quietly, "cats are people too."

"Well … actually …" Jim began. The softness disappeared from Gwen's face like butter on a cat's tongue.

For the second time, Jim decided not to finish his thought.

Instead, as Gwen headed down the front steps, he said, "Thanks for coming."

Jim got the call at his mother's an hour and a half after he arrived in Nova Scotia. "I thought you'd want an update," said Gwen.

Jim had hardly been away from his house longer than he might be on any average day. It hadn't occurred to him to wonder about Molly.

"She seems relatively perky," said Gwen, "but I think she misses you."

"Oh," said Jim. It was all he could think of saying.

"I do hope that woman is calling from her *own* house," said his mother when he got off the phone ten minutes later. "She's not calling long-distance on *your* phone, is she?"

Gwen called every day Jim was away. At the end of the week Jim knew more about the state of his geriatric cat than he would have if he'd been at home. He knew how much water she'd consumed. He knew if *and* when she'd used the litter box.

He knew how long she'd played with her new fur mouse (not long), and how long she'd been sleeping (hours).

Jim couldn't believe how Gwen went on. But if he were being honest, he'd admit that he was enjoying the calls. After a couple of days, Jim and his mother had reverted to the relationship they'd had when Jim was a teenager—when Irene focused on the myriad ways Jim could improve himself.

"You know what would help you out?" Irene asked three days into his visit. "A nice pair of slacks. I think we should go get you a nice pair of slacks."

Jim responded the same way he always responded to her helpful suggestions—with sulky silence.

That afternoon, Irene plunked a small box on the kitchen table. "I bought you some green tea," she said. "Betty says it helps with weight loss. I imagine you've already tried everything else."

A few days after that, she got to the nitty-gritty.

"You know where you could meet some nice ladies?" she said. "The bingo. I meet the nicest ladies at the bingo."

By contrast, Gwen's suggestions about Molly, and she had more than a few, didn't seem so bad.

"I've taken the liberty of making a few changes," said Gwen cryptically on Jim's last day away. Jim didn't ask her what the changes were.

When Jim got back home, Molly was standing expectantly at the front door. When the cat saw it was *him,* her tail dropped and she turned away, clearly disappointed.

"Hey," said Jim, following the cat down the hallway.

It wasn't that he'd expected a warm welcome. Usually when he came home Jim found Molly curled up on the couch. Usually, if she gave him any response at all, she lifted her head with an air of bored indifference. But she *had* been standing at the door, and it bugged Jim that she'd obviously been expecting someone else.

"Hey," he said again.

In the kitchen, Jim found a two-page typed memo taped to the fridge. Gwen had logged all the medication and food Molly had consumed each day.

She had switched Molly to a more expensive cat food. "The feline geriatric digestive system requires some dietary accommodation," she had written.

She'd brought a sheepskin sleeping mat and introduced organic catnip. Jim had to admit that Molly looked better for all the changes. Her coat had a shine, her fur brighter—so orange, in fact, that it reminded him of Gwen's hair.

It was two nights after Jim got home that Molly had her seizure. Jim had opened a beer and was about to sit down to a bowl of chili when Molly got up suddenly from the sofa, stumbled over to a corner of the living room, and began to pant. Her sides were shuddering, her small mouth was open, and her eyes looked glassy and strange. When Jim put his hand on her back, she growled softly. Jim felt a mix of panic and dread wash over him.

He watched the cat shaking and heaving in the corner for a few more seconds and then dashed to the phone. "Gwen," he said when she answered, "something's wrong with Molly."

By the time Gwen got over to Jim's place, Molly had settled. She was still in the corner, but she was lying down. Her breathing was laboured, but her eyes had cleared. Gwen crouched down and put her hand out.

Before long, Molly was sitting on Gwen's lap. Gwen was stroking her ears and whispering to Molly, their two orange heads close, as if they were sharing a secret. Molly began to purr. Then suddenly, with a flick of her tail, she leapt down and headed into the kitchen to her bowl. Gwen sat alone on the couch, her hands in her lap, looking thoughtful.

"You might want to take her to the vet for another checkup," said Gwen. "But there probably isn't much he can do."

Jim nodded.

"You know," Gwen said kindly, "twenty years is pretty remarkable. She's not going to last forever."

"Yeah," said Jim, "I know."

There was a moment of silence, and then Gwen said, "That sure smells good."

Jim offered her a bowl of chili. It seemed the polite thing to do.

So Gwen and Jim sat at his kitchen table and ate together. After a few mouthfuls, Gwen put her spoon down.

"I think what you just did was terrific," she said.

"What?" said Jim.

"Spending a week with your mother," Gwen replied.

"Oh," said Jim, a little taken aback.

"Looking after cats," said Gwen, "even sick cats, is easy. Looking after parents, that's hard."

They were both quiet for a few minutes, and then the conversation began again. Gwen told Jim about her divorce. And Jim told Gwen about Brenda.

"My neighbour Dave's cousin," he explained. "She drives a taxi in Cape Breton. She hooked up with a mechanic from Sydney last spring, so that was that."

Gwen nodded sympathetically.

"It never would have worked out," Jim added. "She hated cats."

They both looked at each other awkwardly. Then it dawned on Jim that he didn't *know* if Gwen had cats.

"I had two," said Gwen. "But I just have one right now."

"How come you don't have more?" asked Jim.

"Oh," laughed Gwen, "I can't have more than two cats at a time. If I had more than two I'd be one of those crazy cat ladies with bright orange hair, wouldn't I?"

After Gwen left, Molly came up to Jim as he stood at the sink, washing the dishes. She purred around his ankles until he bent down and scratched her behind the ears. She looked … smug. Like a cat that had swallowed a canary.

"You big fake," said Jim.

In the days and weeks that followed Molly's seizure, there seemed to be plenty of reasons for Jim to call Gwen. He called to tell her about Molly's vet appointment, and about how much she enjoyed her new sleeping mat. He called to laugh about his mother's latest advice, and eventually he called to invite her for another bowl of chili.

As the year unfolds, Gwen and Jim will see more of each other. Most of the time they'll hang out at Jim's with Molly. Sometimes they'll leave her sitting in the living-room window while they take an evening stroll through the neighbourhood. Despite all the time they'll spend together, despite his mother's New Year's request, Jim won't be thinking of marriage any time soon. Yet when spring arrives, Jim will realize that he and Molly are approaching the twenty-first anniversary of their meeting in the alley. Twenty-one years with someone is no small accomplishment. Even if that someone *is* a cat.

And one day in May, as the Virginia creeper greens the garage walls along the alley, Jim will find himself thinking that maybe he *is* ready to let another person into his life. He would never admit it to anyone but Gwen, but the thought has occurred to Jim that this is what Molly was trying to tell him. And as he and Molly shed their winter coats and seek out sunbeams in the backyard, Jim will stare at Molly and see, not an old tabby in her last days, but the unpredictability of life itself. You befriend a hungry cat. Who wouldn't do that? And twenty-one years later your life is totally different. Twenty-one years later you find yourself thinking about something you never would have dreamed.

SPRING AT UNIVERSITY

Dave's daughter, Stephanie, spent the first three weeks of spring hovering over her laptop, her heart fluttering, waiting for chilly news.

It came, finally, on a Monday morning. And when it did, it didn't come on her computer. It came the way everything comes these days: by text message. Four short words from her friend Scott.

"O'Neill's grades are posted."

They should have been posted weeks ago.

Steph stared at the text and sighed. It shouldn't have been a big deal. She knew her other marks, A's and B's all of them. And she had never, not once, failed a course.

How bad could it be?

Statistics.

That's how bad it could be.

What had she been thinking?

Well, she knew what she'd been thinking. She'd been thinking that if she wanted to do some sort of post-grad thing, a stats course would look good on her transcript.

What didn't make sense was that she'd opted for the *advanced* class, the section designed for engineers and science majors. What sort of misdirected ambition had led her there?

She glanced at her phone.

She had failed statistics. She was pretty certain of that.

Her little spasm of grad-school hubris had probably ruined her chances for grad-school admission.

She stood up, walked across the kitchen, picked up the kettle, and carried it to the sink.

She should have dropped the course. She should have dropped it after the first class.

The warning signs had been as plain as day. Twelve students in a lecture hall that seated three hundred.

Stephanie told herself that the class was empty because the material was famously complicated. She told herself that she was up to the challenge and that the challenge would be good for her.

She filled the kettle and carried it back to the stove. She opened the cupboard beside the sink and removed a blue and yellow cardboard box the size of a pound of butter. Herbal tea. Harmony Comfort Tension Tamer.

She slammed it down on the counter.

In the initial blush of enthusiasm, she'd found the class challenging and fun. Dispersions and tendencies, regressions and boxplots. Unlike everything else she studied, there were rules. All you had to do was apply the rules.

"Statistics," she told her boyfriend, Tommy, early in the term, "is just like Sudoku. I *like* statistics."

And then. And then.

A week later.

Maybe two.

"This is impossible," she said. "I *hate* statistics."

And then there was Professor O'Neill.

"Loony," said Stephanie. "Certifiably bonkers."

He brought his cat to class.

The cat was a ridiculously overweight Cyprus that Professor O'Neill would lug around under his arm like a textbook. He'd wander into class, drop the cat on an empty desk near the front, and there it would lie, twitching its tail like a metronome.

Then Professor O'Neill would begin erasing the blackboard.

"They all do that," said Tommy. "It's like a warm-up exercise. Think of it as academic calisthenics."

Sure. Except there *was* no blackboard to erase. There was a *smart* board.

"Same thing," said Tommy.

"No," said Stephanie. "Not the same thing. You're not listening to me."

Professor O'Neill didn't go *near* the smart board. Professor O'Neill *hated* the smart board. Professor O'Neill used the blackboard that hovered just behind his lectern, unseen by anyone else but him.

"An *imaginary* blackboard?" said Tommy, perking up.

"Yes," said Stephanie, waving her hand in the air as if she were hailing a cab.

"And after he cleans it, he writes on it."

"With *imaginary* chalk?" asked Tommy, hopefully.

Tommy was leaning forward. He was listening intensely. He'd never shown this much interest in *any* of her courses.

"Sometimes," said Stephanie, nodding, "after he writes something, he erases it and starts again."

"When he makes an imaginary mistake," said Tommy earnestly.

It was all so incredibly weird: the empty lecture hall, the cat, the imaginary blackboard, and, of course, the timetable.

Monday mornings at eight. Fridays at four.

How did you get a schedule like that?

"You pick a fight with the registrar," said Tommy.

"Bingo," said Stephanie.

Professor O'Neill and the university registrar had, famously, been waging a feud since the 1970s.

It began, according to legend, the September Professor O'Neill was accidentally mailed a sticker assigning him the registrar's primo parking spot.

Security was dispatched to Professor O'Neill's office to explain the error, and to tell him that he shouldn't actually park in the registrar's spot. But Prof O'Neill continued to pull into the space every morning. He ignored the tickets and notices that began accumulating on his windshield. In fact he left them there, driving around campus with the flurry of indictments flapping in the wind.

According to the story, the apoplectic registrar took matters into his own hands. He arrived at school before dawn one morning and pulled into the space *before* Professor O'Neill. When the stats prof arrived and saw what had happened, he parked in a visitor's spot, waited until the registrar left for the day, slid his car into the disputed spot, and took the bus home.

Professor O'Neill left his car there and got to and from work by public transportation for seven and a half months—until the dean of science retired, and a sign with the registrar's name went up in the dean's old spot. The registrar had conceded, but he hadn't forgotten.

And that's why he scheduled O'Neill's statistics course for the worst possible times. And why the agoraphobic O'Neill was assigned cavernous lecture halls for his handful of students.

It was also why you had to wait until the end of May to see your marks. It was no accident that Professor O'Neill held on to them until the very last moment. The registrar's office had to go through an annual scramble to get them out.

Professor O'Neill was as dull as a donkey. His classes were torture.

After a month, Stephanie came to her senses and tried to switch out—but by then the other stats course was full. She was stuck.

At the end of the next class, Professor O'Neill motioned her to the front.

"I understand you were trying to get out of my class," said Professor O'Neill.

Stephanie froze. Her heart began to pound.

"I'm allergic to cats," she said.

It was patently untrue.

She was petting the cat as she said it.

Professor O'Neill gave her a venomous look.

The very next class he began calling on her—always, it seemed, with the most difficult questions, chuckling when she got them wrong.

"I hate Professor O'Neill," she said to Tommy.

She wasn't the only one. As the weeks marched on, it became clear that statistics was an ordeal for everyone.

The schedule didn't help.

Nor did the hall, which always seemed mysteriously warmer for statistics than for any other class held there. Suffocating, in fact.

The students all sat rows away from the lectern—in random pairings around the huge room, as if they'd been flicked in place by a fountain pen.

The combination of the heat, the time, and Professor O'Neill's tedious presentation made staying awake impossible.

One day, Scott Abbott fell asleep and dropped his pen. He was sitting on the aisle, so the pen clattered down the stairs toward the lectern, step after echoey step. Professor O'Neill stopped talking. He glared at the pen as it rolled toward him like a windup toy; when it stopped at his feet, he glared up at Scott.

And at that exact moment, with complete silence in the hall and *everyone* staring at him, Scott's head snapped backward and he began snoring loudly.

Scott wasn't the first, or the last, to fall asleep during class. Just the most obvious.

As the term wore on, people began nodding off with regularity. So much so that many began class by setting the alarms on their phones to ring a few minutes before the sched- uled end. By February each class concluded with a symphony of beeps and buzzes.

Stephanie's strategy was to bring a thermos of coffee and a large chocolate bar to every class. She rewarded herself with a piece of chocolate for every fifteen minutes she stayed awake. By reading week, she was the only one who hadn't nodded off.

It was a triumph, albeit a small one, but there wasn't much else to cling to. So she clung to it. The course, which had begun with such lofty aspiration, had turned into a disaster. It seemed as if everything about it was cursed.

One Thursday, for instance, Stephanie finished an assign- ment on frequency distribution. Before she printed it out, she took her laptop to a party so that they could use her playlist. Someone spilled a beer on it, and it was fried. She lost her assignment, not to mention her laptop.

She knew Professor O'Neill wouldn't give her an extension without a thorough grilling, and she wasn't about to tell him about the party, so she redid the assignment from scratch and resigned herself to the inevitable deduction for tardiness.

Then there was the midterm. She slept in. Through three alarms. She ran into the class in her pyjamas, well, her pyjama *pants* and one of Tommy's hoodies, her hair mussed and sticking out in patches as if it were trying to escape her head.

"I used to dream about that," she said later.

As she ran across campus she kept thinking she'd wake up and find herself in bed.

She didn't.

She was crying when she got to the exam room. Professor O'Neill took pity on her and let her in. And somehow, though half the class failed, she passed. Barely. But she passed. After that Professor O'Neill stopped picking on her in class. As the second term began, she actually allowed herself the indulgence of hope. Maybe she would get through statistics after all.

Then came April. The oppression of final exams settled over Stephanie, and indeed over the entire campus, like the Black Death.

This wasn't Stephanie's first April at university. She knew the drill. She'd started rationing money in February. And food. So when classes ended, she had both funds and sustenance. But not a lot of either: Cheerios and peanut butter, tuna fish and crackers—unlike the April before, when she'd survived on Mr. Noodles and the occasional foray to a local box store, where she pushed an empty cart up and down the aisles, assembling meals from the free samples.

It was April again. You could feel desperation everywhere on campus.

Student loans, summer cash, cafeteria cards. All used up. All spent. And, all around, the sourness of looming exams and late papers.

Stephanie wasn't broke, though she might as well have been. Her steady diet of cold tuna and milk wasn't making things easier.

And through all this, she had to prepare for Professor O'Neill's final.

Everyone said that thirty percent of those who took the course failed. *He bell-curves for failure,* they said. Whatever he did, Stephanie needed to be sure she wouldn't have to take it again. Once the exam schedule was posted, she triaged each course. She set some of them aside. Maybe she was sacrificing an A for a B, but it beat having a fail on her transcript. And having to do O'Neill over again.

To make everything worse, statistics was, of course, scheduled for the very last day. The weather turned warm and everyone else was finishing. She kept getting texts. *Come to the beach. Come to the bar. Come play tennis.*

With seven days to go, she mapped out a plan that had her studying ten hours a day.

After a few days she had fallen a day and a half behind.

The Saturday before the exam, she decided to pull an all-nighter and see if she could catch up.

"I'll do your laundry," said Becky.

"I'll bring supper," said Janice.

Janice brought two Red Bulls with supper.

"I don't know," said Stephanie.

She drank one at ten p.m.

"I don't feel anything," she said.

Janice handed her the other.

Tommy came over at two in the morning. Stephanie had moved all the furniture to the centre of her room. She was down on her hands and knees scrubbing the baseboards with a toothbrush.

On Monday, with four days before the exam, she felt as if she was going crazy. She had to get out of her place. She went to the library. There was one empty chair. At a table with six other people. She sat down.

The girl opposite Stephanie was chewing her hair. The boy to her right was biting his nails. The guy at the far end, the guy with the blue hoodie, was highlighting every single line in his textbook with a yellow marker. Every. Single. One.

How could anyone concentrate with that going on?

She got up and left.

She wandered around the campus. There had to be a quiet spot somewhere. She tried the cafeteria, but it was full too. She went to the fitness centre and sat in the gym, in the top row of the bleachers. That worked for an hour, until three boys came in and started shooting baskets. She gave up. On her way home, she wandered into the science building.

She took the elevator up to the top floor and walked down a long corridor, past a number of faculty offices and into a big room, some sort of research greenhouse. She found a desk by a bunch of weird plants and sat down.

She opened her backpack. The first thing she pulled out was a roll of toilet paper. She knew enough to carry a roll with her at this time of year. All the stalls were inevitably empty, the rolls pilfered and taken back to some poverty-wrecked apartment. She set the toilet paper down and pulled out her laptop.

She stayed at the little desk until after ten. And went back to it over the next three days. No one ever asked her who she was or what she was doing there. She was making headway is what she was doing. She had never studied for anything as hard as she was studying for this. As the days passed, she began to feel she *might* pass. She began to feel hopeful.

On Thursday night, the night before the exam, she vowed she wouldn't drink anything to stay awake. Not even coffee. She wanted to be rested. She wanted to make sure she got a good night's sleep.

When Tommy came over around midnight she was still up.

She was sitting at the kitchen table in her pyjamas. Her skin was pale and her eyes were dark.

She had papers and textbooks spread out all around her. There was also a jar of instant coffee. And a spoon.

There were little flecks of coffee dust on her lips.

"I'm almost finished," she said.

"I see that," said Tommy, looking at the almost empty jar. He leaned over and gave her a kiss on the top of her head.

She went to bed at four-twenty. When her alarm went off four hours later she sat bolt upright in bed, her heart pounding. This was it.

Professor O'Neill proctored the exam himself. He brought his cat, of course.

Stephanie sat down at the folding table in the cavernous exam room. She stared at the exam when the student helper placed it on her desk upside down. Three pages, stapled. When

Professor O'Neill said "You can begin," she took a deep breath and turned it over.

The first thing she felt was a flush of panic.

The numbers looked like a maze on the page, the formulas seeming only vaguely familiar, like half-forgotten nursery rhymes from long ago.

Her heart started to pound. She made herself read the whole thing from start to finish. She wrote her name and student number on the top of the exam booklet and began question one.

She had no idea how long she was out, but Professor O'Neill was standing beside her desk, glaring down at her, when she woke. She sat up quickly.

"I was just thinking," she said.

They both looked down at her exam book. There was a big drool across the cover.

Professor O'Neill didn't say anything. He shook his head and walked away.

She still had time to complete the exam, but she finished with a sense of gloom.

Stephanie stood up, walked to the front, and handed in her booklet. She was the last to leave. When she did, Professor O'Neill's cat hissed at her. It felt like an omen.

Her fate was sealed. What had she been thinking? No amount of studying would have gotten her through that course.

And here she was, all these weeks later, sitting in her kitchen, staring at her laptop screen.

She took a sip of her tea, shrugged, and typed in her password.

She sat perfectly motionless, staring at the little wheel as it spun around and around.

All those days and all those nights, all the *work,* all the *angst,* had come down to this.

Her student page snapped up.

English Rhetoric, Public and Community: A

Revolutionary Aesthetics: A–

The Sociology of Gender: B+

Islam and the West: A

And there, at the very bottom …

Introduction to Statistics—Advanced …

She felt like a marathoner staggering over the finish line.

Introduction to Statistics?

C.

She had passed. She would graduate.

But with a completely undistinguished and forgettable grade. Neither a shame nor a triumph. Neither a short story nor a novel. A novella. She had written a novella.

"A waste," she said to herself as she flicked her computer off. "I might as well not have taken it."

What she doesn't know now, of course, and what she will come to know in the fullness of time, is that it did matter. It does matter. And it matters a lot.

These things come up all the time in life. Over and over, we're faced with situations beyond our control. Disasters and frustrations, little and big. The clerk on the phone who won't do our bidding. The car that comes out of nowhere, the slow-motion sound of crumpling metal.

And when they come like that, loud and out of nowhere, it is always our choice how we react. Whether we choose to keep moving, head down, steadfast, and do what has to be done, one foot in front of the other, or whether we choose to disassemble.

Soon enough, Stephanie will forget all the formulas she memorized. She has already forgotten most of them. And all the essays and all the seminars she sweated over. Soon they will be gone, too.

But one thing won't.

It is an hour later. It is noon. Her phone is ringing. It is Tommy.

"I got your text," he said.

"I passed," said Stephanie.

"I knew you would," said Tommy. "I'm proud of you."

That was pretty good.

Not that *he* could say it.

But that *she* could.

It wasn't what she'd learned about statistics that mattered. It was what she had learned about herself.

That night, her last night in that apartment, she had two things left in her pantry.

"I'm down to the least common denominator," she told Tommy on the phone. "A pack of Jell-O and a can of sardines."

"What flavour is the Jell-O?" asked Tommy.

"Berry Blue," said Stephanie.

"Perfect," said Tommy. "I'm coming over."

When Tommy appeared, he pulled a Jell-O mould out of his backpack—who knows where he finds these things.

"I'll make supper," he said.

Stephanie said, "Fine. Thanks. Whatever." She was putting on her jacket, about to lug a load of stuff to the laundromat.

When she came home, Tommy met her at the door.

He led her into the kitchen and pointed proudly at a blue mound.

He said, "Sardines in Jell-O."

She said, "My favourite."

"It's perfect," he said as he picked it up. "The sardines look as if they're swimming in water. Especially when you jiggle them."

Stephanie smiled. She took him by the elbows and spun him around, looked right into his eyes, and said, "Did I tell you I passed statistics?"

Tommy said, "Did I tell you that I knew you would?" And then he reached into his backpack and pulled out a bottle.

"I asked the man at the store what would go well with this," he said. "The man suggested aftershave. I chose this instead."

He set the bottle of wine on the table, and then reached into his backpack again and pulled out a takeout roast chicken.

The night was chilly, but not cold. Not yet summer, but no longer spring.

Tommy poured them each a glass of wine.

They held them up.

"You made it," said Tommy. "You did it."

She smiled. And put her glass down.

All was well.

STAMPS

Choosing a hero is a delicate business—one that shouldn't be undertaken frivolously. For the heroes we choose, whether real or imagined, whether from the world of fact or from the pages of fiction, will determine, to a greater or lesser degree, the things that we do, and if we allow them the privilege, the lives that we lead.

Sam and his friend Murphy, not boys anymore but not yet men either, not even *young* men really, are both of the dangerous age of heroes—old enough to recognize a heroic feat when they see one, and young enough to answer the call of who knows what trumpet should it stir them to action.

They are, this day, sitting at one of the little tables in the corner, by the olives, at the back of Harmon's Fine Foods. It is a Saturday. Almost eleven. Sam has been at the little boutique grocery since seven a.m., stocking shelves and making coffees. He is on break. Murphy, who knows Sam's schedule almost better than Sam knows it himself, has, as is his habit of a Saturday morning, dropped in for a visit. The two boys are drinking espresso that Sam made. Mr. Harmon taught him how. But to the old man's horror, Sam has added milk and caramel sauce, vanilla and salt, chocolate shavings and sugar—and run it all through the blender with ice. He has topped the whole sorry mess with whipped cream and cinnamon.

"An abomination," said the greengrocer, shaking his head. "A befoulment."

"It's a frozen caramel latte, Mr. Harmon!"

"An atrocity!" said Mr. Harmon. "If you can use a straw, it is *not* coffee."

"It is *delicious,* Mr. Harmon. You should let me make *you* one."

"I would rather drink Kool-Aid," said Mr. Harmon.

That was ten minutes ago. Mr. Harmon is downstairs in his basement office now, sitting at his invoice-strewn desk, enjoying *his* habitual mid-morning indulgence—a café correcto—and gossiping with a man from Modena who supplies him with a sticky, private-stock, twenty-five-year-old balsamic.

"What's the matter?" says the man from Modena.

Mr. Harmon is frowning at his little coffee cup. It has just occurred to him that the literal translation for his grappa-laced espresso is *corrected* coffee.

"I think I put in too much grappa," he says. "It's tasting … too sweet this morning."

The man from Modena reaches for the bottle of fragrant brandy and tops up his cup.

"Too much grappa," he says, "is not enough."

Directly above them, at the little table by the cooler with the olives and the feta, the boys are still hunched over their drinks. They are talking about Murphy's new hero.

"I thought Ferrari was a car," says Sam.

"Philipp *von* Ferrary," says Murphy. "With a *y*. We are talking *stamps,* not cars."

The man Murphy was so excited about, born Philipp Ferrari de La Renotière, was recognized around the world, by people who know these things, as the *greatest* stamp collector who has ever lived.

"*Ever,*" says Murphy. "*Ever.* His father was a financier—the Rothschilds' arch-rival. He built the Suez Canal. And then one day he locked himself in one of his huge safes."

"On purpose?" said Sam.

"By accident," said Murphy. "It was an accident. He suffocated in there. He literally drowned in his money."

"And *he's* your new hero?" said Sam.

"Not him," said Murphy. "His son, the stamp collector."

The son, Philipp, inherited his father's fortune and lived all his life in Paris, in the house where he was born—a house so fine that today it is the official residence of the French president. And he used his father's fortune to accumulate the greatest stamp collection—

"Ever," said Murphy again. "Greatest in the *world*."

Philipp dedicated three entire rooms—*large* rooms—in his Paris home to stamps, with shelves crammed full of them all the way to the ceiling. He employed three people—full time—to curate his collection while he travelled the world, buying stamps and paying for them with gold.

Murphy was running his finger around and around the froth clinging to the lip of his empty cup.

"I," said Murphy earnestly, "am going to be the next Ferrary."

Just the week before, he was going to circumnavigate the world on a unicycle.

And here he was, a mere seven days later, rummaging through his backpack, which was slung over the back of the chair.

"The thing about being a stamp collector," said Murphy, turning around again, "is that you need only one thing to get going."

"A rich father?" said Sam.

Murphy pulled a huge magnifying glass out of his pack. A thick disc of gleaming glass with a long gold feather-shaped handle.

"A magnifying glass," said Murphy, "gives a person a certain gravitas."

He put the magnifying glass on the table.

"A person like me," said Murphy, squinting at Sam, "*needs* a certain gravitas in his life."

He had removed his glasses. He was polishing them on his shirt-tail.

Sam picked up the magnifying glass and held it between them, staring at Murphy through the distorting lens.

Then he leaned forward and whispered, very quietly, "Have you ever considered that you might be—completely crazy?"

And *that* is when Mr. Harmon appeared out of the cellar— his red face set off by his white shirt and his forest-green apron. Mr. Harmon was carrying two espresso cups.

"I have to get back to work," said Sam.

But he missed his chance. The moment Sam started to get up, Mr. Harmon waved him back down.

"Sit down," said Mr. Harmon. "I want you boys to try something."

He set the two cups of espresso down in front of them and stood back with his arms awkwardly by his sides.

"Go on," he said. "Go on."

Sam peered at his cup suspiciously.

"Mr. Harmon," said Sam. "Have these got alcohol in them? You know we're too young for alcohol."

Murphy had already chugged his.

"Café correcto," said Murphy. "The grappa is way too sweet, Mr. Harmon. It tastes like Kool-Aid. You should try a frozen caramel latte."

They didn't talk about stamps again until the following weekend.

"I have been busy," said Murphy. "Researching."

He was holding an orange cloth-covered book. *How to Start a Stamp Collection.*

Sam took the book and flipped to the title page. It was published in 1930.

"Your research is a little out of date."

Murphy said, "When I'm studying history, I like to get it from people who were there."

Then he leaned back. "Did it ever occur to you ..." he began.

This was classic Murphy. This was Murphy about to do what Murphy loved doing more than anything in the world. This was Murphy about to *hold forth.*

Sam smiled. *This* is why Sam loved Murphy.

Murphy said, "It's been almost two hundred years since stamps were invented. Two hundred years, and they haven't changed in *any* important way. They're still little pictures you stick on envelopes."

Sam nodded.

Murphy smiled.

"Has it not occurred to you," said Murphy, "that they might be the most perfect invention ever? They got them *perfect* on the first go. How often does that happen?"

He was still going an hour later. They had changed venues but not topics. They'd moved from the grocery store to one of the study rooms at the far end of the library. Murphy was lying across the table on his back; Sam was sitting on the chair.

When finally Murphy paused, presumably to take a breath, Sam said, "You understand this is not normal, right? You understand we're supposed to be out skateboarding or something?"

Sam's comment didn't even slow Murphy down.

Murphy said, "Here's the best part. You know *why* they were invented?"

He didn't want an answer. Or expect one. He was happy just to have the audience.

"Mail delivery used to be collect. You paid when you *got* the letter, not when you *sent* it. So everyone wrote coded messages on their envelopes. And people would look at the envelopes, read the coded message, then refuse to pay.

"They had to figure out a way to get people to pay for delivery in advance. Et voilà. Le stamp. Perfectly brilliant."

"What would be perfectly brilliant right now," said Sam, "would be a chicken burrito."

It was another week before Murphy came up with his plan.

"I've got it," he said.

"I knew you would," said Sam.

The morning bell hadn't yet rung. They were doing laps around the ball field.

"Attics," said Murphy. "Everyone has a shoebox of letters in their attic."

Sam said, "They do?"

Murphy stopped walking. He held his arms out, palms up. This was so elementary.

"People keep old stuff in attics. We get into attics, we are going to find *old* stamps. It's the old ones that are valuable."

Lunchtime, the next day. The school cafeteria. Murphy and Sam are sitting opposite each other across a lunch table.

"I printed business cards," said Murphy.

He slid an official-looking piece of card stock across the table.

Sam picked it up and turned it over.

MURPHY KRUGER, it read. ATTIC INSPECTOR.

Sam said, "First off, no one is going to believe you're an attic inspector."

Murphy said, "Why?"

Sam said, "Well, first, because there is no such thing. And second, even if there was, you're too young, and third, you can't go into someone's attic and pretend to be an inspector. That's false pretenses."

"How about *junk removal*," said Murphy, pulling a second card out of his pocket and sliding *it* across the table.

"That would be theft," said Sam.

"Not if they gave me permission," said Murphy.

"But it's not *junk* you're removing," said Sam. "It would be *unethical* junk removal."

Murphy put the cards away.

He had a new one the next day.

MURPHY KRUGER, PHILATELIST.

"Honesty is *always* the best policy," said Sam.

"I made one for you too," said Murphy.

Sam read his card. PHILATELIST ASSISTANT.

The rarest Canadian stamp in existence was printed in 1868. It's a two-cent stamp that features an image of the queen— Victoria—and it's printed on unusually thick paper. It is called the two-cent large queen on laid paper.

There are only three copies known to exist. Although collectors have long believed there must be others.

"In attics," said Murphy. "They're in attics."

Experts say that whoever finds the next two-cent large queen on laid paper will have made themselves a million dollars.

"One *million* dollars," said Murphy.

Murphy and Sam talked about it incessantly. How should they split the million? What would they do with their share? They decided the right thing would be fifty-fifty with the owner. Then fifty-fifty between themselves.

"You deserve more," said Sam.

"A quarter of a million is enough," said Murphy. "It's not good for you to get too much money too fast. Look what happened to Justin Bieber."

He drew up a contract. They each signed it.

They decided to start the following weekend.

It was Murphy's idea to dress up.

"Shirts and ties," said Murphy. "Clothes make the man."

Sam said, "I don't have a tie."

Murphy said, "Borrow one of your dad's."

So the following Friday, after school, they were standing in Sam's kitchen—each of them wearing a too-large shirt that they'd borrowed from their fathers.

Murphy was holding a briefcase. "Magnifying glass and contracts," he said, tapping it.

Then he turned and headed for the door.

On his way he said, "I thought we should start at your house."

Sam said, "We *are* at my house."

Murphy nodded at Sam's mother. Morley was sitting at the desk by the back door. Murphy said, "We'll be right back."

They went out the side door and headed around to the front.

Murphy said, "We have to be professional."

Then he said, "You ring the bell."

Sam said, "Why me?"

Murphy said, "I'm the philatelist. You're the philatelist's assistant."

They went out again the next Friday. It was this second Friday when Murphy got his first stamp.

They found it in Dorothy Capper's house. Dorothy runs the little bookstore a few doors down from Sam's father's record store.

Dorothy, who lives by herself, was delighted to welcome them into her house and give them the blessing of her attention. They sat at the kitchen table and Murphy explained their proposal. She signed the contract, and then she went out to her garage and returned with a box of letters.

"We must agree on one thing," she said. "You may examine the stamps but you must not read the letters. The letters are private."

Murphy nodded solemnly. Murphy said, "We can assure you that we are not interested in your private affairs."

They took the box into Dorothy's basement and emptied it onto the floor. They made a pile of the envelopes and went through them one by one.

They were almost done when they found the torn fragment of brown paper with the blue stamp.

Or Murphy did.

He stared at it through his magnifying glass for the longest time.

"What is it?" said Sam.

"It is beautiful," said Murphy.

Sam crawled over and sat beside his friend.

"It is a miniature work of art," said Murphy.

"Let me see," said Sam, tugging the magnifying glass away.

He was looking at a fifty-cent Bluenose.

Issued in 1929, the Bluenose stamp has an engraved image of the same schooner that sails across the Canadian dime. The stamp is the rich grey-blue of a faded five-dollar bill. The ship, sailing across the stamp from left to right on a windward tack, its sails full, is heeling ever so slightly.

Murphy said, "If you keep staring, you feel like you could crawl right in."

Sam said, "I have been on that ship. I was on that ship in Halifax."

Not the exact ship. A replica. The *Bluenose II*.

The original, the one on the stamp, was a fishing boat. Sleek, fast, and well sailed, it won the international fishing trophy year after year after year, undefeatable, it seemed, until sailing schooners were replaced by motored ones and she was relegated to freighting bananas around the Caribbean. She sank, off the coast of Haiti, in 1946.

The *Bluenose II*, the one Sam had been on, carries tourists out of Halifax Harbour every summer.

"It is beautiful," said Murphy.

I'm not sure whether Murphy meant the boat or the stamp. Not that it matters. He would be right about both. The boat *is* beautiful. And collectors from around the world say that the Canadian fifty-cent Bluenose stamp is one of the most beautiful stamps ever printed. Anywhere. There is something about the blueness, the lines of the engraving, the lines of the boat. The composition and the scale, the sea and the subject.

A beautiful one, in mint condition, might go for three or four hundred dollars. A soiled one, cancelled and creased like the one on the brown paper the boys were looking at, well, you can get one like that for thirty bucks.

They brought it upstairs to Dorothy.

"I want this one," said Murphy.

He had no idea of its value. There was just something about the way it looked.

"You can have it," said Dorothy.

Sam and Murphy went right to Murphy's house and looked the stamp up on the web.

"I knew it," said Murphy.

It was the first stamp in his collection. He put it in an envelope and put the envelope in his book about stamps. He put the book about stamps on the table by his bed.

On Monday after school Murphy went to the bank and withdrew thirty dollars. He met Sam at Harmon's and gave him $7.50. Then he went to see Dorothy. He had a twenty-dollar bill in his pocket.

When he got to Dorothy's store he walked by it and kept going—around the block to Lawlor's drugstore, where he bought a bar of dark chocolate and a bag of chips.

He ate them both. And then he headed back to Dorothy's.

He hung around the back, looking at magazines, waiting for the store to empty. When it did he went over to Dorothy and pulled out the twenty-dollar bill.

"I owe you fifteen dollars," he said.

Dorothy almost didn't take it.

She almost said, "It's not like I knew it was there or anything."

Then it occurred to her that that might be disrespectful.

Murphy, sensing her hesitation, thought, *Go ahead, insult me.*

It was the briefest moment, but they were both aware of it, so it didn't seem brief. It seemed big. It felt awkward.

Then, awkwardly, Dorothy nodded, and Murphy pulled out the bill and she took it and gave him change.

"Thank you," she said.

They signed a contract that said the stamp belonged to him.

And that was that.

Murphy extended his hand, they shook, and he put the piece of paper they had signed in his briefcase with the magnifying glass.

Out on the street, Murphy felt an unexpected surge of exhilaration. There was something about paying for the stamp that made it more precious.

He couldn't wait to get home to check it.

It was his now.

As he hurried along, it occurred to Murphy that it was probably harder for him to hand over his fifteen dollars to Dorothy than it would have been for Philipp Ferrary to fork over a bar of gold.

Ferrary's fortune had been given to him; Murphy had to earn his money shovelling walks and cutting grass.

He admired the French collector's perseverance, but he was feeling something different. It was a feeling he'd never had before—pride mixed with something else, something intangible.

When he got home, he went up to his bedroom and opened his briefcase on his bed. He put the page that Dorothy had signed carefully on his desk. Then he pulled the stamp out and stared at it.

Ferrary was no longer a hero—he was a brother in arms.

And so Murphy's life as a collector had begun.

He couldn't imagine it then, but over the years his feelings for this stamp will be eclipsed by his feelings for others.

Like all collectors (and artists), Murphy will always be in love with his most recent acquisition. His favourite stamp will almost always be his latest—the one that still evokes the thrill of the hunt.

Eventually, he will put his collection away. But memory is patient.

One evening, years and years from now, Murphy will be looking for something, and there, in a box of books in his attic, he will find his long-forgotten, cloth-covered history of stamps. The book that got him going. As he picks it out of the box, it will all come flooding back: he and Sam, dressed in their fathers' shirts, going through the letters on the basement floor, and how he stood in the little bookstore, praying that Ms. Capper wouldn't take his money. And how good it felt when she did.

And as he remembers all that, he will flip the book open, and there, lying between the pages, he will see the piece of torn brown paper with the little blue square and he will feel the tug that he felt that night in the basement when he first saw it.

It is the tug of beauty. The awareness that there are things in the world that move us. Music and poetry, paint perfectly rendered, a building well conceived, big blue skies and big blue moons, and sometimes, when you are very lucky, things so small and soft you would never imagine: a little glimpse, a little smile, the ever so light touch of a hand on yours, and, yes, a little stamp stuck to a little piece of paper that says, if you just look long enough and hard enough, that it is beautiful enough that you could actually climb right into it.

All the beauty stored there, in the tiny picture of the little blue boat sailing across the deep blue sea.

FOGGY BOTTOM BAY

The vestibule between two cars on a passenger train is one of the few spaces in the world of transportation that has remained virtually unchanged. We have flown to the moon and we can scoot around this old earth on the world wide web, but if we want to walk from the club car to the dining car—if we're lucky enough to find a train that has either of those things these days—we still have to lurch through the same accordion-walled rattletrap that our mothers and fathers passed through all those years ago. And when we do, we'll pass the same Dutch doors, the ones that open on the top so that the attendant can watch the platform as the train pulls in or out of the station.

They are the same doors Dave used to lean out of whenever he could get away with it. The prairie was his favourite place to do this, his head out the window, his mind in the clouds. You weren't *supposed* to, of course. Even back then it was against the rules. But back then conductors and porters weren't as fussed by rules as they are today. Today the lawyers have their hands on the throttle, so Dave, with a wary eye to time's heavy hammer, was trying to be circumspect as the train he was on swayed past the Prescott Golf Club and the adjacent village—a short fifteen minutes, by his reckoning, to the town he was waiting for.

The train wasn't going to stop there, so he knew he'd have to move fast.

"Ten minutes," he said to the empty seat beside him.

He sat for an unbearable seven. With one eye on the fields rolling by his window, and the other on his watch. After seven minutes he could sit no longer. He stood up and swayed to the end of the car. When he got there, he checked to see that no one was looking. The coast was clear, so he opened the vestibule door and stepped out into the rattle.

They were coming up on the edge of town already. And they didn't seem to be slowing. He thought they would slow. He stepped close to the door so that he wouldn't be seen from either the car ahead or the one behind. He reached up and unlatched the top lever. It was exactly the way he remembered it. The door swung open and a gush of cool air rushed in. He stepped back, reached into his coat pocket, and pulled out a manila envelope—the kind you might be handed if you had a job that paid in cash. On the front of it, in a neat blue hand, someone had printed *Jimmy Walker, Foggy Bottom Bay, Newfoundland.*

Dave opened the envelope and looked in.

The train's whistle blew. It startled him and he almost dropped the envelope.

He stuck his head out the door. For a moment he thought he was on the wrong side of the train. For a moment he thought he had remembered it wrong.

And then he saw the red-tiled roof, the grey wood building. The Brockville Station. It was just as he had remembered.

The whistle blew again.

"Okay, Jimmy," he said. "Here goes nothing."

He leaned out, and he shook the envelope empty. Then he let it go. He watched the brown paper rectangle disappear—flying away like litter from a car window.

"See you," said Dave.

Jimmy Walker. Foggy Bottom Bay, Newfoundland.

Dave was still a kid the night he and Jimmy met.

They were *both* still kids.

They had met on that very train. Well, almost that very train. They'd been heading in the opposite direction. They were heading east the night they met. On the Montreal train. Dave had been going home. In Montreal you got the *Ocean Limited*. Left at supper, arrived in Halifax the next night. Twenty-four hours, more or less. Jimmy? Well, whenever they got together and started reminiscing, neither of them could remember where Jimmy was going or what he was up to. No good, probably.

It was a long time ago, of course. Neither of them was married yet. Though Dave *was* already touring. Jimmy was working construction in Toronto. Maybe on the CN Tower, maybe something else. Dave wasn't sure. Something high, anyway.

The point is that they were both young, and they both had money burning holes in their pockets.

The moment they saw each other they knew they were kindred spirits. They could just tell. Two boys from the East Coast. One from Cape Breton, one from Newfoundland. Before they knew it, they were sitting in the dining car together. This was in the days when there still *was* a dining car on the Montreal train. Prime rib and linen tablecloths. Waiters in white jackets. And the two of them sitting there like big shots—clattering by the same towns, the same fields, the same marinas, with the sun going down and the tables cleared and a fresh round in front of them. How often in your life are you aware that you're making a new friend while it's actually happening?

As he closed the window, Dave remembered that long-ago train trip as clearly as if it were yesterday. How perfect it had been, perfect as a moment could be, sitting there with Jimmy.

Now, in those days, when the train got to the Brockville Station it used to stop so that it could be split into two trains. The front half would continue to Montreal. The back would peel off to Ottawa. Somehow Dave and Jimmy, who had both taken this train many times before and should have known better, missed the announcement. And you've got to know, there was more than one.

So when they finally got up and tried to walk back to their seats, they got about four cars along, opened the door, and instead of *their* car, all they could see was a mile of empty track. Their half of the train, the front half, the Montreal half, had left without them.

Neither of them could see any benefit in going to Ottawa. The only thing that seemed to make sense was to get off— there in Brockville—and that's what they did. They got off, and they went into the station.

It was nine o'clock. At night.

The stationmaster told Dave that the next train to Montreal, which was the overnight train, wouldn't be along until four in the morning. He said *he* was going home to bed, but Dave and Jimmy could sleep on the waiting-room benches if they'd like. He would lock them in.

When Dave walked back to Jimmy and tried to explain that to him, Jimmy pointed at the guy *he* was talking to. "This is Roy. We're going to Roy's house."

Roy happened to be at the station buying a ticket for the next day. While Dave was dealing with the stationmaster, Jimmy had made friends with Roy, and Roy had invited them over. "You can watch TV in the basement," he said.

They ended up in the kitchen. Roy's wife fed them chili. They drank beer, ate chili, and talked until just after three, when Roy poured them into a cab.

As they slid through the sleeping town, Jimmy said, "That was just like home. All the parties are in the kitchen in Foggy Bottom. And the best ones are like that one. When some fellow's boat breaks or something and he just shows up."

That sort of thing happened all the time when you were around Jimmy.

You made memories.

As I mentioned, or more to the point, as it was written on the envelope that Dave threw out the window, Jimmy was from Foggy Bottom Bay. Which is to say, Jimmy grew up as a bayman.

His daddy was a bayman too. And his mother. They were baymen all the way down in Jimmy's family, which meant Jimmy grew up loving the grey salt smell of seaweed and the grinding crash of the surf on gravel. That's how he used to describe it to people from away, *the grinding crash of the surf*. Jimmy had a way with words. He would tell you all about the bay, and all about the town, and the meals his mom would feed you if you came home with him. Fish and brewis, moose and brewis, jiggs dinner, and turr.

"Oh," Jimmy would say, "a turr in the oven is such a sweet thing."

Which, of course, is something *only* a bayman could say. Because if you've ever been in a house when there's a turr in the oven, you know it is not a sweet thing at all. It is a gamy thing. Nothing like a turkey. A turr does not fill your house with thoughts of Thanksgiving.

"Well, it fills my *heart* with thanksgiving," Jimmy used to say. "Not to mention my stomach."

Jimmy was a bayman to the core. And though he did move around some, he loved nothing better than to sit down at a table with a Black Horse in his fist and tell stories.

"Now," he would say. "Did they learn you about the margarine war in Upper Canada?"

Jimmy thought of himself as a student of history, but like everything about him, Jimmy's take on history was not from the mainstream.

Jimmy loved his history from the margins.

"The ting is ..." According to Jimmy, anyway.

Well, the thing is that margarine was outlawed across the Dominion of Canada soon after Confederation.

"In 1886," Jimmy would tell you.

Except for a spell during the butter shortage of World War I, you couldn't make or sell margarine in Canada from 1886 until pretty much the 1950s.

"Because they wanted to protect your dairy farmers," Jimmy would say. "But we didn't have no dairy farmers to protect at home. So we didn't have no margarine laws."

And then Jimmy would sit back and tell the story of his two uncles who used to smuggle margarine into Halifax.

Eversweet or Good Luck or whatever the popular brands were back then.

"And when we comes into Confederation, are we going to give up our Eversweet? Not on your life," Jimmy would say. "Not on your life, my son."

So the business of margarine became part of the terms of Confederation.

"It's right there in the Newfoundland Act. Term 46, if you care to check.

"We could make it, but we weren't allowed to sell it to the mainland. And that was some good margarine, my son. It was made of fish oil, that margarine."

Jimmy, like many people who have a thing for history, had a thing for trains, too. It was Jimmy who, long after it had stopped running, hatched the plan for taking another ride on the Newfie Bullet.

The Bullet was the narrow-gauge railway that ran across Newfoundland and was shut down, torn up, and replaced by the hated Roadcruiser.

"Roadcruiser," Jimmy would say, rolling his eyes. "That'd be a bus in English."

Then he'd cock his head, take a pull of his Black Horse, and say, "You know, you can read all about the Bullet in the Bible."

He'd leave that hanging there for as long as he thought he could (Jimmy had excellent timing), and then he'd smile slowly and add, "Yup. Right in the Bible. Right there where it says, *The Lord made all things that creep and crawl.*

"Twenty-seven hours and twenty-three minutes," said Jimmy. "St. John's to Port aux Basques. Averaged twenty miles an hour."

It was Jimmy who discovered that when the Bullet was mothballed they sold the engines, the cars, and even some of the rails to a scattering of South American dictators—in Bolivia, Chile, and Nicaragua. It was Jimmy who organized the trip down there. Although in typical Jimmy style, something happened along the way, and they ended up on a cattle ranch in Argentina and never even *saw* a train. But that's a whole other story.

"Yeah," said Jimmy. "There was a misunderstanding at the border."

Which border was never clear.

Anyway, Foggy Bottom, the bay where Jimmy was born and raised.

If you haven't been there, you've no doubt been to places like it. It is no more than a handful of houses strung along the shore road—the odd lane drifting into the hills on the right, or down to the water on the left, each lane connecting a few homes and then doubling back to the road along the way. There are no sidewalks or numbers on the houses. In the phone book everyone has exactly the same address: Foggy Bottom.

Half the houses are the square, flat-roofed, two-storey cottages you see on postcards; the other half are new bungalows.

When Dave met Jimmy on the train that night, Jimmy had just bought a lot from one of his smuggling uncles. For a dollar.

That's what you'd do in those days. Get a cheap lot from someone in the family and then build your bungalow bit by bit—as you could afford it. Soon as it was finished, you got married. You might have a kid or two before, but you got the bungalow finished before you walked down the aisle. Getting married before the bungalow was built would be a sin.

They were still fishing in the bay when Jimmy was a boy. Everyone worked with the fishery—the men in the boats, and the women and kids in the plants. Anyone who grew up in Foggy Bottom could clean a cod so fast you'd swear the fish had zippers.

So Jimmy built his bungalow, and married Rhonda, and had a couple of kids. Jimmy and his family lived pretty much like his grandfather had lived: they put moose into the freezer, snared rabbits, and went berry picking with the neighbours— bakeapples and partridgeberries. They fished in the summer and cut wood in the winter. You don't need a whole lot more.

And if times were hard, if the fishing was poor or you needed *extra* cash, you could work at one of the American bases.

And then the Americans disappeared. And so did the cod. And soon after that, all the men did, too.

Jimmy went to Toronto and worked construction. He and Dave would collide from time to time.

One night they were sitting outside a little club when Jimmy waved his beer in the direction of the street.

"Reminds me of Newfoundland," said Jimmy.

Dave stared at the stream of cars pelting past them. "The traffic?" he said.

"The roar," said Jimmy. "The roar of traffic. Sounds like the sea."

"Really?" said Dave.

"Well, not as peaceful, for sure," said Jimmy. "But still."

After Toronto, Jimmy headed west. I don't want to say that Dave and Jimmy lost touch, because there is a certain kind of friend with whom you never lose touch. It doesn't matter how long it's been since you last saw them, could be years, you're still in touch—because you're connected by something that is more fundamental than sight, more basic than conversation. But there was a stretch, maybe ten years, when they didn't see each other.

And then one day out of nowhere, they ran into each other at the airport.

"Alberta?" said Dave.

"Just for a year or two," said Jimmy. "I've been working at Fort McNewfoundland."

He was driving a truck in Fort McMurray. If you want to call it a truck. Jimmy's rig was more than two storeys high and weighed a million and a half pounds fully loaded. More like driving a house than a truck.

"Still boggles my mind," said Jimmy. "Every day."

Jimmy worked twenty days on and ten days off. The company flew him home to Newfoundland and back for his time off. He was bused from camp along with everyone else to a private airstrip. You had to wait on the bus until your number was called. Once you heard your number, you'd walk, not run, walk across the tarmac to the plane. There were no assigned seats, and no one wanted to sit in the middle for the eight-hour flight to the Rock. So even though everyone on the bus was an adult, there were rules: no running on the tarmac, no pushing, no shoving.

At first Rhonda would come and pick Jimmy up in St. John's, and they'd drive home to the Bay. But that was crazy—an eight-hour flight across the country and then another five for the drive. Jimmy would be curled up in the backseat fast asleep while Rhonda was blinking away behind the wheel.

So they moved to St. John's.

"It's not so bad," said Jimmy.

But Rhonda was lonely when Jimmy was away. And she wouldn't go down into the basement at night even though that's where the TV was. Said she felt scared down there. It was different in the city than in the Bay. In the Bay she knew the neighbours. They were her friends.

Jimmy put in a security system and that made her feel better.

"I'm only working out West for the money," said Jimmy.

He could make double what he could make at home.

Jimmy tried to stay on Alberta time during his week off. He said it made the transitions easier—living in Newfoundland and Alberta at the same time.

Rhonda would go to bed and Jimmy would stay up, walking around the neighbourhood at midnight, taking the dog down by the water. He'd stop at the Tim's, hook the dog outside, and go in to have tea or a bun. There was a girl there who'd slip him a muffin for the dog.

That's what Dave and Jimmy talked about the last time they met. About the travelling back and forth, and how St. John's was prospering. They also talked about how it was getting harder and harder for Jimmy—to have one foot here and one foot there.

Sometimes, he said, on those long nights he'd head up to Signal Hill for the sunrise.

"It can be awful pretty," said Jimmy. "The sun coming out of the sea. Everything turning orange."

Then Jimmy said, "You know what surprised me?"

Dave shook his head.

Jimmy said, "The northern lights. I thought they'd be some show up there in Fort Mac. But they're better at home. At home they dance around like crazy. Up there they're just streaks in the sky."

That was one of the last things they talked about: the northern lights.

Because then Jimmy died. Two months ago now. Dave didn't even know Jimmy had been sick.

Dave went to the funeral. He'd been to Newfoundland before, but that was the first time he'd been out to the bays.

He arrived in the afternoon and went for a walk all around. There was an iceberg in the harbour. It was the first time he'd seen an iceberg, and it was more beautiful than you could imagine—not only for all the huge angles of it, but for the colour—it was as much blue as white—like a sculpture from a modern museum, just floating there. He walked down to the stone beach and stared until he got cold. The waves on the beach were just as Jimmy had described, the rattle of stone in the water, the grinding surf.

He thought it was going to be unbearably sad. But these things are never as sad as you imagine.

There was a gathering at Jimmy's house the night before. Someone had a guitar, and there was music and stories and, eventually, laughter. He told the story about the night he and Jimmy met and how Jimmy found them a place to go when they were abandoned in the station.

"That was Jimmy," said Jimmy's wife, Rhonda. "Always turning everything into a party."

He got Rhonda to draw him a little map, and the night before he flew home—which he spent in St. John's—he set his alarm for five a.m. and struggled up and went for a walk, headed down Water Street, stopped in at the Tim's on Duckworth and then up to Signal Hill for the sunrise.

He thought it would be a way to get close to Jimmy—to say goodbye—but it all felt a little flat. The neighbourhood was just another neighbourhood. The Tim's was just another Tim's. Without Jimmy's infectious enthusiasm, it turned out to be the saddest part of the trip.

"What about the sunrise?" asked his friend Kenny when he got home and was telling him about it. "Was it all molten and gold and pouring out of the sea the way he said?"

"Yeah, that part was right," said Dave. "It came up slow and beautiful, just the way he described it. It was the most beautiful thing I've ever seen. Or I imagine it was. It was pretty foggy, so I couldn't *actually* see it. But I imagine it was."

It was while Dave was in Foggy Bottom that Jimmy's wife gave him the envelope he would carry on the train. After the service. Everyone got one. Well, not everyone. But Dave saw more than a couple of guys with them. The little manila envelope came with a regular-sized white one—a letter-sized envelope.

"Open the white one first," said Rhonda. Then she said, "But wait till later."

So Dave put both envelopes in his coat pocket, and when he got back to the B and B he sat on his bed and opened the white one as Rhonda had told him. It was from Jimmy. Handwritten instructions.

Take the train to Brockville, it said, *and sprinkle them at the station. That was a sweet night. And I am glad for it. Lucky to have known you. Love you bro.*

So Dave changed his flight. Instead of going right home he went to Montreal and got on the train. And just before Brockville he got up and pretended to walk to the washroom. He looked around, and when he saw no one was watching, he went out into the vestibule and opened the top half of the door and scattered some of Jimmy Walker's ashes out onto the tracks.

"See you, Jimmy," he said.

A true bayman. And like all the baymen before him, blown away by the wind of these so-called modern times. A little bit of him here, and a little bit there. That's how he had lived his life, and that's how he was taking his leave. The rocks and the rails, the sea breeze and the train whistle were all mixed up now. A train clattering along the steel rails like surf on a stone beach, the train whistle blowing in the lonely night like a horn in a fog. Over and over, the foggy days and the long dark nights. Dave shut the door and stood there in the vestibule. He took a deep breath and let it out slowly. That's when it hit him. How much he would miss him.

THE ONE AND ONLY MURPHY KRUGER

The bank branch where Murphy had his account shut its doors. Although it wasn't really his account. It was an account his parents had opened for him when he was born.

When the notice arrived, Murphy withdrew his money—all of it: $74.58. And he and Sam headed off to the bank nearest their school. Murphy was going to open his first *real* account.

The new branch was a bank of the old kind—on a corner, heavy of limestone—built back when money whispered instead of shouted.

"I would like to see the manager," said Murphy.

People who work in banks are taught not to make assumptions. They are told apocryphal stories about clerks who have insulted shabby millionaires. About huge accounts that have walked in, and then, just as quickly, *out* of a branch.

The lady at the desk inspected Murphy. It was *possible* the boy had an inheritance. One could never be certain. She pointed to a couch.

The boys waited for ten minutes for the manager to appear. She was a stylish woman, more pearl than limestone.

"My name is Moira," she said, holding out her hand.

"Murphy Kruger," said Murphy. "Kruger with a *K*."

The manager smiled, but under force of habit, said nothing more. She stood there and waited for Murphy to speak. It was a power technique—you made your visitor speak first.

But the silence was getting uncomfortable.

"How can I help you?" she said at last, a little bewildered that the silence, which always compelled adults to talk, hadn't compelled this odd-looking boy to anything.

Murphy looked around diffidently.

"Perhaps you would like to come to my office?" said the manager, who was both trying to regain control of the situation and avoid the curious eyes of her tellers.

Murphy nodded, followed her, sat down, smiled, and got right to the point. "If I open an account in your branch and do my banking here, will you throw in a safety deposit box?"

The manager blinked.

She'd been trying to size Murphy up, something she was usually good at. She would not be occupying this office had she not a good eye for people. But there was something about this boy she couldn't put her finger on. Something disarming.

He was a little—she will almost say *different* when she tries to describe him to her assistant later in the day, though she will edit herself, consider *odd* instead, before finally settling on … *wonderful*.

"He's quite—wonderful," she will say.

But that will be later.

Murphy was still sitting across from her, and had just asked for a free safety deposit box (something that no one had ever asked for before), and something about him, which the young woman can't put her finger on, was making her want to give it to him.

Murphy was peering at her through his black-framed glasses, his ears and his shirt-tail *both* sticking out.

The manager said, "Why do you need a safety deposit box?"

An obvious stall. And really none of her business.

Murphy took off his glasses and wiped them on his shirt-tail.

"Do I need to tell you that?" he asked. "Are these not private matters?"

The manager blinked again. She *had* lost control. To her credit, it amused rather than upset her.

She shrugged and allowed the smallest of smiles.

"Of course," she said.

Murphy nodded.

The truth is that Murphy was *unsure* why he needed a safety deposit box. The truth is he'd just finished reading a book about an international jewel thief. There was a safety deposit box involved. Murphy wasn't even certain he knew what a safety deposit box was.

"I need a place for my stamp collection," said Murphy. "And certain other valuables."

That he had only one stamp in his collection seemed unnecessary to bring up.

As to the other valuables, they were as follows: a coin from the year he was born, a stone he found on a school trip in the shape of an arrowhead, his first pair of glasses, and a cheque from his grandfather for twenty-five dollars that he didn't want to cash until he knew for certain his grandfather was solvent.

"I don't want him to be sent up river for cheque kiting," he explained when Sam had asked about that.

"Cheque kiting?" said Sam.

"You know," said Murphy, "paper hanging. Playing the float."

He wasn't about to tell the *manager* about his sketchy grand-father, or about his arrowhead, so Murphy came up with the stamp thing and then sat there, like a jewel thief.

And for reasons she didn't fully understand, maybe it was simply that she found Murphy completely charming, the manager asked Murphy for his address and typed it into her computer.

"This is a little out of the ordinary," she said as she fished for something in her drawer.

"I hear that a lot," said Murphy.

The manager found what she was looking for—an index card.

"I need you to sign this," she said.

And she slid the card toward Murphy.

Murphy's heart began to pound.

Suddenly *Murphy* was the one off stride.

Murphy didn't *have* a signature.

An hour later Sam and Murphy were sitting at one of the cast-iron tables at the back of Harmon's Fine Foods—back by the briny tubs of feta and olives, in the grocery store where Sam worked.

They were drinking a coffee concoction that Sam had frapped in the blender and topped with whipped cream and caramel sauce.

Murphy's had the benefit of a tiny shot of grappa that he'd snuck from the bottle in Mr. Harmon's desk drawer.

The boys had been sitting at the table for half an hour. Murphy had not stopped talking.

"I can't believe I let this happen."

To be precise, he meant *not* happen. What he could not believe was that he had arrived at this stage of his life without a signature.

"It is such an oversight," he said.

When the manager had pushed the little index card across her desk and asked him to sign it, Murphy had realized the significance of the moment right away.

She wanted his *official* signature. And he didn't have one. He had only ever printed his name. But he knew he couldn't print it now. And he knew something else. Something earth-shatteringly important. The way he wrote his name on that little white card would stick with him for the rest of his life.

He looked at the manager and then he looked at his watch.

"Oh my goodness," he said. "I have another appointment. I'll come back and sign another day."

"It's not our fault," said Sam to Murphy. "They should have taught us in school."

"Signatures?" said Murphy.

"Cursive," said Sam.

"They *used* to teach it," said Murphy. "But they stopped."

"How come?" said Sam.

"They use it when they're writing about us."

It was the next morning. First period was social studies. Murphy was hanging over his notebook with his tongue poking out the side of his mouth—the picture of concentration. But Murphy wasn't concentrating on social studies. Murphy was writing his name over and over on the back pages of his notebook. At recess Sam and Murphy examined what he'd done.

He had hundreds of versions. He'd tried up-and-down lettering and slanted lettering—both forward and backward. He'd tried versions with his middle name and versions with just his initials. He had a page where all three of his names were joined to make one word and a page where they were broken into three.

He had even played with the spelling.

M-u-r-p-h-e-e.

"It's good," said Sam.

"I think it makes me look like a dog," said Murphy.

They both considered this for a moment.

Sam nodded in agreement.

"It does make you look like a dog."

Right away Murphy shot back, "What kind of dog?"

And that, of course, was the nub of the problem, the whole mess of the matter.

Because Murphy *wasn't* just writing his name. If that was the case he could have put an *X* on that index card and been done with it. It was far more than writing his name.

His signature was a declaration. His opportunity to tell the world who he was.

The problem, of course, was that Murphy had no idea who he was.

The next day they were in the library—in their favourite study room, the one at the far end of the corridor with the window that overlooks the park. They had set up camp.

"Look at this one," said Murphy. "I like the way it goes below the line."

Murphy had accidentally written a version where the tail of the *y* dove down and back like an underwater swimmer and underlined the whole of his first name, before it circled around—bisecting the bottom of the *p* on its way—and then swooped up and looped over the line again to begin the *K*.

"It makes you look like a president," said Sam.

And there they were again, back at the heart of it. *Was* he a president? Or was he a dog?

The problem with the opportunity of choice is that it affords you the opportunity of choosing wrong.

"Then you change it," said Sam, who was lying on his back, on the floor under the table.

"You can't just *change* it," said Murphy, who was lying on the tabletop.

"If you change your signature," explained Murphy, rolling over and peering over the table's edge, "you can be denied the necessities of life. Things like health care, even education."

The back pages of his notebooks were covered with all sorts of attempts—exuberant versions with swooping capitals and curlicue consonants. Modest lowercase versions worthy of a poet.

"Look at this one," said Murphy, sticking his open notebook over the table. "What do you think of this?"

Sam, who was beginning to tire of the exercise, grunted.

"I don't know why this has to be so complicated," he said.

"What if I become famous?" said Murphy, dropping off the table. "What if I have to sign it over and over? What if people collect it?"

"You can never read autographs," said Sam. "If you get famous you can just scribble it. Like that one." He was pointing to a black scribble on the corner of a page.

"That one was if I decided to be a psychopath," said Murphy.

The next afternoon, at the end of last period, Murphy was standing by his desk shoving books into his backpack when Mrs. Bailey, the school secretary, came into their room.

"Mr. Kennedy," she said, "I need you to sign the attendance form."

Murphy stopped what he was doing and stared.

Everything going on around him faded from his awareness—all the kids, all the clatter—until all there was was Mrs. Bailey walking in front of the chalkboard, holding the attendance record in front of her, and Mr. Kennedy picking up his pen. Everything was moving in slow motion, until Mr. Kennedy signed. He wrote with a flourish. Did it take a second? Maybe less. No more. The pen hit the paper, things speeded up—a wave of his arm, and it was done.

Murphy caught up to Sam by his locker.

"Did you see that?" he said. "Did you see that? I hadn't even thought of it. It never occurred to me."

Sam said, "I have no idea what you're talking about."

It wasn't only *what* you wrote, it was *how* you wrote it. It wasn't your official signature unless you could do it at the speed of light.

That night after supper, Murphy asked his mother.

"Do you have an autograph?" he said.

His mother was doing the dishes, but he had a paper, and a pen, and he made her sign—her wet hands dripping.

"Can you sign your name?" he asked his dad a moment later.

Both of his parents went fast. Everyone went fast. And something else. Everyone was messy.

It was far more complicated than Murphy had ever realized. He was never going to figure it out. He would never have a signature.

"I don't understand the big deal," said Sam.

They were walking through the park, not sure where they were actually going, vaguely toward Harmon's, or maybe the arena.

"I want it to be clear," said Murphy. "Yet I want it to have a certain …" His voice trailed off.

"A certain what?" said Sam, who was becoming impatient with the way Murphy wasn't finishing his thoughts.

"A certain *mess*," said Murphy. "Plus I have to be able to do it fast, *and* I have to be able to repeat it perfectly every time, and also it has to have something … something …"

There it was again.

"Something what?" said Sam.

"Something special," said Murphy.

"Because *you* are so special," said Sam, landing it halfway between a question and sarcasm.

"No," said Murphy. "Not because I'm special. Because … Because …" He started lost, but then he pounced—like a cat landing on a fly. Like he'd just had some important insight.

"Not because I'm *special*," he said. "But because *I am the only Murphy Kruger.*"

"Mr. Caverhill," said Murphy. It was the next afternoon. It was the end of the day again. Mr. Caverhill teaches English. The classroom was empty. Murphy had lingered.

"Mr. Caverhill, when a person signs his name to something, like an autograph, or on a bank form or something, do they just move their fingers and their hand? Or are they supposed to hold the fingers still and move their whole arm?"

Two weeks had passed since Murphy's first visit to the bank.

It was Saturday afternoon.

He called Sam.

"I'm coming over," he said.

He sounded panicked.

They went up to Sam's room.

"Shut the door," said Murphy. "I want to show you something."

Murphy sat on the bed and held out his hand.

There was a lump, just before the first knuckle on his middle finger. A lump, and a valley, and then another lump.

"It's where I hold the pen," said Murphy. "I think I've given myself a tumour."

It went on like this for weeks.

"What about this one?" said Murphy.

"It looks like a girl's," said Sam.

"Okay, this one."

It was like looking at paint chips. After a while everything seemed the same—everything equally good or bad. And it was impossible to tell one from the other.

There was the signature, for instance, where the K was in the shape of a star.

And the one with a smiley face in the head of the p.

There was the one Murphy copied from his father.

And the ones that came from nowhere at all.

And then, out of the blue, there was one that was perfect.

"This is it," said Murphy.

Until he turned up the next morning and pointed out the fatal flaw.

"It's impossible to forge," he said.

"Isn't that what you'd want?" said Sam.

"If you only think of yourself," said Murphy dismissively. "I have to think of others. I have to consider my unborn children."

"Good point," said Sam.

Murphy was back at square one.

But Murphy finally got it. He went back to the bank on a Tuesday, this time by himself. He appeared at the manager's office and stood by the door.

"I'm ready," he said.

The manager smiled and pointed at the chair. She'd thought she wasn't going to see him again.

They talked for a while, and then she opened her desk drawer and got out an index card again. Murphy reached into his pocket and pulled out an old fountain pen he'd found in his father's desk. He'd bought a new package of cartridges for the occasion. Peacock blue.

"I've been practising my signature," he said. He inhaled, closed his eyes, and then opened them. He signed on the exhale.

Truth be told, it was a piece of graphological thievery. He'd stolen the *M* from his mother and the *K* from his dad. He'd taken the *p* from an author's signature he'd seen on the web. The *y* was his—the swooping tail that swam back and underlined everything, the one that came by accident in math class.

Murphy signed, and then sat back, looking at what he'd done. It wasn't his best. He'd done better at home. He wanted to ask for another card so that he could do it again, but before he could, the manager reached out, picked up the card, and said,

"That's a very nice signature."

"I know," said Murphy.

Murphy kept practising, and the more he practised, the faster he got.

"It's like a coat of arms," he told Sam one day. "Or finger-prints. Not having your signature is like not knowing yourself. You should get one too."

Sam said, "I have been practising."

And Murphy said, "It'll come. The perfect version is out there somewhere. You just have to find it. And when you do, it's like finding yourself."

It became Murphy's habit to go to the bank every Friday.

Whenever he earned money, or was given money for his birthday, or whatever, he'd change it into five-dollar bills and put them in the safety deposit box. He fastened them together with a small black clip.

He loved the seriousness of it. The long metal blackness. The ceremony of the opening and the closing. The bank's key and his. But what he liked best was the signing of the card. His signature stacking up upon itself week after week, gaining gravitas as the weeks passed.

When he was done, when he'd put what he needed in, or taken what he wanted out, he would visit the manager. They would sit in her office.

It was Murphy who introduced her to café correcto. She kept a bottle of grappa in her bottom desk drawer especially for these Friday meetings.

"You understand we really shouldn't be doing this," she said.

"Don't worry," said Murphy. "People are always saying that to me."

It was Murphy who told her about the Blue Nile app. This was maybe six months before the company went public.

"You should buy stock," he said. She did. And did rather well by it.

Their ritual continued for about two years, until the manager was transferred. The week before she left, she went into the computer and fixed Murphy's account so that he'd never be charged for his safety deposit box.

With her gone, however, Murphy slowly lost interest in the box. He had a debit card by then. And eventually he forgot about the safety deposit box altogether.

It will come back to him years from now. He'll be telling someone about his early adventures with stamps, and he'll remember how, for a brief while, he kept his very first stamp at the bank.

"In a safety deposit box," he will say.

He'll go back to the branch a week later, fully expecting it to be closed, or if it was open, fully expecting them to look at him quizzically. Instead, a woman, younger than him, will examine his ID, open the gate, and lead him behind the counter into the little room at the back. There she'll pull out his index card from the grey metal box where they keep these things and hand it to him.

And he'll stare at what he wrote on that afternoon so long ago. The swooping *y* and the borrowed *M*. His mother and father suddenly present in the quiet room.

He will pull a pen from his pocket and sign again, a quick flourish, no more than his initials, really: *MK* and a little squiggle. He'll hand the card back to the young woman, and she'll peer at it.

"Your signature has changed," she'll say.

And he'll laugh.

"That was a long time ago," he'll say, referring to the signature on the card. "Things were more complicated then. Or I was anyway."

The young woman will hesitate, staring at the card for another moment, and Murphy will say, "It's okay. It's still me." And he'll take the box into the little cubicle where he used to sit and open it alone.

The only thing in it will be the cheque from his grandfather. He'll pick it up and stare at the signature. *Murray* Kruger, with a swooping *y*.

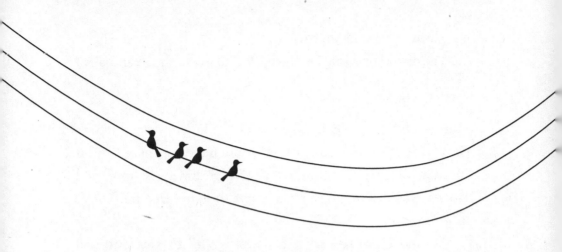

HELEN MOVES IN

It had been a long time coming. It's not like it came out of the blue. It had been coming for years. It had started with the car. Helen had that accident. That must have been ... phew! Ten years ago? She'd kept driving—for a while. But eventually she'd stopped, thank God. Then, last winter, she had the fall. And now? It was hard to put your finger on it. It's not like there was some big change. It was just— Morley had to face it: her mother was old. It had been a long time coming, but at the same time, it seemed to happen all at once, and Morley was worried.

She took Helen to see Dr. Keen for a checkup.

"I'm worried about her," she said.

Dr. Keen called the next afternoon.

"There is nothing I can do," he said.

"I knew it," said Morley. "What is it? Tell me."

You could almost hear Dr. Keen shrug over the phone. "Your mother has the dwindles."

"The what?" said Morley.

"The dwindles," said Dr. Keen. "We all get them. Eventually."

Morley and Dave had talked about this for years. It was Dave's idea. Not hers. She never would have suggested it. But there it was. Helen shouldn't be living alone anymore, and Morley was driving to Helen's house to invite Helen to move in with them.

She had practised what she was going to say. She had practised it out loud in the car on her way to work, and on her way home. She had practised it in front of the bathroom mirror, and she was still practising now, on her way to talk to her mother.

It was a delicate matter. She didn't want to sound patronizing. She didn't want her mother to feel as if she needed—rescuing.

She had to give her mother the space she needed to maintain her dignity. But she also had to be firm.

Morley had practised so much that it all came out in a big awkward rush.

"It would be good for all of us," she said. "You could help out. With both Dave and I working, it's … it's hard. We could use the help. Or I could."

Helen was dazed.

She was staring at her wedding ring. How many years since Roy had died? Was it almost twenty? She'd never *tell* anyone, but she had come to enjoy the freedom of living on her own. She glanced around her kitchen: there were dishes in the dish rack. Maybe she was no longer the housekeeper she was when Roy was alive, but she sort of enjoyed that, too.

Sure, she was lonely sometimes, but she had her friends—even though many of them had moved from the neighbourhood.

"Mom?" said Morley.

"I'm sorry dear," said Helen. "I was just thinking of your father."

She still isn't over Dad, thought Morley.

Helen reached out and patted Morley's arm. She didn't want to leave her house, but her daughter was practically begging for help.

Morley obviously couldn't manage anymore. It was hardly a surprise. It was ridiculous what she was trying to do. Run a home and work full time. It was nonsense. Capital *N*.

Helen said, "All right, dear. I'll help out."

It's what you do when you have children.

Though you'd think by the time you were in your eighties they would leave you alone.

The plan was she'd rent her house so that she could move back when things settled down, when Sam went to university. But she got an offer. And the agent said, "You know, that's a good offer." So in the end, she sold.

There is a room, upstairs, at the back of Dave and Morley's house, that has its own bathroom. Helen moved into the room at the back. Her bed and her bureau. It wasn't perfect, but there was nothing about this that was perfect. It was workable.

"I don't know," said Helen on the day before the move. "This makes me nervous." They were at Helen's house, packing the last of her stuff. "I'm not sure if three generations are supposed to live together. It seems—*unnatural*."

Morley said, "Don't be nervous, Mom. It's going to be *so* much easier."

Maybe for you, thought Helen.

She came on a Sunday.

She always came for Sunday dinner, so it almost felt normal. They had dinner, as they always did. And she washed the dishes, as she always did. But then, instead of getting into her coat and getting into the car so that Dave could drive her home, Helen hung up her apron, and there was an awkward moment, the three of them standing in the kitchen, until Helen said, "Well then, I think I'll go to my room."

"Sleep tight," said Morley. "I'm going to make lunches for tomorrow."

Recently, on Sundays, after Helen left, it has become Morley's habit to re-wash the dishes. Not all of them, but a lot of them. Helen's eyesight is not what it used to be. She misses things.

And so Helen went upstairs and Morley waited in the kitchen with her ear cocked, waiting to hear her mother climb safely into bed before she tackled the dishes.

It seemed to take forever. What could be taking Helen so long? What could she be doing? Morley wandered around the living room peevishly. It had been over a half an hour, and she could still hear her mother moving around.

Helen was just as fussed—pacing around her bedroom, wondering the same thing about Morley. If Morley couldn't put three sandwiches together in forty minutes, no wonder she needed help running her house. What could possibly be taking so long?

Finally the noises from upstairs quieted, and Morley turned on the tap. She was working on a wineglass when Helen reappeared.

They both stared at the glass in Morley's hand. And then Morley followed Helen's gaze over to the dish rack. It was full of dripping dishes.

Neither of them said a word about the dishes. Instead, Helen said, "I was wondering if there's any toothpaste."

Morley said, "I'll get some."

Monday morning was its usual rush and panic: Morley trying to make breakfast, Sam trying to wake up. Neither of them meeting with much success.

Dave was wandering around looking for his backpack, his sunglasses, the blue folder with the leather thing. The kitchen smelled of orange juice and burnt toast. And in the middle of it all, Helen wandered downstairs in her house-coat, oblivious.

"Have you made the eggs yet?" she asked.

Sam looked up happily. "We're having eggs?"

"No. No eggs," said Morley. "There's no time for eggs. Eat your toast."

Helen stood in the middle of the kitchen and frowned. But she didn't say anything.

It was clear that she was going to have to get up earlier from now on so that she could make this family a decent breakfast.

Morley sighed and dropped more bread into the toaster. Now she was going to have to get up early enough to make her mother eggs.

"I made tea, Mom," said Morley.

Helen was sitting at the kitchen table beside Sam, staring at his bowl of yogurt.

Now what, thought Morley. But she didn't ask.

"Here," she said instead, putting the teapot down in front of her mother.

Helen seemed to snap out of her reverie. As she reached for the teapot, she stole one more glance at her grandson's breakfast. She had no idea that her daughter had let things unravel so much. Ice cream in the morning? She would see about that.

And so passed the morning. They were like four horses in one harness, all of them pulling in different directions.

Stamping, bucking, and snorting.

And then everything came to a crescendo. The horses whinnied and ran off, and just like that, in the snap of your fingers, the kitchen was like a racetrack at the end of the day. Deserted and quiet.

Just Helen.

Helen alone at the table with her pot of tea. The cat, somewhere nearby. Or maybe not. It was always hard to tell.

"Oh my," said Helen.

The first thing Helen did, once everyone was gone, was go upstairs and get a cardigan. It was freezing in the house.

She found the thermostat in the hall and turned it up. She would turn it down before everyone came home. Then she wandered around and closed all the blinds. She didn't like the idea of strange people staring in at her.

After lunch she napped in her room with the paper in her lap. Then she came downstairs and made herself another pot of tea and took it to the den to watch *Coronation Street*.

The television, or what was left of it, the screen part of the television, was attached to the wall.

Helen looked around the room. The rest of it, the guts of it, was nowhere to be seen.

Helen stared at the screen carefully, searching for a knob or a button so that she could turn it on.

The television didn't appear to have knobs or buttons.

She ran her hand around the edge of the frame to see if she could feel something.

All she could feel was *nothing*. She stepped back and scratched her head. She saw the remotes lying on the bookshelf beside the screen. There were four of them.

Helen's heart sank.

Helen was afraid of remotes.

She had read an informative article in the *Reader's Digest* about remotes. According to the article, they were the most germ-ridden objects in hotel rooms.

She didn't stay in hotels often, but the article had made a fierce impression. She had vowed that if she ever found herself in a hotel she would never, under any circumstances whatsoever, touch a television remote.

The *Reader's Digest* had explained that no one ever cleaned their remotes.

Well, that was something she could do right now, wasn't it?

But she'd have to be careful. At her age, something as simple as a cold virus could take her out in a matter of days.

Helen went downstairs. She found a pair of rubber gloves under the sink. She put the gloves on and went back and picked up the remotes. She was careful to hold her breath while she was handling them.

She dropped them—one, two, three, four—into a plastic bag. She held the bag away from her body as she carried it.

It occurred to her that she'd seen other remotes in the house as well. She might as well do them all at the same time.

She started at the top of the house and worked her way methodically down to the kitchen. It took her forty-five minutes. When she got downstairs and emptied her bag onto the kitchen table, there were twelve remotes lying there.

Air conditioning remotes, heating remotes, stereo remotes. She lined them up carefully on the top shelf of the dishwasher.

It seemed wrong, however, to run the dishwasher for barely half a load. She went back upstairs. She came back with two computer keyboards, an infra-red mouse, and Sam's iPod.

She set the dishwasher to sterilize.

Then she collapsed onto the largest chair in the living room. That was a good day's work.

Morley was the last one home that night. She walked in through the back door. The house was unusually quiet.

And unusually dark.

All the curtains were closed.

It was hot, too.

"I'm home," she called.

There was no response.

She yawned.

She found them in the living room—all of them—sound asleep. Helen in the chair with her legs stretched in front of her and her head drooped on her chest. Dave curled up on the couch. And Sam sprawled on the floor. Morley almost sat down with them. *Give your head a shake,* she thought. Instead she turned down the thermostat and started preparing dinner. First thing she did was open the dishwasher. That woke them.

The thing with the remotes was a bad beginning. Helen could see that her daughter's family needed help, but she began to question whether she was the one to provide it. They had such peculiar ways of doing things. It was unreasonable for them to expect her to understand them. Helen decided that she should draw the line—she'd do the dishes and she'd dust, but she'd leave the rest to them.

Instead of searching out chores, Helen began to spend her time as she did at home—doing crosswords and talking on the phone to friends. In the afternoon, after her nap, she went for walks around the neighbourhood. She didn't say anything, and she wouldn't have seen it this way herself, but those walks were small acts of defiance. Helen was asserting herself. She was telling her daughter that she didn't want to be a housekeeper.

Of course, that's not the way Morley interpreted it.

"I saw your mother again this afternoon," said Mary Turlington. "She seemed lost."

The idea of her mother walking aimlessly around the neighbourhood scared Morley.

"Mom," said Morley. "Where were you this afternoon?"

Helen hadn't been paying any attention—she had just walked for fifteen minutes and then come back.

"I have no idea," said Helen.

Oh dear, thought Morley.

Helen was enjoying her walks, but she tired easily. One afternoon when she'd ventured a little far, she flagged a taxi to take her home. She told the driver that she was trying to learn her new neighbourhood and asked how much it would cost to drive around for a while.

She got lucky. The driver was from Somalia. He felt guilty about having left *his* mother when he came to Canada.

He didn't charge Helen. He arranged to pick her up the next afternoon when business was quiet. They drove around the neighbourhood, telling each other their problems.

It was Dave's friend Kenny Wong who spotted her.

"See," said Kenny the next afternoon. "Very same time every day. They just seem to drive around in circles."

Morley was convinced her mother was losing her marbles, not to mention a fortune on taxis. The only thing she could think of doing to keep her at home was to keep her busy. She drew up a new list of chores.

"These are the things you could do," she said. "These things would really help."

It was lunch. They were sitting at the kitchen table.

Helen's heart sank as she ran her finger down the list. She felt overwhelmed.

"I could do these things," she said.

But she didn't mean it.

Morley had decided that if grease spots on her dinnerware were the cost of her mother's dignity, she would live with grease. And so would her family.

She sat Dave down and explained all this.

When she finished she said, "Are you okay with that?"

Dave said, "I have no idea what you're talking about. What are grease spots?"

And so Helen got to work. She washed supper dishes, pruned Morley's garden, and took on the laundry.

"I wish she would let me relax," said Helen to her friend Ruth. "I wish I could take it easy. I've earned it."

"She doesn't seem to be able to relax," said Morley to Dave. I wish she could relax. She's earned it."

But they didn't say these things to each other.

"You should move to my retirement community," said Ruth to Helen. "I have my own place and they have dinner in the dining room if I want."

"She needs me," said Helen. "It's hard for her—the kids, the job. David."

When she was a girl Morley used to love to watch her mother iron. The hiss of the steam, the spray of water, the peaceful perfection of the folded piles. When she thought of her mother, she always thought of ironing. She added ironing to the list.

So Helen started ironing, too.

And so one morning Sam stood in his bedroom calling for his mother.

"My jeans are weird," he said.

The jeans were hanging stiffly from his hips.

There was a sharp crease running down the middle of each leg.

"I can't bend my legs," said Sam.

According to the list, Helen cooked dinner on Thursdays. Morley didn't say anything after the first or the second week, but she did on the third.

"You know you're not supposed to eat liver anymore, Mom. They say it's not good for you."

Helen snorted. "The next thing you know they'll say the same about cheese."

Then she turned to Sam, who was pushing a piece of grey meat around his plate.

"Don't you worry, Sam. Dig in. Enjoy!"

Helen was trying her best, God knows, but the truth is she didn't want to cook family-sized meals anymore; she wasn't even sure she wanted to cook at all.

"I really want to help," said Helen to Ruth one afternoon on the phone, "but honestly, who irons these days?"

Ruth said there was a laundry service available at her retirement residence and that she had a cleaner come in every other week to do her floors and bathroom. There was a bridge night and a movie night. And a community dinner every night of the week if you wanted.

Helen sighed and looked at the basket of socks waiting to be sorted. What on earth was her daughter's family doing with so many socks?

In the end she stayed four months.

All things considered, it ended well. Better, really, than anyone could have hoped.

One afternoon Helen looked at Morley and said, "We need to talk.

"My friend Ruth is lonely," she said. "She needs my help. I think I should move in with her."

Morley sat up straight.

Morley knew the place. A good place. You got your own kitchen and a living room. Helen would have her own space. And meals whenever she wanted.

"It will be difficult," said Morley, measuring her words carefully. "Without you."

"Well, that's obvious," said Helen.

"What?" said Morley.

Helen put her hand on her daughter's arm. "You do a good job, sweetie," she said.

And so she went. And Morley, who had spent her life leaving her mother, for the first time had to watch her mother leave instead.

TANK OF TRANQUILITY

Occupational hazards are obvious for people who work in certain occupations—on high-rise construction, for example; on a police force, or at a nuclear plant. But there are hazards in the quieter professions as well. Pity the poor accountant who can't help but keep a running record of everything in his life: totalling the cost of all the spoiled milk and unread newspapers. The lawyer who sees nothing but lawsuits wherever she turns. Or the poor shopkeepers, whatever shops they keep—they all fall victims to their own goods.

Dave's friend Dorothy Capper has bought so many books from her own bookstore that she can barely fit a guest into her guest bedroom. And Kenny Wong, who runs a café down the block—Wong's Scottish Meat Pies—Kenny can't resist a deal on a case of produce. How many eggplants have to spoil in his walk-in cooler before Kenny learns *his* lesson?

And then there's Dave. Owner of a second-hand record store, Dave spends a good quarter of his working life poking around flea markets and garage sales, church basements and record shows, making *him* vulnerable to what might be the most insidious occupational hazard in the world—the impulse purchase.

Set *your*self loose in the sort of places Dave frequents, and see if *you* don't come home with the odd lava lamp or abused pair of cowboy boots. See if you don't find yourself, like Dave, huddled under the fire escape at the back of your store— where you could have found him one wet November after- noon—signing a packing slip *here,* and *here,* initialling *there,* acknowledging the receipt, safe and secure, of a large wooden crate. A crate large enough that it took three guys to wrestle it out of the back of the cube van idling in the rainy alley.

"It's bigger than I thought," said Dave.

The guy with the clipboard shrugged and said, "Where do you want it?"

After a few more words and thirty dollars changing hands, the three guys picked up the crate again and lugged it through the back door of Dave's store—lurching down the narrow hallway to the storage room, Dave leading the way.

"Careful of the step. Watch the door."

The men were pros. They pocketed their thirty bucks and didn't ask what was in the box. Which was just as well, because Dave was self-conscious about that and wasn't inclined to say.

It took him a good half hour to pry the crate apart. When he was finished, he stood there in a mess of wood planks and shavings, staring at a sleek fibreglass box that looked like some kind of space capsule.

He tore off the instruction manual that was taped to the top and spent the rest of the afternoon sitting by the cash register reading it carefully. It seemed simple enough. All he had to do was fill the box with tepid water and salt.

Dave had just bought a second-hand sensory deprivation tank. And he had gotten it for a steal. His only problem was that he wasn't sure who he could tell.

A few days after it arrived, Dave was at Kenny Wong's café, sitting on his regular stool at the end of the counter, poking at a bowl of Kenny's rice pudding.

Kenny was sitting at his desk, where he'd been sitting most of the morning—more or less in the middle of the café, tilted back on his wood chair, his feet up on the paper-strewn desk top—talking on the phone or talking to customers, or sometimes both at the same time.

He was on the phone now. And Dave was waiting for him to get off.

The lunch rush was over. They were the only two in the café.

Even though Dave was excited about his tank, he still hadn't told anyone about it. He was intrigued, and had been for years, by the claims he'd read online of tank-imposed, otherworldly bliss—but he was also self-conscious. He didn't want people thinking of him as, you know, all new age and crystal-weird.

He hadn't told anyone, but he was going to tell Kenny as soon as Kenny was off the phone. Because he needed Kenny's help.

Just as he finished his pudding, Kenny hung up. Dave put his spoon down and said, "Where do you get your salt, anyway?"

Kenny, head down and pawing through a stack of paper in front of him, waved absentmindedly at the cupboard behind the counter. Then he paused, frowned, and looked up. Kenny was suddenly thinking, *Was there something wrong with the rice pudding?*

He called Bobby.

"Bobby. Get out here!"

Bobby, his afternoon chef, *makes* all the desserts.

Dave said, "No, no. I mean where do you *buy* your salt? Who supplies you?"

Kenny waved Bobby off, looked at Dave, and said, "You looking for a deal? How much salt do you want?"

Kenny thought they were kidding around.

Dave said, "About eight hundred pounds."

Now, if you're feeling unsure about something you've done, as Dave was, shy or uncertain about how others might receive it, chances are when you share your secret, your story is going to drift from the realm of information exchange into the world of hyperbole, justification, and rationalization.

Kenny said, "You need *eight hundred* pounds of salt?"

Dave said, "It's for my float tank."

Kenny said, "You're kidding me, right?"

And Dave took flight.

"Floating," said Dave, "is like a return to the womb. You climb into a tank and stay in there long enough, you're going to lose touch with your arms and your legs, and before you know it you're going to be nothing more than a kernel of pure awareness floating in the inner-verse."

"The inner-verse?" said Kenny.

"You close that soundproof lid and lie back," said Dave. "And you're floating on water denser than the Dead Sea. And for the first time in your life, your brain will be free of stimulation and stress."

Kenny didn't say anything.

Dave leaned forward dramatically and said, "One hour in a float tank is as good as four hours of sleep."

He was making stuff up now. He was riffing on vague memories he had from his online research.

"We get *two hours in a tank*"—he was waving his spoon in the air—"we wouldn't need to sleep at all. Think of everything we could get done."

"We?" said Kenny.

"Think of all the extra time we'd have if we didn't have to sleep," said Dave.

Kenny cocked his head, eyed his friend, and said, "You have never struck me as a guy who is exactly short of time."

No doubt about it, Dave was overselling the idea. Especially when you consider that he'd never floated himself, and had no idea what he was talking about. But as I said, he was feeling self-conscious about the tank. He was unsure about the thing. And uncertainty is a certain fertilizer for conviction.

Besides, there was something else going on.

Dave has a touch of claustrophobia. And as enticing as he made it sound, as enticing as it might be, the thought of floating in a dark, coffin-like capsule terrified him. What if he fell asleep and flipped over and drowned? Or worse? What if he went insane and came out stark raving mad? Maybe he would find the inner peace that they talked about online, or maybe he would come out convinced he could talk to shrubbery.

That, of course, was why he really bought it. We are all drawn to things that terrify us. Don't touch? We reach out. Don't look. We do.

Oh, Dave wanted to get in that tank.

But what he really wanted was for Kenny to take it out on a test drive.

That's why he was laying it on so thick.

And it worked.

By the time he was finished, Kenny wanted to try it too.

They bought sixteen fifty-pound bags of salt and picked them up in Kenny's truck.

And a week later, early on a Friday morning, they hooked up a hose to the sink in the washroom of Dave's store, ran it across the hallway to the back storage room, and filled the tank with warm water.

It took all day for the salt to dissolve.

Just before four that afternoon, Dave called Kenny. "It's ready," he said.

Kenny changed in the washroom. He darted across the hall with his belly protruding over his little Speedo.

Dave was standing beside the tank with the lid open.

"Be my guest," he said.

Kenny reached in to feel the water.

"It's warm," said Kenny.

"It's perfect," said Dave.

And so Kenny climbed in. Kneeling awkwardly at first, and then slowly lowering himself onto his back.

Dave was watching every move.

"It's easy," said Kenny. "It isn't hard at all."

It was just like lying on a bed—except wetter.

Kenny said, "Close the lid. I want the total experience."

Dave closed the lid. He stood beside the tank in the suddenly silent room.

Almost immediately he felt his heart rate accelerate, his mouth get dry, his palms turn cold and clammy. He knew immediately what was going on. He was suffering the onset symptoms of sympathetic claustrophobia.

He lasted five uncertain minutes before he tapped on the lid.

"You okay?"

Did he hear a muffled "Okay" from inside the tank? It was hard to tell. It was like talking to a can of peas.

Five minutes later, he tapped again. This time, however, it was more a rap than a tap. This time he hit it as hard as he could.

And this time Kenny opened the door and stuck his head out. Kenny was blinking. He looked like the dormouse in the teapot from *Alice in Wonderland.*

He also looked peevish.

"I was just checking," said Dave.

Kenny said, "*I* was just letting go. I'm not going to be able to get into this if you keep interrupting."

And so, feeling a little reassured, and a little foolish, Dave turned off the storage-room light and left—shutting the storage-room door behind him. Alone in the darkness, Kenny ducked down and closed the tank door behind him as if he were getting into a submarine.

A half an hour went by, then another. Dave cracked the door and peeked in. He wanted to knock on the tank, but he didn't.

Inside, where it was dark and soundless, Kenny was floating on his back in the soft, salty water—his legs and arms extended as if he were making a snow angel. Although he'd been in there for an hour, it felt like only fifteen minutes to Kenny. But Kenny was beginning to feel that he'd had enough. He was refreshed, and rested and calm, but he was also pruney and his mind was starting to drift back to work and a food order he needed to call in. He decided to give himself fifteen minutes more, so Dave wouldn't think he couldn't take it.

Another hour went by. Kenny had had enough. He was wrinkled and bored. He was hungry.

He reached up in the darkness and felt around for the handle to open the tank door. Now that it was time to get out, he suddenly had a touch of claustrophobia himself. He found the handle and pushed. The door didn't budge. He pushed harder. Still nothing.

When things go wrong—when nuclear plants melt down, or buses full of the faithful leave the road, when disasters happen, that is—it is seldom the result of some big thing; it's always a chain of simple things, almost all of them avoidable.

Outside, a mere foot from his head, Brian, who works part time at Dave's store, dropped another milk crate of records on top of the tank. Brian is used to strange things popping up in Dave's storeroom: a huge papier mâché sculpture of Frank Sinatra, a rusting phone booth, once, even, a coffin.

No one had said anything to Brian about a flotation tank.

Brian set the crate of records, the sixth, down on the lid of the tank and went back into the store to get the seventh and last.

Inside the tank, Kenny brought his knees to his chest, put his feet on the door, and pushed with all his might.

Without warning, Kenny's back slipped on the slimy, salty bottom and he spun rapidly around so that his feet were where his head should have been and his head was where his feet belonged. He tried to flip back, but the salty, pitch-black tank hadn't only disoriented him; it had left him tired and clumsy. He managed a half turn, slipped again, and found himself wedged across the width of the tank, knees bent, head pressing against the side. He wriggled and squirmed and batted his hands around. The water sloshed back and forth, washing over his nose and mouth. And most horribly, into his eyes. He felt his heart begin to pound erratically. He willed himself to stay still, to stop thrashing about, and then he slowly contracted his knees into his chest and bent his neck and slithered around until he was lengthwise again. His eyes were burning so intensely that he couldn't open them, not that it mattered. He couldn't see a thing in there anyway.

You'd think it would be impossible for Dave to forget Kenny. You'd think Kenny would be the only thing Dave was thinking of that afternoon.

But we all forget things. Sometimes we forget important things. It happens when other things come up. And other things had been coming up all afternoon. Soon after Kenny had crawled into the tank, a fellow had walked into the store with *seven* milk crates of soul albums to sell. It had taken Dave a while to sort through them so that he could make the fellow a reasonable offer. Right after that, one of Stephanie's old friends had come in, looking for a birthday present for her father. And then, just before closing, Morley had phoned to remind him that they were going to dinner at the Lowbeers'. He promised he wouldn't be late. And now—he was.

In his rush, he just *forgot.* He locked up and he left. Simple as that.

He quit the shop—leaving Kenny wedged in the fetal position at the bottom of the tank, cursing like a strangely foul-mouthed infant.

Dave remembered Kenny an hour and a half later.

He was sitting at the Lowbeers' dining room table.

Gerta carried in two beautifully plated filets of pink salmon.

"I cooked them *sous-vide,*" said Gerta.

Which means sealed in plastic and immersed in warm water.

"It's quite remarkable," said Gerta. "You leave anything in warm water long enough, it will eventually cook—cook right through."

Dave stared at his piece of fish and said something unspeakably inappropriate.

Carl's jaw dropped.

Gerta's hand flew to her mouth.

Morley sighed.

And Dave bolted from the table and the house. Ran right out the front door.

Gerta poked at the salmon on the plate in front of her and then looked at Morley and Carl.

"It looks fine to me," said Gerta.

Dave was already out of earshot. Dave was pounding along the dark streets, racing through the neighbourhood toward his shop.

It was possible that Kenny hadn't noticed his absence. It was possible that the hours that had passed had felt like minutes to Kenny.

Dave threw open the front door of his store and sprinted toward the back room. As he passed the cash register he was praying he'd find a mellow, transformed Kenny Wong—Kenny wrapped in a towel, waiting to describe some ethereal, other-worldly experience.

What he found was $500 worth of salt water leaking through the floorboards and crates of soul records scattered everywhere.

And a noticeable absence of Kenny.

Dave gave Wong's Scottish Meat Pies a wide berth for a day or two.

But after a few days, he knew he had to face the music. He screwed up his courage and headed for Kenny's café. He went early and found Kenny alone, behind the counter, unloading the dishwasher.

Dave sat on his regular stool.

The last one in the row.

"I guess you've been wondering where I've been," he began.

Kenny shrugged.

Dave said, "Well, I'm here to apologize."

Kenny was unexpectedly gracious.

He turned and picked up the coffee pot from the warmer on the counter behind him. He poured a mug of coffee and put it down in front of Dave.

"Nothing to worry about," said Kenny. "All's well that ends well."

Then he looked up and down the countertop.

"Hey," he said. "Could you grab me a basket of creamers?"

Dave got up from his stool and headed for the big walk-in fridge.

He couldn't believe this was going so well.

Dave opened the big fridge door and gazed around the shelves—at the red-netted bags of carrots and potatoes, the bucket of broccoli. The boxes and boxes of eggplants.

"You have enough eggplant in here to sink a ship," he called.

The creamers were at the back.

He stepped over a crate of lettuce and around a flat of tomatoes. He reached for the little cardboard box.

And that's when he heard the big cooler door click shut behind him.

He hopped back and reached for the handle with a sinking heart.

Just as he expected, it was locked.

What he didn't expect was to find an envelope with his name on it taped to the inside of the cooler door.

It was a sympathy card.

"Thinking of you in your time of trouble," it read.

Inside, Kenny had written, *"Don't worry, I won't forget you."*

Dave had just enough time to read that before the fridge light snapped off.

He sat down on the crate of lettuce.

At least he wouldn't starve.

He sighed.

He'd known this was coming.

They had always made it clear that you should forgive your enemies.

But no one ever said anything about friends.

HOME ALONE

It's the end of an autumn day. Morley is walking home from work, which is not something Morley often does. There's usually too much to be done at both ends of the journey, and seldom enough time for pedestrian luxuries. But she's walking tonight, and she's chosen a roundabout route—a route that takes her through the park and, consequently, past the local arena, where—don't kid yourself—Morley is going to stop and buy a bag of kettle corn.

Morley fell under the spell of the sweet, salty treat six months ago. And it has become a monstrous addiction. She would gladly forgo any meal of the day for a bag of kettle corn, and, truth be told, has on more occasions than she would care to admit.

There's something about the ping of the salt mixed with the kindness of the sugar. She glances at her phone. She really doesn't have the time, but she can't stop herself now. Besides, the little detour isn't only about the sweet temptation of corn. It's also about taking her sweet time. Morley knows what's waiting for her at home.

To wit, her son, Sam, and her husband, Dave, and a conversation about the weekend ahead—and what should and shouldn't happen.

But I'm getting ahead of myself.

Morley is trying to tarry, and we should allow her that indulgence. Let's tarry with her. Let's watch as she wanders along the shady neighbourhood streets, her bag slung over her shoulder, preoccupied with the mortal sin of sugar and salt.

That woman is rich, wrote Thoreau, *whose pleasures are the cheapest.*

Well, of course, he didn't write that exactly. He wrote that *man* is rich—but I don't think he would object to the rewrite.

That woman *is* rich. But also oblivious, so lost in her simple pleasure, so dedicated to her compulsion, that she doesn't notice, until it's too late, her neighbour Bert Turlington standing on the sidewalk just ahead of her, his little dog, Tissue, straining at the end of a long retractable leash, pulling desperately in the opposite direction, away from the park, which is where Bert and Tissue had been heading, and more importantly, away from Morley.

Tissue is a teacup Pomeranian: small, white, a little bit yappy but mostly pleasant enough, except— Morley hides the bag of popcorn in her purse.

"Tissue," she calls, holding up her empty hands. "All gone."

Too late.

Tissue *saw* the popcorn.

Morley looks at Bert ruefully and crosses to the other side of the street.

"Sorry," she calls.

"Dang," says Morley, doing the only thing she *can* do: walking on.

What just happened wasn't really Morley's fault. Tissue's response was an echo from a night, long ago, when Bert, never one to be accused of patience, peeked into a pot of popcorn and an un-popped kernel blew across the kitchen. Tissue, a mere pup at the time, bounced after it like a tennis ball, hoovered up the unexpectedly hot kernel, and stood there holding it in her mouth, tail wagging proudly.

Until the kernel exploded.

Tissue has had a fear of popcorn verging on the psychotic ever since.

Morley knows that. And if she hadn't been so preoccupied, she would have tucked the bag of kettle corn out of sight. It was careless. It was the sort of mistake addicts make.

But Morley is going to get over it pretty quickly. She has just arrived home. She is reaching for the front doorknob.

Upstairs in his bedroom, Sam is pacing anxiously.

Sam just watched his mother come up the walk. His best friend, Murphy, had made it clear: he should give her a moment to transition before he goes downstairs.

They're going to have a talk. Sam has been gearing up for it all week.

Sam had handed himself over to Murphy for coaching. Murphy is well versed in the psychological strengths and, more importantly, weaknesses of parents.

Their preparations are about to be put to the test.

Dave and Morley are going out of town this weekend. There is a wedding. Sam is about to put the case to them that he's old enough to stay home—alone.

Dave is actually okay with the idea. Dave long ago decided that being a parent means losing most of the major battles. Parenthood, he believes, is an endless war of rearguard actions, retreats, and regroupings.

"Until what?" said Morley.

"Until there is nothing more to lose," said Dave. As if losing were an achievement.

"But it is," he said. "As long as you're losing, you're still in the game. That's what's important. Being in the game."

Morley doesn't see it that way.

More to the point, Morley doesn't think Sam is ready to stay home alone.

She is clear on this, and she's expecting Dave's support.

She scrunches up her bag of corn and tucks it away. She walks inside.

It's a tricky thing to negotiate, the war of independence. Both sides approach the battlefield full of righteous conviction—but righteousness always conceals uncertainty, and conviction is never far from doubt.

Are you ready?

Here comes Sam, bounding down the stairs, determined to spread his wings. And there is Morley, waiting in the kitchen, just as determined to clip them.

You have to understand: Sam is still her baby. He may be at that awkward age where he's no longer young enough for a *babysitter*. But he's still young enough that— Well, let's listen, shall we?

They're sitting at the kitchen table now.

The battle has begun without us.

"A babysitter?" says Sam.

Morley has just suggested someone—not *exactly* a babysitter, more a house-sitter and cook—who might spend the weekend not *with* him, exactly, but in the house, at the same time.

"Oh," clarified Sam. "Someone *like* a babysitter."

He said this exactly the way Murphy had drilled him.

It was hard to be sure whether he was being sarcastic or just emphatic.

"Why didn't *I* think of that," he said.

Sarcastic.

Morley felt her anxiety rising.

This was not going as smoothly as she'd hoped.

"How about Caitlin?" said Sam.

"Caitlin?" asked Morley.

Caitlin is a girl in his class.

"Caitlin," said Sam, "does *lots* of babysitting."

Okay, point made. Score one for the teenager. He was too old for a babysitter.

Sam had been worried his parents would make him come with them—to stay in the hotel room while they were at the reception.

"They won't," predicted Murphy. "They don't want you there. They want time away from you. Have you no appreciation of how obnoxious you are?"

Murphy was right. They didn't even bring the option up. In fact, the entire discussion was playing out *exactly* the way Murphy had predicted.

Sam began to tick through a speech he and Murphy had been practising all week.

"Mozart was composing piano solos when he was eight," said Sam.

"Tatum O'Neal won an Oscar when she was nine."

He had someone for each year, from eight to sixteen. He'd just done twelve when Dave jumped in and threw him off stride.

"Tanya Tucker recorded *Delta Dawn* when she was thirteen," said Dave.

Morley glared at him.

"It's true," he said.

Then he remembered which team he was supposed to be on and muttered a barely audible "Sorry."

It was too late. Battles turn on a dime. That was the ten-cent moment. They all felt it, although they all pretended not to. Sam nodded at his dad and kept going, ticked off fourteen and then moved in for the kill.

"When she was fifteen," said Sam, pausing dramatically, "which is my age, incidentally"—that was a Murphy flourish—"Anne Frank had written the final entry in her diary."

"And on a lighter note," said Dave, forgetting himself again, "when *he* was fifteen, Eubie Blake was playing piano in Baltimore brothels."

Both Sam and Morley turned and stared at him this time.

"Oops," said Dave. "May I retract that?"

It was all over, of course. But the conversation continued for ten more awkward minutes.

Of all things, the argument that finally won the day was little dog Tissue. Morley had promised that they'd look after Tissue that very weekend, forgetting, when she did, that it was the weekend of the wedding. Sam, of course, had used the oversight to his advantage.

"Someone has to look after Tissue," he said.

And so, as Murphy had predicted, Sam prevailed. Dave and Morley would go to the wedding and, for the first time in his life, Sam would stay home alone. No alcohol. No friends. Except, of course, and this was part of the plan, for Murphy. Murphy could come over. They could order pizza and watch movies.

And everything would have worked wonderfully, no doubt about it, except Murphy got sick and couldn't come.

And *that* is how Sam found himself, somewhat unexpectedly, home alone for the first time in his life. Hoisted, as they say, on his own petard.

He'd been alone before, obviously. But he'd never been alone overnight, which means he'd never really been home alone.

The afternoon had been unremarkable. He biked to the library and hung out for a while. But everyone had gone home. And then he had to, too.

As he pushed his bike into the garage and headed for the side door, he looked at the dark, quiet house and felt a twinge of anxiety, and for the first time, *alone*.

While Sam was nervously walking into the house, Dave and Morley were pulling into the parking lot of the country club where the wedding was about to begin. As they came to a stop, Morley flipped down the sun visor to check her lipstick.

Then she checked her phone.

"Did he call?" asked Dave.

Morley shook her head and handed him her cell and the little silver tube of lipstick.

"Do you mind carrying these?" she said.

"I'm sure he's fine," said Dave as he slipped the phone into his pocket.

Sam started making dinner as soon as he got inside: a meat and two vegetables.

For the meat he would grill some beef—in the convenient hot dog format. For the first vegetable he chose potatoes—in their handy chip form.

Two wieners and a bag of chips.

For his second vegetable he would make corn—popcorn.

Dinner done, the echo of anxiety returned.

He walked around the house to be sure he was alone.

Then he went down to the basement and settled in front of his Xbox.

While Sam battled battalions of attacking zombies, Morley and Dave made their way to the reception.

"Maybe we should phone him," said Morley.

Dave patted the cell phone in his pocket.

"Let's let him have his freedom," said Dave.

Two hours later, Sam went upstairs to find every light in the house off. He had never seen the house so dark. There was always someone upstairs. There were always lights on. It scared him a little. He phoned Murphy. Just to see how he was.

Murphy said, "You have nothing to worry about. The highest percentage of break-ins happen in the summer."

Sam said, "But it *is* summer."

Murphy said, "Technically, perhaps. But as far as I'm concerned, summer is pretty much over once Mercury rises into Virgo."

The wedding ceremony was a tad precious. The bride and groom wrote their own vows. The bride's mother gave her daughter away—her father relegated to marching glumly up the aisle carrying a bouquet.

"If he was going to be the flower girl, he should have had a dress," said Dave.

As Morley and Dave waited for their turn in the receiving line, Morley reached into Dave's pocket and pulled out her phone.

"I'm going to call him," she said. "Just to say hi."

Dave took the phone back and returned it to his pocket.

Morley said, "I just was going to say hi."

Sam headed up to bed at ten—an hour earlier than usual. As he lay there on his back, covers pulled to his chin and little dog Tissue lying beside him, his room felt unfamiliar, dark and creepy. The house was creaking and groaning like a wooden ship in a storm. Why had he never noticed the way the house creaked before?

Sam stared at his phone on the table beside his bed. Maybe he should call his parents and check on them—make sure they were okay.

Morley poked at her dinner and only half-listened to the speeches. She was thinking that if something went wrong at home, she'd never forgive herself. But when the toasts began and a waiter glided by with a tray of champagne, Dave plucked two glasses off the tray and handed one to his wife.

"To Dave and Morley," he said quietly.

Then he added, "And weddings in far-flung places."

Morley sighed and brought the glass to her lips.

And then the band began, and people started dancing, and her concerns began to fade. Before Morley knew it, she and Dave were dancing. And somewhere there on the dance floor, she let go. Her children were independent and capable. And that meant she could be independent, too.

Sam picked up the phone from the bedside table and punched in his mother's cell number. But he didn't push Send. He didn't want his parents to get the wrong idea. He didn't want them to think he couldn't make it alone.

Instead he lay there, staring at the numbers on the screen. Fifteen minutes ticked by, then another thirty. It was almost midnight. He'd been in bed for over an hour and a half. He was still staring at the phone screen.

He had just remembered a conversation he'd overheard between his mother and father. They'd been away—the entire family—and had come home to find a window on the main floor wide open. His mother was chastising his father for not locking it, and his dad had replied—defensively no doubt, the way any of us might have replied under the circumstances—*Leaving the window open is no big deal. If someone really wanted to get into this house, there are a million ways they could do it.*

This is what Sam remembered as he lay in his bed in his creaking house. There was another noise downstairs. A moan, or a groan, or a something.

Something that sounded like—zombies!

Sam sat bolt upright and pressed Dial.

He counted the rings: one, two, three.

When he heard the line click over to the answering machine, he hung up.

Why hadn't his parents picked up?

The only answer that made sense was that his parents were lying dead on the side of the road.

Now he was more worried about his parents than the burglar downstairs.

Okay. It was possible that they were still at the reception and couldn't hear the phone ringing over the band. He'd wait half an hour and phone them again.

He lasted eight minutes. Still no answer. That made it official.

He was an orphan.

He phoned his sister.

She didn't pick up either.

He left a message.

"Call me when you get this. Mom and Dad are dead."

He didn't know what else to add, so he hung up.

He felt bad for being so abrupt.

He called back.

He said, "It's me again. They were in a car accident."

It made him feel better to share it.

He lay there another half an hour.

He remembered his mother telling him that if he couldn't sleep he should read for a while. He had never tried it. Her advice was easier to accept now that she was dead.

He sat up and turned on his reading light. That's when Tissue, who was still on the bed with him, started to growl.

Sam was transfixed. He stared at the silhouette of the little dog standing on the end of the bed, glaring out into the hall, growling at whatever was out there.

He looked around the room. He wasn't going down without a fight. His tennis racket was propped against his desk. He picked it up and climbed out of bed.

On the way out the door, he scooped up Tissue and stuffed her into the kangaroo pocket of his hoodie. The dog could sense something was terribly wrong. She whimpered and shivered all the way down the stairs and into the kitchen.

Sam had to calm her down or she was going to give him away. He looked around for something to distract her, and there on the counter was a bowl with the remains of his popcorn.

Tissue is not a big dog.

She does not have a big brain and is not capable of complex thought. But when Sam shoved the handful of popcorn into his hoodie pocket, the little dog had a moment of complete clarity.

She understood precisely what was happening.

She was about to be blown to smithereens.

She erupted out of Sam's hoodie with a yowl and, in a blur, clawed her way up his chest and over his shoulder. She made a beeline for the stairs and disappeared.

When she got to Sam's room, Tissue dove under the bed.

Sam slid under a second behind her.

It was almost eight the next morning when Morley woke up. And the first thing she thought of, the very first thought that entered her mind, was how great it was to have gone an entire night without checking on her son. Dave was right. They had entered a new stage in their lives. Their daughter, Stephanie, had been living on her own for a couple of years. And now Sam didn't need her every waking moment. He was fine, and she could lie here and wonder about what she'd order from room service for breakfast. She could take a swim in the hotel pool before they headed home.

She rolled over and saw her husband sitting in the bed beside her, staring at her phone.

There were sixty-three missed calls.

"I turned the ringer off before the service," said Dave.

There were no messages.

And there was no answer when they called Sam back.

They threw their stuff into their suitcases, ran to the car, and shoved everything in the trunk. They peeled out of the parking lot, spraying gravel behind them.

They called their neighbour Jim Scoffield from the road.

"Something has happened to Sam," said Morley. "He's not answering the phone. Can you go and check?"

Jim called back twenty minutes later. He'd gone over and rung the bell, but there was no answer. He couldn't find his copy of their house key anywhere. Should he call the cops? What should he tell them? What should he do?

"Don't panic," said Dave. "We'll be there before you know it."

So, there they were, a Sunday morning, not yet nine, hurtling down the highway. Morley was in the passenger seat leaning forward, a huge bag of kettle corn in her lap. She had packed it for a moment just like this. She was eating it with the compulsive distraction of a chain smoker.

Half an hour later they careened around a corner and screeched to a stop in front of their house.

They found Jim pacing in the driveway.

But there was no sign of Sam.

Anywhere.

His bed had been slept in, but *he* was gone, and so was the dog. They searched the house in rising panic. They were about to call the police when Dave heard a scratch and a snuffle coming from Sam's room. He found boy and dog fast asleep and wedged under the far corner of Sam's bed.

After a brief conference, Morley and Dave and Jim tiptoed out of the house and went out for breakfast. Morley and Dave stayed out until they were sure Sam would be up and about.

They never asked about the sixty-three phone calls. And Sam never asked why they had come home early.

It was clumsy. They all knew that. But new beginnings are often clumsy.

IN THE WEEDS

A Saturday morning in early April. The sky still dark. You can tell by the puddles that the wind is up to no good. It is a morning so wet and grey and so devoid of hope that all over town people are getting up, looking out their windows, and crawling back to bed. What was the use? A day like that, you might as well move to St. John's.

The tulips in the garden in front of the municipal building, which had come up a good three inches during the week, spent the night trying to burrow back underground.

But Dave's daughter, Stephanie, is out—skirting a puddle in front of the garden, heading for work.

If you could see her face, under her hat, you would see that Stephanie is on the verge of tears.

Her cell phone had rung at seven-fifteen. She'd thought it was her boyfriend, Tommy. Tommy was away at some science fiction convention. Something to do with Isaac Asimov. Who else would phone at seven-fifteen in the morning? Tommy was probably just going to bed. Her heart fluttered as she fumbled for the phone.

"Tommy?"

It was her boss, Mark.

He didn't wake her, did he? He was sorry to call so early. Listen, could she come in? Could she cover the morning shift?

"What about Allison?" said Stephanie, lying on her back, her eyes still closed. Allison was supposed to do Saturday mornings.

"Allison called in sick."

Surprise surprise.

Exams had just ended. *Everyone* was out last night. She should have seen this coming.

Of course, she could have said no. Except Stephanie didn't do that. And she wasn't about to start now. *Especially* now. On her *last* day. What did they say about showing up? Showing up was everything. And showing up was what Stephanie did. Maybe the only thing she was any good at. She showed up.

She wasn't supposed to go in until noon. She was only supposed to work lunch and dinner. She'd been planning on sleeping in. Instead, she got out of bed and made coffee. And now she was pounding past that wind-whipped puddle in front of the municipal building, heading for a fourteen-hour shift. Heading to work in the sure knowledge that it was going to be a miserable day. She'd already expected a day of yelling and conflict and almost certain failure. Now it included Saturday morning. The worst shift of the week. An appropriate beginning for her last day.

There is nothing to do on a Saturday morning at the East River Grill except to make pot after pot of coffee, and get paid next to nothing for doing it. No one tips for coffee.

"What *I* do," said Peter, the server in section two, "is I only put every second cup through the till. I throw every other cup in the tip jar. Everyone does that in the mornings," said Peter. "You should do that too."

Not *everyone*. Stephanie didn't do it, though she wasn't sure whether it was because she thought it was wrong or because she was afraid she might get caught.

It would all be over on Monday anyway. Stephanie was going home on Monday—where she'd have to decide about a job for the summer. She was utterly exhausted. She needed a rest. Maybe she'd go tree planting again. Or maybe she'd go to Banff with Becky. She had to decide soon. She was tired of being asked about her plans. She was tired of not having an answer.

When she got to work and found the restaurant door locked, she smiled for the first time that morning. She reached into her pocket and pulled out her keys. It made her feel important to have her own key.

She unlocked the door, went in, and headed behind the bar to flick on the lights.

She went to her station and turned on the computer. A map of the restaurant lit up the screen. Her tables were in red. The others were in blue. She had section B3. B for in the bar, three for farthest from the kitchen.

She took her two coffee pots back to the bar, filled them with water, and got them going. Before the coffee was finished, Mark came through the door.

"Geez," he said. "It's brutal out there."

He came over and poured himself a cup of coffee from one of her pots. You were allowed as much coffee as you wanted.

Stephanie pointed at the bowl of creamers beside the terminal and Mark shook his head. He said, "Brutal night."

The front door opened. A man wearing a fur hat walked in and stood there uncertainly. They weren't supposed to open for twenty minutes. Stephanie picked up a menu and headed over.

Stephanie began working at the East River Grill just before Halloween.

It was less than minimum wage, but she'd heard that you could clean up on tips. She'd thought about trying to get a job doing research for a professor or working in an office, but working in the restaurant meant she'd have her days free for class. *How hard could it be to be a waitress?* she'd thought.

A lot harder than you'd imagine, it turned out. She almost didn't make it through the first week.

They were supposed to give her a week of training, but guess who phoned in sick on Stephanie's first night? She covered for Allison on her *first* day, and here she was, covering for her on her last.

She handed the guy with the fur hat the breakfast menu.

Her first night had been a disaster. That was the night a kid dropped his retainer into his basket of fries and no one noticed until Stephanie had cleared the table. When she returned with the bill, the agitated mother had launched into a lecture on responsibility and the boy was slouched over the table, looking as if he was about to burst into tears. Stephanie ended up digging through the garbage to find it.

The man with the fur hat said, "Two eggs over easy, home fries, brown toast, extra butter."

Stephanie said, "Would you like orange juice or maybe a cappuccino?" She nodded her head slightly as she said "cappuccino."

The man said, "Uh. Sure."

He didn't sound sure.

As Stephanie punched in his order she was still thinking of that first night. There she'd been, not two hours on the job, her arms up to the elbows into the greasy waste bucket by the kitchen door, digging around in the remnants of other people's half-eaten meals, when she unexpectedly closed her hand around the slimy retainer, let out a whoop, and—

If you're going to *fully* appreciate the catastrophe that is about to unfold, I should tell you a little bit about Chef.

The most important thing is that he went to cooking school with the famous Brock Godkin. The guy who started, well, Bluberry, among other places. The guy with the TV show and the bestsellers. The six-foot-six guy with the tousled hair and the movie-star grin. The guy the reviewers write about, who everyone talks about, who never did anything special when he and Chef were at school together. In fact, Chef did better than Brock Godkin ever did at school, so you tell me why *Brock Godkin* had a TV show while *he* was slaving away at the East River Grill as if he were being held hostage at a McDonald's.

Chef was obsessed with Brock Godkin. Or with Brock Godkin's notoriety. Or, more to the point, with his own lack thereof. Every Tuesday morning he'd arrive with a new creation—something he'd dreamed up over the weekend that was going to shift the spotlight onto him. Filet of venison in a licorice reduction. Beetroot sherbet. It would go up on the specials board, and by the end of the night, when not one single order had come in, Chef would storm around the kitchen, foaming and spitting and berating the servers. *They weren't pushing hard enough. They were trying to sabotage him.* A few days later the item would be off the menu, and no one would ever mention it again.

That night, Stephanie's first night, it was a crayfish gumbo with okra, chilies, andouille sausage, and a raspberry finish. Chef had worked on it all week. Mark had talked a reviewer into coming and Chef was bouncing around the kitchen in anticipation. As he lifted the gumbo off the stove, he was actually humming.

He was carrying the pot across the kitchen to the warming station while Stephanie was on her knees, digging in the garbage for the retainer. When she found it, she jumped up with her arms in the air. It was something she wouldn't do today—a quick, unpredictable movement in a crowded kitchen filled with hot liquids and hotter tempers. But it was her first night, and she had just solved a big problem.

Or that's what she thought.

When she found the retainer, sticky and slimy, bits of mashed potato and parsley clinging to the metal wires, she threw her hands in the air, jumped up, and smashed into Chef.

The gumbo went flying.

If Stephanie had known *then* what she knew now, she would have just gone home.

Stephanie hadn't had the nerve to say one word to Chef before then. But now she was talking.

"Sorry, sorry," Stephanie said as Chef let out a wail.

"Sorry, sorry, sorry," she said as Chef picked up the pot and threw it down.

"Sorry," she said as Chef picked up the pot and threw it a second time.

So Stephanie started picking up the crayfish. Chef left the pot on the floor and said, "Let me help you." He took a handful of crayfish from Stephanie and began hurling them around the kitchen. Then suddenly Chef went still. He squatted down on the floor and lowered his hand sadly into a pool of gumbo. And as he squatted there, he started to cry. Which was far worse than the yelling.

Stephanie kept her head down and no one said a word. Everyone had *their* heads down, everyone suddenly intensely focused on their own business. Of course, there was no time for a mop and bucket, even if Stephanie knew where they were kept, and it was impossible to completely clean up the terra-cotta tiles or whatever they were. So she kept scooping the stuff up with her hands. When she was finished there was still a thin layer of gumbo smeared all over the floor.

For the rest of the night, the tiles were so slippery that you couldn't walk safely. The only way to get from the dining room to the line where you put in your order was to skate across, sliding along, never lifting your feet from the floor. As the night wore on and the spray from Pamu's dishwasher mixed with the gumbo smear, the floor got greasier and greasier. By nine o'clock people were carrying orders in one hand and using the other to grab onto racks and trolleys to keep themselves upright.

Any other night, Stephanie would have been fired on the spot. But they were short staffed, so they couldn't fire her. She couldn't believe it when she thought about it now.

She got a second shift.

She arrived determined to make amends.

She brought in a recipe.

She walked right behind the serving line, the stainless-steel counter with the heat lamps that divides the servers from the cooking staff, and handed Chef the recipe. She said, "I think you should put more basil in the tomato sauce. See, in this one it says a third of a cup of fresh basil."

She was trying to reach out.

Chef stared at her for a long time, and then turned around so that she was staring at his back. He said, "Get out of my kitchen."

That should have been the end of her, except *Robin* took her under her wing. Robin said, "She's okay. I'll train her."

Robin taught her everything.

It turned out Stephanie wasn't supposed to even *talk* to Chef. Stephanie wasn't supposed to talk to any of the cooks behind the line. And she certainly wasn't supposed to *go* behind the line.

"Are you kidding?" said Robin. "*Never*. Never go behind the line. Unless you have a death wish."

When things were hopping, there could be five servers working out front, all with five or six tables each. At an average of four people per table, that's a possible 120 problems. All of which had to be solved in sequence.

That was the pivot's job. You took your orders to the pivot. The pivot called them out.

The pivot was like an air traffic controller.

Stephanie teamed up with Robin in section one for a week, which is what should have happened at the beginning.

Robin had worked in the industry for years. She was a lifer. She was actually an actor, but she understood *everything* about serving.

"It's one of the toughest jobs in the world," said Robin at the end of Steph's first week. The Grill was closed. There were no customers left. They were sitting in Robin's section. Table two. Right in front of the fireplace, best table in the restaurant. They were polishing off a bottle of Californian Pinot Noir that table five hadn't finished.

Robin topped up their glasses.

It was Robin who showed Stephanie the ropes. It was Robin who sat beside her at the staff table in front of a big pile of napkins and taught her to roll cutlery: knife, fork, fold, fold. Knife, fork, fold, fold.

Stephanie learned everything from Robin.

It was Robin who taught her the Sullivan Nod.

The Sullivan Nod is a subliminal technique developed by a restaurant consultant named Tom Sullivan. He came up with it to increase the sale of appetizers.

"Does it really work?" asked Stephanie.

"Not *all* the time," said Robin. "But a *lot* of the time. It has been proven.

"If they choose apple pie for dessert," said Robin, "you say, *'Would you like ice cream or cheese with that?'*"

Robin nodded her head as she said "cheese."

Cheese cost more.

She did it again.

"Would you like ice cream or cheese," her head bobbing up and down almost imperceptibly.

"Just a little one," she said. "Sometimes they nod right along with you."

"Don't you feel guilty?" said Stephanie.

"Honey," said Robin, peering at the empty bottle of Pinot, "we get paid less than minimum. A bigger bill means a bigger tip. Besides, they *want* the cheese. They just don't want it to be their fault. They *want* you to talk them into it."

Robin got Stephanie over the hump. And slowly Stephanie was accepted. Or more to the point—taken for granted.

By Christmas she was pulling three shifts a week. Unlike the other temps, she never missed one. She showed up, and kept her head down.

The job seemed to get into her bones. At Christmas dinner, when she carried the potatoes to the table, she heard herself say, "Can I get you anything else?" At the school cafeteria, she had to stop herself from whisking away everyone else's trays when she'd finished eating.

She *dreamed* about it: Chef slamming the bell, Pivot calling out orders, everyone running about. Once she woke up in the middle of the night and found herself standing beside the kitchen table in her apartment holding a pitcher of water.

And now it was her last day.

Breakfast was slow, but lunch was frantic.

She got a family with four small children. She was headed for the kitchen as the children and their parents plumped through the front door. By the time she got to their table, two of the children were already tearing apart sugar packets, and the baby in the high chair had launched her sippy cup across the room.

The baby's name was Harmony, and she was two years old. The great pleasure in Harmony's life seemed to be dropping things from the high chair to the floor: cutlery, her napkin, the salt shaker. She had plenty of things to drop. Her mother kept handing them to her.

When Harmony got her meal, spaghetti and meat sauce, she started flinging handfuls of spaghetti.

Meanwhile there was the woman at table twenty-eight. The woman at twenty-eight was snapping her fingers.

When Stephanie got to her, the woman didn't say a word. She just sat there and stared at her plate. Stephanie stared too—without saying a word. It was passive-aggressive, but the woman had snapped her fingers. Stephanie was going to make *her* talk first. She would have waited her out if it had been quieter, but over at twenty-six one of the boys had crawled under the high chair, and Stephanie could see him unscrewing the lid from the ketchup bottle.

"Yes?" said Stephanie.

"This," said the lady, "isn't a chicken breast."

Stephanie blinked at the chicken breast. She didn't have a clue what to say.

"Chicken breasts," said the woman, "have bones. There are no bones."

"It's boneless," said Stephanie.

The woman looked up at her and nodded.

"Exactly," said the woman.

They stared at each other.

Stephanie cleared her throat.

She said, "It's supposed to be boneless."

She threw in a Sullivan Nod for good measure. The woman's lip curled. The woman started to raise her voice. "What do you take me for? Do you take me for an idiot? There's no such thing as a boneless chicken."

Stephanie picked up the plate and said, "I'll tell Chef."

Andy was the pivot that Saturday afternoon. He was standing in front of the line opposite the fry man and the grill man. Andy said, "Up on fourteen. Up on twelve," and then he looked at Stephanie and said, "You're kidding, right?"

Stephanie shook her head.

Andy said "I need two fries" to the fry man, and then he turned back to Stephanie. "She wants bones?"

Stephanie nodded.

Chef walked over and said, "What's the matter?"

Andy held the plate out and said, "She wants bones."

Chef glared at Stephanie.

Stephanie said, "Not me. The woman at twenty-eight."

Chef had spent an hour deboning and butterflying all the chicken. He didn't say a word. But his face began to change colour. First to pink, and then to red and then to a deeper red.

"She wants bones?" he whispered. Stephanie wished he would just yell. Instead he grabbed his hair and began to hop around in a circle, pulling at his hair and moaning.

Now everyone was staring at Stephanie as if *she'd* done something wrong. She was about to explain but remembered the family at twenty-six and bolted.

The father was waving the bill impatiently as she came through the kitchen door.

As for Harmony, Harmony was holding her spaghetti-smeared doll over the edge of her chair and grinning. As soon as she saw Stephanie she let the doll go and started to cry. Something inside Stephanie snapped. She walked toward the table pretending she hadn't seen anything, and she ground her foot into the doll's face.

Harmony gasped.

"Oh my goodness," said Stephanie, lifting her foot, "I am so sorry."

Ten minutes later, as Harmony was being carried out, Stephanie and the little girl locked eyes over her father's shoulder. Harmony glared at her. Stephanie stuck out her tongue.

That was lunch. At dinner the touchpad on the screen in Peter's station misaligned. Mysteriously, the touch function shifted one item to the left, which meant that when Peter touched "hamburger" on his display it came out as "salmon steak" on the pivot's printer. Of course, no one realized this right away. It took about an hour to figure it out, and by then Chef was moving from his chopping block to the stove, weeping noisily. Pamu the dishwasher was sitting glumly on the edge of the sink, eating fries.

Even Andy the pivot, unflappable Andy, was leaning against the heat lamps, head buried in his hands, refusing to talk.

The kitchen had ground to a halt.

Peter was beside himself. The people in Peter's section were beside themselves.

"We're in the weeds now," said Robin as she and Stephanie waited in front of the line.

It was Andy who pulled it together. Andy began to yank order slips from the cooking station. He put everyone's orders on hold as the cooks scrambled to catch up in Peter's section. It was a logical move, but it meant that pretty soon all the other servers were on edge too.

Of course it was one of the busiest Saturday nights in weeks. Before long everyone was shouting. Servers screaming at Andy, Andy screaming at Chef, Chef screaming at everyone. Orders appearing so fast there was no room for them under the heat lamps. Andy yelling "Pick up thirteen, pick up twelve, pick up twenty-one! Come on: pick up, pick up, pick up!"

There was smoke from the grill hovering in the air, blended with tempers, sweat, grease, the smell of fear and all of it, everything, seasoned by the fine spray coming out of Pamu's dish pit.

The servers walked into the screaming and started screaming themselves. Then they walked out carrying an order as if everything back there was calm and perfect.

Stephanie didn't scream. Instead she flew wordlessly from table to table, from bar to kitchen, as if she were some kind of manic wind-up doll. She picked up orders and set down drinks in a blur. She scraped spaghetti out of high chairs, plucked soggy napkins off the floor, wiped melted ice cream off the tables. She smiled when she didn't feel like smiling, and said "Enjoy your meal" when she really meant "Why can't you people eat at home?"

On the way past the bar, she scooped up ice cubes and dropped them down the back of her blouse to stay cool, just as Robin had shown her.

"I *hate* fresh ground pepper," said Robin as she pounded past Stephanie. She was juggling three enormous plates and a pepper grinder the size of a baseball bat.

At midnight, Stephanie was sitting at the staff table in the kitchen, her eyes glazed and her jaw slack, exhausted but unable to stop moving. Her section had emptied first. She was folding napkins, doing roll ups.

Her feet were aching. But she didn't dare take her shoes off. She knew that if she did she wouldn't be able to get them back on. Her calves hurt and her knees hurt.

She looked up.

Robin was standing there. Stephanie realized that she'd stopped folding. She hadn't folded anything for a good five minutes. She had been sitting there staring at—who knows, at nothing.

Robin sat down. "Your last night," she said. "How does it feel?"

"I don't know," said Stephanie. It was the truth.

Chef appeared at the table. "Here," he said, dropping half a baguette and a plate of duck pâté in front of each of them, then heading behind the line again.

Robin raised an eyebrow at Steph. "I think that means you're welcome back in September."

Stephanie nodded.

"What are you doing when you get home?" asked Robin, reaching for a roll up.

"I don't know," said Stephanie. "Maybe tree planting? Maybe Banff? I wish people would quit asking."

Robin nodded. "What about next year?"

"I don't know," said Stephanie, a little quickly.

There was an awkward pause.

"Sorry," she said. "It's just, you know, I always thought that when I graduated I'd go into law. And now I don't know. I know I'm not going into law. But I don't know what I want anymore."

Robin smiled. "Except you know you don't want to work in a restaurant."

Stephanie shook her head. "Absolutely not. No. I mean. Sorry. I don't mean it like that."

"That's okay," said Robin. "I never thought I wanted to either. But it turns out I'm good at it. And I happen to like it."

"You're super good," said Stephanie.

"You're not so bad," said Robin.

Stephanie went over to get a pitcher from the counter and brought it back to the table. She poured them both a glass of water. "Yeah. But—"

"But you don't want to be a waitress the rest of your life."

"I guess not."

They sat there for a moment without saying anything. Then Stephanie nodded and said, "Thank you."

Robin waved her hand dismissively, then wandered over to the kitchen door and peered out into the restaurant.

"Hey," she said. "Someone just came in. Will you handle it? Go tell him we're closed. I'm done."

Stephanie was done too. But she didn't say that. Robin had never asked *her* for anything. She got up and headed for the door.

It was always odd at the end of the night. To see the dining room with the lights up, the tables empty, all the disorganized chairs, the cluttered tables, the half-finished coffees.

She pushed the door open and stood there.

She couldn't see a soul. Kathie was the only one left. Kathie behind the bar, counting out. Kathie waved. Stephanie threw her an exaggerated shrug. And Kathie pointed at section one. Robin's section.

The guy was sitting at table two. The table by the fireplace. He had his back to Stephanie. There was something about the way he was sitting that seemed oddly familiar—like maybe she had served him before.

She gave Kathie a big nod, like, *Okay, I'm on it,* and she headed over.

She was halfway there, halfway across the room, looking at the table, thinking, *I know this guy,* when she sensed they weren't the only ones in the section. She felt a movement to her right and she stopped, turned, and looked. It was Pamu. The dishwasher.

He said, "Madame?"

And she forgot all about the guy at table two, because Pamu was standing there with a dishcloth over his arm like he was a headwaiter or something.

Pamu said, "May I show you your table, Madame?"

The whole moment is a bit of a blur. The next thing she remembers, they were standing by table two and Pamu had pulled out a chair and the guy who'd been sitting there was standing up. And it was Chef. Pamu was holding out the chair opposite him and Chef was motioning for her to sit down, and she sat, and then she looked up at Pamu and then at Kathie, who was walking across the room toward them with a bottle of wine, and Chef said, "I hope you don't mind. You were a little late. I took the liberty of ordering for you."

Andy was coming through the kitchen door. And everyone was behind him. They had a chicken liver and unagi terrine. The unagi was so sweet and the chicken liver so creamy. Japanese and French. Who else but Chef would think of combining them?

When they'd finished it, Chef said, "You will have to excuse me."

He went into the kitchen and came out ten minutes later with a platter of raviolis. Big raviolis, the size of your palm, filled with cheese and floating in melted butter—the pasta airy and as light as a cloud.

He had made ginger cake with lavender ice cream for dessert.

Stephanie looked over at Chef and said, "That was delicious."

He smiled at her.

It was the first time Stephanie had ever seen him smile.

She felt encouraged.

"I think you might have— I mean, this is really good. Maybe you have something here. Maybe you've hit your stride."

"Maybe you have too," said Chef.

Then he was standing up, raising his wineglass. "I want to make a toast," he announced.

"To Stephanie …"

"To Stephanie, who is not defeated by her mistakes, who never abandons her workmates, and who can stand the heat in the kitchen."

Everyone applauded. It was her last night there. It was the first time she felt as if she was one of them.

Someone said "Speech," and someone seconded the motion.

So she stood up and said, "I have learned so much from you guys. I'm going to miss you all."

She meant it.

They were applauding as she sat down.

Someone said, "See you in September."

Steph nodded as if to say yes, but then she stole a glance at Robin. Robin gave her an almost imperceptible shrug.

"I'm going to miss you," she said quietly to Robin about half an hour later as they were clearing up.

"Well," said Robin, "you know you're welcome for dinner any time you want."

"Thanks."

"On one condition, of course."

"What's that?" said Stephanie.

Robin smiled. "That you leave a decent tip."

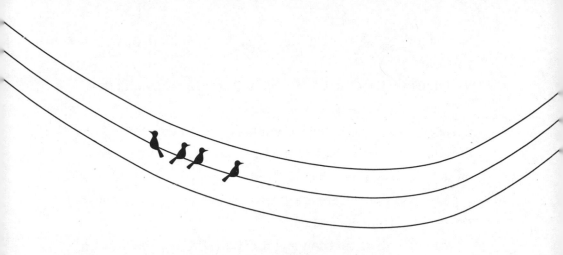

PRINCE CHARLES

It was the softest of summer mornings—a Sunday in the middle of August—and Dave, in jeans and a T-shirt, was lying on the couch. There was a coffee at his elbow and a pile of magazines were strewn about. It was, in other words, a scene of serenity and repose, a holiday of sorts, a retreat.

And then Morley appeared and said, "I think we have mice."

She might as well have announced the house was on fire.

Dave levitated. He lifted right off the couch.

He went from the horizontal to the vertical in such a blur that if you'd been there, if you'd seen it with your own eyes, you surely would have been unsure about what transpired. You might have asked yourself, *Did he just go right over the back of the sofa?*

It sure seemed like it.

One moment he was lying there as peacefully as a man could lie, the very personification of summer, and the next he was standing, staring at his wife, his agitation positively palpable.

"I think we have mice," Morley had said to horizontal Dave.

"No we don't," he said, vertically.

He almost sounded belligerent—as if he were accusing her of fabrication. He *looked* belligerent—vertical, but semi-crouched—as if preparing for a fight.

But it wasn't belligerence. It was fear. Or more accurately—terror. Dave is terrified of mice.

You might think that coming from Cape Breton, coming from Big Narrows, Cape Breton, Dave would have long ago made an accommodation with rodents. After all, Big Narrows is more rural than urban. Most people heated with wood when Dave was growing up, many still do, so there are wood lots, and wood piles, and maple bushes, and farms. There are barns, and deer in the pastures, and bear on the mountain, and plenty of things rodentia. You might think that having grown up in the middle of all this, Dave would have accepted the presence of mice.

But there had been an incident.

"I was eight," said Dave.

Actually, he was twelve. He was twelve years old. And he woke up in the middle of a dark night—

"Dark and *stormy* night," said Dave. "It was stormy. Thunder and lightning."

But it wasn't the thunder and lightning that woke him, it was the sense that there was something on his face.

He was asleep—deep asleep—and he tried to *stay* that way. He brushed at the thing the way he might have brushed at, say, a moth, which is what he thought it was, until he realized through the fog of that long ago night that it was a furry rather than a fluttery thing. A mouse, not a moth. And he had a surge of adrenalin unlike any surge he'd had before or has had since. He snapped awake, and there was a swat and a flurry—a fumble of boy and bedclothes—and then there was utter silence. Deep, dark, alone-in-the-middle-of-the-night silence.

And Dave reached out in the still of it and turned on the lamp on his bedside table.

Somehow he'd moved *so* fast, *so* suddenly, *so* unexpectedly that he'd plucked the thing off his face. He was sitting there staring at his clenched fist, too afraid to open it and too afraid not to.

He's had nightmares about that moment for years. Gangs of giant mice corner him in his closet—pick him up and pass him around.

But that was later. What happened next that night was that he called his parents.

And he called in a way that caused them to come running. When they got to his room, they found him sitting in his bed, holding his clenched fist as far away from the rest of him as he possibly could.

His mother sat down on the edge of the bed and began to stroke his hair. His father stood by the door.

Dave said, "I-have-a-mouse-in-my-hand-it-was-on-my-face-and-now-it-is-in-my-hand."

His mother said, "Sweetie, you're dreaming."

Then she said, "Open your hand. You'll see."

So he opened his hand.

"See," said Dave.

His mother screamed.

And Dave, in his surprise, threw the mouse.

It landed in his mother's hair.

She didn't react well. It's hard to know, all these years later, whether it was the actual encounter with the mouse or the encounter with his mother that led to Dave's intractable dread of rodents.

But now, perhaps, you can be more understanding of why, when Morley came downstairs and said *We have mice,* it was terror, not belligerence, that responded.

Of course, once the idea that they might have mice was introduced, the sorry slide into sleep disturbance began, followed, predictably enough, with episodes of sleep-deprived craziness.

Morley, it's worth pointing out, hadn't actually seen any mice. But there was plenty of evidence. Once you started looking, it was everywhere.

At first, Dave *tried* to affect a light-hearted nonchalance.

"Maybe those aren't mice," he said when she led him into the kitchen and pointed at the counter. "Maybe we have an infestation of poppy-seed bagels."

But he knew better. He could hear them scurrying around—in the walls, or ceiling, or wherever it was they were scurrying.

They made their first sighting a week later. Another Sunday, just before supper. They were in the kitchen. Dave was sitting at the table going through old mail. Morley was standing by the stove.

Something grey and peripheral scurried along the baseboards.

"Did you see that?" said Dave.

"I'm not sure," said Morley.

"I am," said Dave. And he stood up and reached for the car keys.

"No napalm," said Morley.

"What about traps?" said Dave.

"Humane traps," said Morley.

John Wayne once said that courage is being scared to death and saddling up anyway.

Morley said, "Since when did we start quoting John Wayne?"

Dave said, "Since things got serious."

It was the next night.

It was bedtime.

Or it was bedtime for Morley. Dave wasn't going to bed quite yet. Dave was saddling up.

Instead of pyjamas, Dave had slipped into black jeans and a black shirt. He had a flashlight clipped to his belt and a pair of night-vision goggles on his forehead.

"You want to catch a mouse," said Dave, "the first thing you have to know is where to put your traps."

He leaned over and kissed Morley on the forehead.

"Go to sleep," he said.

"Be careful," she said.

Dave nodded earnestly.

He'd completely missed the sarcasm.

He sat at the kitchen table like a marine on perimeter duty. He breathed softly, but made no other movements. He knew that if he sat long enough he would vanish and things would appear. Sure enough, they did.

The first thing came from under the radiator. He didn't spot it right away, of course. It came too quietly. A whisper, a twitch; a suggestion of grey, a shadow of movement. But he sensed it. He *saw* it a few moments later. Scurrying along the wall by the window. Little staccato bursts of movement. Its tail was sticking up in the air, its bulging eyes gleaming in the green glow of his night goggles.

And so it was confirmed.

They had mice.

He watched it make its mousey way across the kitchen— hugging the baseboard, under the window, behind the fridge, right to the cat bowl. Of course. The cat bowl. It was so obvious he had completely missed it.

Five minutes later, it was back again. But now there were two of them. The mouse from behind the radiator had been joined by a mouse from behind the stove. The stove, and the radiator, and now a third from the pantry. Three at once.

Two more in the basement. A sixth in the upstairs bathroom. They were infested.

At four o'clock Dave crawled into bed, exhausted and shaken.

He set up traps the next morning. He caught three on the first night. Catch and release.

"Where did you release them?" asked Morley.

"The Turlingtons'," said Dave.

He was kidding.

He had taken them to the park.

But the trick to getting rid of mice, of course, isn't getting them out. The trick to getting rid of mice is figuring out where they're getting in.

"We have to seal up the house," said Dave, who had spent the morning crawling around outside.

"Where *are* they getting in?" said Sam.

"Dryer vent," said Dave. "They chewed through the mesh."

The thing is, a mouse can wiggle through the most unimaginably small space. All a mouse needs is a slit the height of a couple of dimes. Dave got a caulking gun and caulked every crack and crevice.

"Tight as a drum," said Dave to Sam.

"Of course you know what that means," said Sam, unhelpfully. "It means you haven't only sealed them out, Dad. You've sealed them *in*. It's like a horror movie."

"We've done this in math," said Sam that night at supper. "It's called a progression. You start with one pair. And they have six babies. Assume half of them are female. And assume *they* each have six babies. There is a formula."

He ran upstairs and came back with a calculator.

He sat down and began to happily punch in numbers.

Sam said, "Roughly speaking, all things being equal and rounding things off, we are talking, in six months ..."

Sam frowned.

Sam said, "Wait a minute. That can't be right."

He began again.

"You start with a pair. They have six babies."

A minute later he looked up and grinned at his father.

"Roughly speaking," said Sam, "in six months we should have over ten thousand mice."

So there they were—middle of September. One month, give or take, into Sam's progression. Sealed into their house with who knows how many breeding mice.

And the mice were getting increasingly bold.

They had begun to see them during the day. Something out of the corner of their eye—after dinner or just before bed—flashes of grey, sometimes real, sometimes imagined. It was impossible to tell the difference.

They gave it a name. PPMS. Phantom peripheral mouse syndrome.

It was beginning to feel as if they were under siege. As if mice were parachuting into their home.

They'd be having breakfast and one of them would stop mid-bite and point at a tiny head popping out of the toaster, or through one of the burners in the stove.

They found stashes of Cheerios and cat food in their shoes and pockets, slippers and drawers.

Morley was the first to find a body. It was in the lint trap of the dryer. Only the tail was showing. She thought it was a hair elastic. It took a couple of firm tugs before she discovered that the "elastic" was attached to a mouse.

One day she came home and found Dave crossing the kitchen on two kitchen chairs, moving one and then the other.

"Get me my cat," said Dave.

But Morley had her hands full of groceries.

Galway was in the living room, curled on the couch.

"Come on, old girl," said Dave. "The game's afoot."

Dave carried Galway into the kitchen and placed her on the floor so that her nose was against the baseboard. And he waited.

"Soon," said Dave.

He and Morley were sitting at the kitchen table, each with a cup of tea.

Fifteen minutes became twenty.

"Come to mama," said Dave.

And come the mouse finally did.

It skittered along the baseboard until it saw the cat—and came to a skittering halt, as if it were a cartoon mouse. As if it had just skittered up to the edge of the cliff. It stopped skittering and it stared.

Galway lifted her head and stared back.

Everything in the kitchen ground to a halt.

No one was moving. Not Dave. Not Morley. Not the cat. And certainly not the mouse.

"Stalemate," whispered Dave.

"I'm not sure I like this," whispered Morley.

Then the mouse ran between the cat and the baseboard. Actually brushed Galway's nose. And Galway didn't move. Not a whisker.

"Did you see its ears?" said Morley.

"Like Prince Charles," said Dave.

Suddenly one of their mice had a name.

Prince Charles.

It took another week before Dave called for help.

And of course of all the exterminators in all the world, *he* got the one who loved mice.

Duane.

Duane, who brought his homemade picture book and sat them down at the kitchen table. Duane in his blue sweater vest opened his picture book and said, "You need to understand a mouse's life."

As if he'd been sent by the mice. As if he *worked* for them.

"What no one seems to understand," said Duane, "is that you could easily remove some of the big players off the top of the food chain—and I'm not suggesting this would be a good thing—but you could let them go, let them go extinct, and the world, the natural world, wouldn't notice. The world would continue pretty much as it is."

Duane flipped the page of his book. A picture of a polar bear. A picture of a panda. Then he flipped again. Now he was holding up a picture of a mouse. A mouse that looked strangely like Prince Charles.

"But rodents," said Duane, "you remove all the rodents from the world and there would be problems. Big, big problems."

Duane snapped his fingers.

"Things would starve. And I am talking about things that are more lovable than mice. Feathered and furry things. Things like foxes and owls."

"But there are no owls in this house," said Dave.

Duane wasn't about to concede his point.

Finally, however, Dave was able to persuade him to sell them some poison.

"You don't have to put it down," Duane said as Dave walked him to the door.

"Stockholm syndrome," Dave said to Morley when he came back.

Morley was peering at the box of poison.

"Don't worry," said Dave. "It's humane poison. I checked."

Things improved, albeit slowly.

The scurrying diminished. The nibbling stopped. And one by one the mice disappeared. Until there was only one mouse left.

One that seemed to have a resilience the others lacked.

"Prince Charles," said Morley.

Prince Charles, who had read Galway so perfectly that night and would now perch on her bowl and help itself to her food while the cat held back and waited her turn.

Prince Charles, who seemed to be there to stay.

Everyone seemed ready to accommodate the mouse. To accept it as one of the family. It seemed to have earned its place.

Dave said, "I'm okay with that."

It was just the one, after all.

It became clear a few nights later that he was not okay with it at all.

They were finishing dinner when he leapt from the table and began swatting his thigh.

"Help me!" he screamed. "Help me."

There was a mouse running up his leg.

He could feel it under his pants.

He was standing there, in the middle of his kitchen, tugging at his belt with one hand, squeezing the mouse so hard with the other that he couldn't believe it was still struggling.

"Help me," he screamed again.

His pants were at his ankles.

But now he'd kicked his pants off and was gripping them in his fist, the mouse trapped in the folds of one leg.

It was like that night so long ago, when he was a boy in bed, calling for his parents, except now he was standing in his kitchen, a grown man in his underwear, struggling with his own pants. Driven by terror and instinct, he did the same thing he'd done when he was a young boy. He hauled his arm back and threw the mouse as hard as he could.

As the mouse (and his pants) sailed away from him in one tangled mess, he realized what his horrified wife and son had already realized. That it wasn't a mouse at all. It was his vibrating cell phone.

They all watched as the bundle of pants and phone arced across the kitchen, over the island and over the counter, exploding through the window and sailing out into the yard.

He put out the traps again that night.

Prince Charles had clearly been able to resist the peanut butter that had been the downfall of so many of his brothers and sisters. Dave had read somewhere that mice love chocolate.

So he gave chocolate a try.

When he got up the next morning, Prince Charles was sitting blissfully in the bottom of the trap, his little whiskers covered in hazelnut-caramel truffle.

No one else was awake.

Dave made coffee and pondered his next step. He put the trap on the windowsill and stared at it. When Morley came down she stared at it too.

Dave said, "They say drowning is the most humane death."

Morley looked horrified. She'd been thinking they should get a little mouse cage, with a drinking bottle and a little dish for cat kibble.

Dave said, "Give your head a shake."

After breakfast he put the trap in his backpack, intending to bike over to the park where he'd left all the others. But when he got there, all he could think of was—

"Duane," said Morley when he came home. "His name was Duane."

The exterminator.

If mice were nature's daily bread, setting Prince Charles free in the park was like opening the pantry door. Dave had sat on a bench with the backpack beside him and (not for the first time) wondered about his moral inconsistency. The way he would indulge his cat but would eat a cow. Kill mice, and coddle a hamster. Fret over his kids, and not the children of others. The only thing that explained any of it was the most irrational thing in the world. Love. Or if you wanted to slide it down a notch, compassion. And when did he start loving mice? Where did that come from?

It came from the law of proximity, of course. We love the things that are closest to us.

But if you love the one, must you not love the many? And where would that leave you? What would that mean?

Today it meant that he picked up the pack and put it on his back. Then he went home and got his car. He stopped at the store and put a sign in the window. OPEN AT NOON, it said. And he drove out toward the airport.

He went to the racetrack—as rural a place as he knew in the city. They still let you walk around in the barns. And so he wandered around, past all the sleek horses, past all the spiffy stalls.

He was waiting for the moment when he'd be alone. When that moment finally came, he opened the little trap and gave it a shake.

Prince Charles fell from the cage, landed on the concrete floor, ran around in an almost circle, started toward the door, turned and skittered into a stable, and disappeared under the straw.

Dave stood there, the trap in hand, half expecting Prince Charles to come back and wave or something. But of course he didn't come back.

The law of proximity had come and now it was gone. The spell was broken. The mouse was in the straw, and Dave was just another guy late for work.

He shrugged and put the cage back in the pack. He nodded at a stable boy as he headed out of the barn, back to the car and the uncertain world in which he lived.

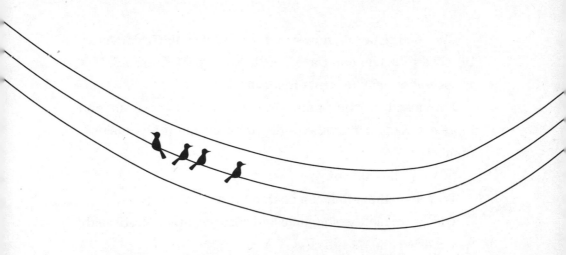

JIM'S SUMMER TRIP

A summer night can settle on the city with the softness of snow—the rustle of leaves, the chunking of sprinklers, the humming of insects—summoning neighbours to do what suits summer best. Absolutely nothing.

One early summer night, Dave's neighbour Jim Scoffield was sitting on his front porch with nothing to do.

Dave wandered by.

"Beer?" called Jim from the shadows. "Tea?"

It is Jim's habit, on summer evenings, to sit out there like that.

He knows it's unlikely that anyone will see him through the shadows of the railings and ivy. Mostly he sits and watches the summer parade. Occasionally he waves it in.

"Not sure I have time," said Dave. Meaning for a tea or a beer. But he wandered up the walk nonetheless.

"Sam is going to the movies," said Dave. "I said I would drive him."

Once on the porch, however, the idea of summer conversation overtook him and Dave sat. "Let me check," he said. "Let me see what time he wants to leave."

Jim picked up the phone from the arm of his chair and lobbed it softly across the porch. Dave caught it and dialed a number.

"It's me," he said softly.

Then something that Jim couldn't hear.

Then, with plenty of volume and some surprise, "But I said *I* would drive him."

A pause. "Okay. Okay. I know."

And Dave shrugged and threw the phone back to Jim.

Sam had already left.

"Took the subway," said Dave. And then he said it again, "I said *I* would drive him."

And so with a second shrug Dave settled on the railing and Jim said, "I'll get the tea."

It had been happening more and more often—these moments with Sam.

Dave hadn't noticed them at first, but now that he *had,* it was clear to him that the moments were adding up.

One morning, in the spring, right out of the blue, Sam had said, "Don't make my lunches anymore. I would rather make my own lunches."

"Why?" said Dave.

Dave and Morley had been making Sam's lunches for years.

"You don't know what I like," said Sam.

And then, exactly the same with the laundry.

Dave was wandering around collecting clothes for a load. And Sam said, "I don't have anything."

"You must have *something*," said Dave. "I am doing darks."

"You shrunk my T-shirt last time," said Sam. "I'll do my own."

Which left Dave on Jim's porch. Fretting. Thinking that he should have said something right at the start. If he'd said something right at the start, maybe he could have nipped things in the bud.

"Nipped what in the bud?" said Jim, who had reappeared carrying a couple of glasses.

"Your tea," he said, handing one to Dave.

A shot of Lagavulin. Sixteen years old. Neat.

Dave fell into the chair opposite Jim, took a sip of whisky, and sighed. He wasn't planning on mentioning it. To anyone. Least of all to Jim. He'd decided *against* asking for advice. He'd already made up his mind anyway. He didn't want anyone changing it.

But there they were. Night was settling. And Jim was not the advice-giving type. Jim didn't have kids of his own. He once told Dave it was his one big regret.

Jim would be neutral. Dave could tell Jim, and there would be no advice to take, or worse, to ignore.

So he took another sip and said, "I'm pretty sure it wasn't Sam's idea. I'm pretty sure it was his friend Murphy's."

Jim cocked his head.

"Murphy," said Dave. "The kid with the glasses and the ears."

Of course it didn't matter whose idea it was anymore. The important thing was to put a stop to it.

They wanted to go to Nova Scotia for the summer.

"To Cape Breton," said Dave. "To visit my mother."

For a number of summers now, Sam and Murphy had gone for a week or two and stayed with Dave's mother, Margaret. The first few summers, Dave had driven them down and hung around. The past few, they'd gone by themselves.

"So what's the problem?" said Jim.

"They flew," said Dave. "They flew to Halifax. I put them on the plane. My mom picked them up."

"And?" said Jim.

"They want to go by train," said Dave. "It's a two-day trip."

Jim said, "Did I ever tell you about the summer I was eleven?"

Then he said, "Let me top up your glass."

To understand Jim's eleventh summer, you need to know something about the ones that came before.

Jim's father left when Jim was a baby. He grew up with his mom, Irene. Though back in those days everyone called Jim's mom Sparkle.

Before she was born, someone gave Irene's soon-to-be older sister a book about a cat who was having kittens.

"I'm having a baby just like the cat in the book," explained Irene's mom.

The cat was called Sparkle.

Irene's sister got everything muddled. When her mother came back from the hospital with Irene, Irene's sister said, "Where's the kitten? Where's Sparkle?" She thought her *mother* was having a kitten too.

Irene grew up to be a nurse. And Irene and Jim lived in the Annapolis Valley, in Nova Scotia. One of the prettiest places you can imagine, all the little towns strung out along the river like beads on a necklace.

"We lived on the south mountain," said Jim. "More in the country than in town."

Dave interrupted. He said, "Hold on a sec. I'm worried about Sam—I think I should call and make sure he made it."

This time Jim didn't offer Dave the phone. Jim just kept going.

"One day," said Jim, "I was maybe five, I missed the school bus. It used to stop right out in front of the house, and I missed it. And I came in crying. I said, 'I missed the bus.'"

"Sparkle shrugged and said, 'You're going to have to walk, then.'"

"She made you walk?" said Dave.

"We didn't have a car," said Jim.

"And we *had* walked before. So I sort of knew the way."

"How far?" said Dave.

"Two or three miles," said Jim. "I had to cross the river and cut through the Pattersons' farm. And then through town."

"That's pretty impressive," said Dave.

"I impressed myself," said Jim. "The fields at the back of the farm felt as wide as the ocean."

"Were you scared?" said Dave.

Jim shrugged. "I did it two, maybe three times a year after that," said Jim. "You know what I used to look out for?"

"Dogs," said Dave.

"Not dogs," said Jim. "And not strangers, either. Worse."

"Worse than dogs and strangers?" said Dave.

"Far worse," said Jim. "Eight-year-old boys."

For his eighth birthday Sparkle got Jim a bike.

"I had complete freedom," said Jim. "I used to ride it all over the place. By the time I was nine I'd been everywhere."

Dave was fiddling with his drink, thinking about the boundaries he'd set for Sam when Sam was *ten*. As far as the main street—but not across it. No farther than the park.

"There were no boundaries," said Jim. "None."

Dave was staring at the phone again, about to reach out and pick it up, call Sam for just a quick check-in, when Jim, who could, apparently, read minds, slipped it under his chair.

"He's fine," said Jim.

The winter Jim was eleven, there was a school trip to Quebec City.

Jim missed the trip.

"I'm not *sure* why," said Jim. "I think we couldn't afford it."

To make up for the missed trip, Sparkle suggested that Jim go to Winnipeg that summer.

Sparkle had a sister there.

"And I had cousins," said Jim.

"To tell you the truth," said Jim, "I always wondered if she might have had a boyfriend. I always wondered if she maybe wanted some time alone.

"Anyway. I didn't care. Still don't. I was excited to go.

"I had a paper route," said Jim. "So I paid for half and I made all the arrangements. Bought the tickets and everything."

Tickets. Plural. Because you have to take three separate trains to get from Halifax to Winnipeg.

Jim bought the tickets and packed his own suitcase. Sparkle packed the food.

"I had enough for a few days," said Jim.

"Some fruit. Some cheese. A couple of bottles of Sussex ginger ale. I can still remember what my bag smelled like. Peanut butter and jam sandwiches don't travel well when you pack them against an orange. A peanut butter sandwich turns into a baseball mitt when you pack it beside an orange."

The trip still takes four days and three nights. You cross two time zones.

"The time changes were my first problem," said Jim.

"I switched my watch when we crossed the New Brunswick border. And then I forgot I'd done that and switched it again when we got to Montreal."

He had a couple of hours in between trains in Montreal. His plan was to go and see the Montreal Forum. He thought he would meet Rocket Richard.

He put his suitcase in a locker at the station and set off. When he got to the Forum he checked his watch. Which was an hour off. It said *quarter to five*.

"I nearly blew a gasket," said Jim.

"I was sure I'd missed my train. I thought I was going to be stranded in Montreal."

He ran back to the station in a panic. He went to the ticket counter and jumped up and down to get the guy's attention.

"He was pretty dismissive," said Jim. "He told me I had *plenty* of time."

Jim bought a snow globe at a little store in the station.

"I still have it upstairs," said Jim. "Want to see it?"

Dave shook his head. "It's okay," said Dave.

He caught the flick in Jim's eyes and added, "I'm sure it's beautiful."

Of course Jim didn't have a berth.

"We couldn't afford a berth," said Jim. He had to sleep in the coach. In his seat.

"It wasn't so bad," said Jim.

One night he snuck into the dome car and fell asleep in the very front seat. When he woke they were stopped on a siding in northern Ontario. They were waiting for a freight. There was a lake and a little bridge over a stream. The sun was just about to come up. He had never seen a sky like that. It was as if it were melting. And if that wasn't enough, a deer and her fawn came out of the trees and stood there and stared at the train for a magical moment. Magical except there was a lady sitting beside him he'd never seen in his life, and he had his head on her shoulder.

He didn't know what to do. Terrified, he didn't move a muscle.

But she must have sensed him stirring. She said, "You awake?," as though it was perfectly normal. Then she asked where his mother was.

"I lied," said Jim. "I told her my mom was downstairs. I was afraid she was going to have me thrown off. Whenever I saw her after that, I'd hide in the bathroom.

"Once I saw her coming through the cars and I sat down beside another lady and pretended *she* was my mother."

Then there was the soldier.

"He bought me a bag of chips at the snack bar," said Jim. "I was scared to take them. But I was also hungry."

There was a town where the train went right down the main street.

"It was the middle of the night," said Jim. "I woke up in my seat and looked out the window and saw all these stores right against the window. It was like a dream."

Somewhere the next day a boy his age got on the train.

"I saw him on the platform. He was travelling with a lady I thought was his mother. She turned out to be his aunt.

"He got on the coach before mine. I just knew he was going to be trouble. And that night when I came out of the bathroom, he was waiting for me.

"I didn't want him to know I was alone. I told him I was the conductor's son.

"The next morning when I woke, he was standing by my seat. He said he knew I was lying. He said he'd asked the conductor. And then while we were looking at each other, and I was waiting for him to do something, the soldier came by and asked if we wanted to finish his bag of chips. We shared the chips, and we became best friends. We hung out for a day— ran all over the train.

"The boy stole a chocolate bar from the snack bar and we went into the washroom and ate it.

"I never shoplifted because I didn't want to get caught. And I didn't like taking stuff that wasn't mine. But I liked it when others did it."

When the boy and his aunt got off the train, Jim watched them from the window.

"I remember them standing on the platform and seeing his aunt point the way. I remember thinking I had no one to tell me which way."

"You had to look after yourself," said Dave.

Jim sat there on the porch in his checked shirt and straw fedora. He smiled and pushed the hat back. "That's right," he said.

And so Dave changed his mind. And Sam and Murphy went to Cape Breton by train. Alone. On the day they left, Dave packed them food and drove them to the station. Sam didn't complain about the food.

Dave's plan was to park and go in with them to make sure they got off on the right foot. At least if they got *off* on the right foot he would have done everything he could. When they got to the station he had another change of heart. He pulled up to the sidewalk instead of into the parking lot.

"Well," he said.

They got out and stood by the car, two impossibly young boys with two impossibly large packs at their feet.

"Well," said Sam.

"Well," said Dave.

Murphy rolled his eyes, looked at the two of them, and picked up his pack.

"Well," said Murphy.

And that was that.

Dave hugged Sam, and then he said, "Come on, Murphy. You might as well be family. Give me a hug."

It was an awkward hug. Murphy's glasses fell off. But Dave was glad he hugged him. And as he stood and watched the boys walk under the huge stone arch of the station's front door—watched them joining the river of other travellers—he felt as if he had done the right thing.

Until disaster struck.

They were just about out of sight when he saw something fall out of Sam's back pocket.

It was hard to tell, but he was pretty sure it was his train ticket.

"Uh oh," said Dave.

He stared at the white envelope lying on the ground—and at his son walking blithely on. Surely this was the hand of God. Surely this was God's way of telling him that this enterprise was doomed. A disaster waiting to happen. Surely this was God begging him to put a stop to it.

He spun around and held out his keys and locked the car. Then he whirled back and headed off. His eyes were on the envelope—the ticket or whatever it was.

Everything in his being told him to hurry, to hurry. He didn't run, but he was moving.

He took only three steps.

Something stopped him.

Jim Scoffield's voice.

"I remember coming home," said Jim. "And I remember how excited I was to see my mother. She came to meet me at the station. *I* saw her before *she* saw me. She was standing at the end of the platform scanning the crowd. And at that moment, when I saw her and she hadn't seen me, I knew that I was coming home a different person than I was when I left—like I'd been away at university, or maybe to war."

That stopped Dave. Dead in his tracks.

When are you supposed to let your children march off alone? When are you supposed to let them learn from their mistakes?

"Now or never," muttered Dave.

So he stopped. And waited until he could barely see them. Their backpacks bumping in and out of sight. It took every ounce of self-control he had ever asked of himself. But he stayed put as they disappeared.

I wish I could tell you that as he stood there, he saw them stop suddenly. Saw Sam reach and pat his back pocket and then retrace his steps and retrieve the ticket. I would love to tell you that. But that's not what happened.

In Dave's imagination it went like that. And then he imagined this.

He waits. He waits until he knows they aren't coming back, and then he waits a little longer. And only then does he walk, tentatively, toward the paper—still lying there in the crowded station entrance. When he gets to it he realizes it isn't a ticket, it's an envelope, a letter or something.

He looks down at it, and as he stands there looking at it, a man with a briefcase bumps him, and then a woman with a suitcase brushes by, and he can feel their annoyance at him standing there in their way, in the middle of things. So he bends over and scoops up the envelope.

There is one word written on the front. "Dad."

He doesn't open it until he gets back to the car.

It is a handwritten note.

Hey Dad, it reads. *That was a test.*

Congratulations.

You passed.

I knew you would.

We'll be fine

You don't have to worry

Love. Your son, Sam.

And as he sits there in the car with the note in his lap, he tears up.

Tears of relief.

He reads the note and his worries evaporate—*just like that.*

That's what he imagined as he stood there staring at the entrance to the busy station.

But that's *not* how it ended.

The real ending wasn't nearly as good.

But it was good enough.

As Dave stood there imagining the envelope addressed to him, he watched the man with the briefcase, the man he imagined bumping into him, bend over and pick the paper up.

It wasn't an envelope.

It *was* Sam's train ticket. He didn't know that for sure, but from where he stood it sure looked like a ticket.

He watched the man hold the ticket up in the air and call out to the boys. And then he watched Sam stop, turn, pat his pocket, and run back. He watched him say something to the man, point at Murphy, take the ticket and shake the man's hand. Then he watched Sam turn and run—catching up with Murphy just before they both disappeared.

They had made it over the first hurdle. *From* the car, *through* the door of the station, by the skin of their teeth. It had been a close call. But they'd made it nonetheless. And they had made it the way Dave had made it over so many of the hurdles he'd cleared over the years. They had made it with the kindness of a stranger. That is the way of the world. It is full of kind strangers. They would be fine. Dave wouldn't be, but they would. And that would have to do.

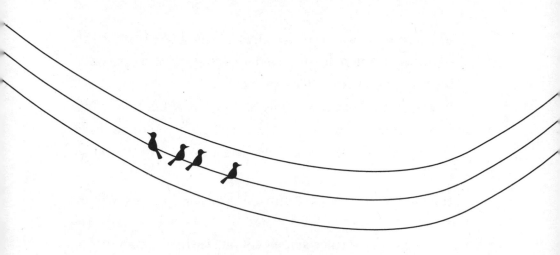

SAM'S FIRST KISS

Murphy had told him exactly where to be.

They had gone over it again and again.

"You go *past* the theatre," said Murphy. "And then the coffee shop. And the shoe store. Five stores in all. One, two, three …"

"Five," said Sam, interrupting.

"Right," said Murphy. "*Past* all five. And then there's the alley on your right."

"And I go down the alley," said Sam.

"Right," said Murphy.

"And there are three fire exits down there," said Sam. "And I go past all three, and around to the back. And as soon as I turn the corner …"

"There's a door," said Murphy. "On your right."

"It's a brown door," said Sam.

"Reddy-brown," said Murphy.

"And I wait there," said Sam. "I wait by the door."

That's where he was now, waiting, in the alley, behind the theatre, beside the reddy-brown door. Although he would have described it as a rusty door himself.

It was a Thursday. It was July. It was just about noon. The first features were an hour in. He wasn't *supposed* to be there for twenty minutes. He was early—because he didn't want to be late.

On the way over he'd run into Lyla Douglas. Lyla was Willow Cassidy's best friend. Willow was a girl in Sam's class. He hadn't seen Willow since school got out. He had spent most of July trying to bump into her.

Biking by places where Willow might be. The pool, the park, the library. Nothing worked. This afternoon he was going to bike by Willow's house. Except Murphy had made plans for him.

There was a bang. Sam jumped. The sound of metal against metal. One of the fire exits. An usher wearing a white shirt and red jacket came around the corner carrying a big bag of garbage. He threw the bag in the dumpster. When the usher spotted Sam, he stopped and stared at him, looking Sam up and down.

So what Sam did was turn and walk away, in the opposite direction, as if he couldn't have cared less about the rusty door. He came back five minutes later. The coast was clear. He knocked on the exit twice, just as Murphy had told him, and said the password softly.

"Open the pod bay door, Hal."

Nothing happened.

When the door finally did open, Sam almost missed it.

Because Murphy hardly cracked it. Anyone could have missed it. In his defence, when he noticed, he played his part perfectly. He ran back to it, gave it a tug, and slipped in. Well, okay. He forgot to check if anyone was watching. But no one *was* watching, so that worked out okay.

And now he was inside, squinting in the dark theatre hallway.

Murphy was nowhere to be seen. So Sam did what he was supposed to do: he turned left and went down the hallway to the men's room.

Murphy appeared three, at most four, minutes later. He was holding out a ticket stub. He said, "Here. In case anyone asks."

Sam gazed at the stub and smiled.

Murphy grabbed both his shoulders, gave him a shake, and said, "Louis, I think this is the beginning of a beautiful friendship."

Sam, who didn't get the reference, put the ticket stub in his pocket and said, "*That* was amazing. An usher came out and everything."

Five minutes later they were in the lobby, in the arcade, at the back, on the left, behind the candy counter—the side with all the pinball machines, not the driving games. Standing beside the claw machine. The crane. They were leaning against the glass case, staring at the pile of prizes—at the mountain of plush toys.

"See," said Murphy. "See it?"

Murphy was pointing to the very back. Sam was shaking his head.

"Under the little panda," said Murphy.

There. Barely sticking out of the pile of stuffed animals was the corner of a Niriko 16.

"It has the touch screen," said Sam, "and Optix Two."

Murphy nodded.

"My precious," said Murphy. "My precious."

Murphy had begun to circle the game.

"We have to move the panda," said Murphy. "And probably the basketball."

One of those miniature souvenir basketballs. Murphy, who'd returned to the front of the machine and had his hands on the joystick, pushing it left and right, said, "We move the panda and the ball—we have a clear shot."

Sam said, "No one *ever* wins these games. They're rigged."

Murphy said, "Yup. They're rigged. The difference between you and me, and everyone else, is—I know *how* they're rigged."

Murphy had been coming to the theatre every day for a week. Instead of watching movies, Murphy had been studying the game.

"It's like a slot machine," said Murphy. "It's programmed. It pays off every hundred games. Every hundred games the claw holds on. The rest of the time it's programmed to drop the prize on the way to the chute. I'm waiting for the hundredth game."

Sam said, "So why do you need me?"

Murphy said, "You're going to guide me in. I still have to get the claw on target. See the mirror on the back wall? I keep overshooting."

And so they sat there, behind the candy counter and the pinball games, where they could watch the game and no one could watch them.

Murphy had a paper. Every time someone played the game he made a mark on his paper.

At 1:35 a man came up and stared at the prizes just the way they had. He didn't look like a wealthy man. He looked like the kind of man you might see driving a taxi. Or in a movie theatre in the middle of the day.

He walked around the machine and then over to the candy counter. He came back with a handful of quarters. He lined them up on the machine.

Sam leaned toward Murphy and said, "You worked out the morality of this?"

Murphy stared at him.

"Letting him play," said Sam, "when we know the outcome."

Murphy took off his glasses, pulled out his shirt-tail, and started to polish the lenses.

Murphy said, "You mean, have I considered the *ethics*."

Sam could feel his heart sink. "Whatever."

Murphy put his glasses back on and reached for his paper.

Murphy said, "I didn't program the game."

It was three o'clock.

They were like a pair of detectives on a stakeout.

And like detectives everywhere, they were starting to get on each other's nerves.

"How much have you spent so far?" asked Sam.

"That's hardly the point," said Murphy.

"What's the point?" said Sam.

"The point," said Murphy, "is getting a Niriko 16 for a quarter."

"But you've spent way more than a quarter already," said Sam.

Murphy looked at his paper.

"Sixty-three down," he said. "Thirty-seven to go."

"This is ridiculous," said Sam.

"It's called delayed pleasure," said Murphy. "And you just picked up the marshmallow. And, as I have explained, more than once, the ability *not* to pick up the marshmallow is an indicator of future success. In just about everything. You should restrain yourself."

"I'm trying," said Sam.

"Try harder," said Murphy.

Five minutes later Sam said, "I didn't pick up the marshmallow, by the way. I just pointed out that this is ridiculous. You told me we were going to the movies."

"What we have here is a failure to communicate," said Murphy. "We *are* at the movies."

Murphy was waving his hand around his head.

"Except," said Murphy, "this is better. This is for real. Plus, for some of us here, it has the added benefit of delayed pleasure. You want more popcorn, perhaps?"

Sam nodded.

Murphy worked a popcorn bag out of his pocket and carefully unfolded it. He handed the bag to Sam.

On his first day Murphy had discovered that if you buy the family-sized popcorn you got free refills. He had rescued the bag from one of the cinemas.

"From where, exactly?" said Sam.

"From the floor," said Murphy. "It's one of the benefits of a movie theatre. A movie theatre is the last place in the world where littering is socially acceptable."

Sam took the bag and wandered over to the candy counter. He had already been twice.

He waited, as Murphy had instructed him, timing himself so that he'd be served by a clerk who hadn't seen him already.

It was only when he was standing at the counter that he realized he'd chosen the guy from the alley.

He smiled at him and handed him the bag. The guy didn't blink.

Sam waited until the clerk had turned and begun to shovel the bag full of popcorn and then quietly, under his breath so that no one could hear, he said, "Hasta la vista, baby."

Five minutes later he was back again, sitting beside Murphy, eating his popcorn—using his tongue to pick up the kernels and pull them into his mouth, like a horse with a feed bag.

"What number are we at?" he asked once too often.

"At the same place we were five minutes ago," said Murphy peevishly. "Why don't you go watch a film. I'll come get you when it's time."

So Sam stood up.

As he walked away, Murphy said, "Enjoy your marshmallow."

There were twelve cinemas to choose from. He went back to the refreshment stand and decided to follow the next person who bought popcorn to whichever one they were watching.

So now he was sitting near the back of a smallish room, with his feet up on the seat in front of him, waiting for a film to begin, with no idea what it was going to be, when out of the blue Lyla Douglas and Willow Cassidy waltzed in and sat down right in front of him.

He brought his feet down and looked at the back of Willow's long dark hair, thinking, *Of all the theatres in all the complexes in all the towns, she walks into mine.*

He was pretty sure the girls hadn't spotted him. But as the lights dimmed Lyla turned and smiled.

"Hey Sam," said Lyla. "What are *you* doing here?"

And then the most unbelievable thing in the world happened. Lyla Douglas and Willow Cassidy stood up, walked back, and sat beside him.

He was at the movies. And there was a girl beside him. And it was Willow Cassidy.

Out in the lobby Murphy had finally made it into the eighties. He checked his watch. It had never taken half this long. A couple of the theatres would be turning soon. He yawned. He stood up and stretched. With any luck he'd hit a hundred plays within the half hour.

Meanwhile in the theatre, Sam had stopped watching the movie.

He and Willow were holding hands.

Well, not *technically* holding hands. Their hands were touching. He is not sure when it began. He missed the transition from not touching to touching, but ever since he noticed, he'd stopped following the movie.

Sam had never held a girl's hand before. Never. Ever.

Oddly, just before he noticed it, he'd been wondering how one might go about that. Did you ask? Did you say, "Do you want to hold hands?"

Or did you just do it? And if so, how did you do it? And why didn't he know this? Surely everyone else knew this. He felt like an explorer making his way through a murky forest without a compass.

How come he didn't have a compass?

And that's when he noticed their hands were touching. Ever so lightly, but touching—no doubt about it.

Had he done this? He didn't mean to. Was it possible that his hand was acting as an independent agent?

Or had Willow done it? Could that be possible? And more importantly, now that he was aware of it, what should he do about it?

What he wanted to do was move his hand closer. Ever so slightly closer. Would that be … harassment?

He sensed that Willow was looking at him.

Whatever you do, don't look, he told himself. *Don't move a muscle. Just breathe. Keep your eyes on the screen and breathe. Breathe in. Breathe out. Lean forward. Concentrate.*

Maybe he should move his *hand*. Not far. But which way? Maybe away. So they weren't touching. But just a couple of centimetres away, so they were still in range. See if she followed.

His whole body was tense. He'd stopped breathing.

He sucked in a lungful of air. Okay, wait. What was that? Something had just happened. What just happened? Willow had just said something. Willow Cassidy, who was sitting beside him in the theatre, was talking to him.

"Lyla wants a drink," she said. "We'll be back in a moment."

The girls stood up. Sam felt as if everyone in the theatre was looking at him. And so he leaned forward. His chin in his hands. If he stared at the screen they would lose interest.

It seemed like an eternity before Willow returned.

He didn't actually see her come back, just sensed her settle beside him. He didn't look. He kept his eyes on the screen. But he had a plan.

He was going to go for it. He was going to reach out and hold her hand. He was going to count to five, and on five he would do it.

One. He began to move. Moving his hand, intending to rest it on the arm of the chair. Why was he scratching his cheek. How did that happen? Two. Come on. Move. Three. He dropped his hand down on the armrest.

He felt Willow's hand move back.

Hurry. Hurry. He had to hurry. Don't let her get away. Four. Five. Come on. Do it. Six.

He reached out.

He grabbed Willow's hand.

Omigod. He did it.

Oh no.

She was trying to pull away.

He tightened his grip. He had to let her know that he meant it. He was squeezing her hand as tight as he could.

It worked. He could feel her relaxing.

He was holding her hand. He was holding her hand. He was in a theatre with Willow Cassidy, and they were holding hands. He was. She was. They were.

Okay. Calm down.

Something was happening. Willow was patting his arm with her free hand. What was he supposed to do now?

He reached out and did the same to her.

Now she was tapping on his shoulder.

Oh my gosh they were making out! He was making out with Willow Cassidy. He was about to get kissed.

Sam had never been kissed before.

He couldn't believe this was happening to him. All he could think was, *Why isn't Murphy here to see this?*

Here we go, thought Sam. And he shut his eyes, turning toward Willow

"I love you," he whispered.

Probably he didn't say it out loud. Probably he thought *I love you, Willow.* But he thought it with all his heart.

And then he leaned closer.

He felt a hand on his face, pushing him away, and he opened his eyes.

He was staring at Murphy.

It was Murphy's hand he was holding. It was Murphy he was about to kiss.

Sam yanked his hand free and jumped up.

"Sorry. Sorry. Sorry," he said.

Now everyone in the theatre *was* looking at him. He sat down.

Murphy reached out and put his arm around Sam's shoulder. He pulled Sam close to him and whispered in his ear.

"It's okay," said Murphy. "Love means never having to say you're sorry."

Then he said, "It's time."

On their way out of the theatre, they passed Willow and Lyla coming in.

Willow said, "I got you popcorn. Are you leaving?"

Murphy affected his best Austrian accent and answered for him. Murphy said, "He'll be baaack."

And so Murphy and Sam swanned back around the candy counter. Back to the game that had brought them there. And Sam stood on the side, the way they'd practised.

"Okay," said Sam, looking at Murphy.

"Okay," said Murphy. And then he smiled and rubbed his hands together and said,

"Play it, Sam."

And then he said, "After I put the quarter in we have thirty seconds. After thirty seconds the claw goes to the chute. It's automatic."

"And this is game one hundred, right?"

"This is game ninety-seven," said Murphy. "We have three practices. You ready?"

Sam nodded.

Murphy put the first quarter in.

Murphy said, "The centre of the claw should be right over the panda's neck."

As he was talking he pressed the joystick to the left. The claw began its jerky trip across the mountain of toys.

"Stop," said Sam. "Back a bit."

"Twenty seconds," said Murphy.

Sam had his face pressed to the machine, his breath fogging the glass.

"Forward," said Sam. "Back."

"Ten seconds," said Murphy.

"We're there," said Sam. "We're home."

Murphy said, "There's no place like home."

And he took a step back and held his hands in the air. Palms out. *Look at me.*

He put his hands back on the stick, and the crane began its tricky descent. The prongs flopped onto the panda. They opened. And closed. They raised into the air. Empty.

"Ninety-eight," said Murphy, digging a quarter out of his pocket.

They have changed positions.

Sam is on the joystick.

Murphy is spotting.

And look! Willow and Lyla are walking toward them.

"Pay attention," said Murphy.

Murphy's face is pressed against the glass.

The claw has begun to move.

"Not yet," said Murphy. "Left."

The girls were beside them now, standing by the machine, watching. Watching Sam's hands on the levers.

"Too far," said Murphy. "Go back."

When you get to the heart of any matter, everything is measured with a microscope. For at the heart of any matter, it's the small things that count. But when the thing you're measuring is the space between a boy's heart and a girl's heart, there is no microscope to measure that.

"Okay," said Murphy. "You're there. You're there. Round up the usual suspects."

Sam shook his head and gave the joystick one last touch. The claw shifted ever so slightly and then shuddered and began its descent.

It's always the things we can't have that we want. The prize behind the panel. The girl in the other room who doesn't know your name.

Down the claw went. Down, down, down.

"I'll get you, my pretty," said Murphy. "And your little dog too."

The claw flopped on the belly of the bear and rested there for a moment. Then it started up again. This time it had the bear in its grip. This time the bear lifted unsteadily out of the pile of plush prizes and swung jerkily in the air. The four of them, the two boys and the two girls, stared at it in wonder.

Sam was beaming.

The girls were clapping.

Murphy was frowning.

It wasn't supposed to work like this. The claw was supposed to drop the bear and clear the way for the next try.

But it didn't drop it. The panda was swinging in the air; the claw was hovering over the chute.

Sam looked at Willow, shyly. Willow was beaming at him.

Stories never end like this. The boy never wins the prize. The girl never gets the bear. But this one does. And Sam will tell it often over the years. The story about the afternoon he and his friend Murphy snuck into the movies, and how they waited until the exact right moment before they put a quarter into the crane game and how they won the panda bear.

It dropped into the prize slot with a thud.

Murphy was standing beside the machine with his mouth hanging open.

Willow said, "You won the bear. He won the bear. It's so cute."

Sam reached down and pulled the bear out.

And without thinking, he held it out to Willow.

"Here," he said.

Willow took the bear and hugged it, and then the most extraordinary thing happened. She leaned forward and kissed Sam on the cheek.

It was his first kiss.

They walked out of the theatre together, standing awkwardly on the sidewalk, all of them squinting in the afternoon sun.

Sam said, "You guys want to do something?"

Willow said, "Lyla's mother is picking us up."

And so they said goodbye.

"Thanks for the bear," said Willow.

"See you later," said Sam.

"Call me," said Willow.

"I don't understand," said Murphy as they headed off, the two boys bumping down the sidewalk, Murphy shaking his head, lost in thought. "I must have miscalculated. Or something. Something went horribly wrong."

"Nothing went wrong," said Sam. "It was perfect. It was absolutely perfect."

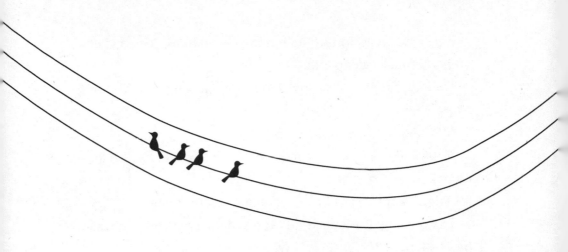

CRUSHED

The invitation arrived by post.

Dave, who comes home for lunch most days, was the first to see it. It was addressed in his *daughter's* handwriting.

"And the first thing I thought," he said, *"before* I opened it, I mean, was wedding. I thought they were getting married."

The envelope certainly stood out from the bills. Flecked and fashioned from handmade paper.

"Did it not occur to you they might have mentioned something?" said Morley. "I mean, before they sent us an invitation. She *is* our daughter."

When Dave did open the envelope, what he found was a piece of torn paper with a photographic negative stapled to it. There was nothing written on the paper. But if you held the negative up to the light, there was a message.

It *was* an invitation, though *not* to a wedding. To a gallery. An invitation to an opening.

Tommy, Stephanie's boyfriend, was having his first big show.

"It's very impressive," said Morley.

"Crushed?" said Dave. That's what it was called. The exhibition, I mean. *Crushed.*

"I don't know," said Dave. "It sounds weird to me."

The opening was scheduled for a Monday evening. It was a bit of a haul to the gallery. Maybe two and a half hours door to door. But they *were* going to go, of course.

"Do we have to?" said Dave.

Dave's resistance was neither whimsical nor frivolous. It was, rather, quite the opposite—the upshot of a long ago but unforgotten trauma lingering from the night when he was burned badly by the heat of avant-garde art.

We all experience trauma, of one sort or another, at one point or another in our lives. If we're fortunate, these upsets leave us stronger than they found us. When we're lucky, we're forged, as they say, by fire.

But fire can consume as easily as sustain. And sometimes, when we're burned, all we want to do is get out of the kitchen.

It was a rainy night in New York City, a long time ago.

Dave was on tour, managing the postmodern Czechoslovakian music group Pulnoc—a spinoff from the history-changing Plastic People of the Universe.

And one of the group, or one of the people travelling with the group—it's hard to remember, and anyway he'd rather forget—was seeing a girl named Tish. There was a lot of talk about Tish. The closer they got to New York City, which is where Tish lived, the more it became "Tish this" and "Tish that."

Tish was a "mixed media" artist—whatever that meant. Dave felt it would be rude to ask. Anyway, he'd see soon enough, because they had all been invited to Tish's opening.

On the night in question, Dave set off with everyone else to a Soho gallery.

The art show was in a second-floor loft, a large open space with exposed iron beams and rough brick walls. When they got there the room was packed.

And hanging from the beams at the centre of the room were ten Plexiglas cubes. Each was the size of a guitar amp. The first one looked as it it was filled with burnt Kleenex. Dave bent down to read the card on the easel beside it. It said BURNT KLEENEX 2.

The fact that he'd recognized the subject did not give Dave any measure of confidence. It confused him. And the more he looked, the more confused he got.

Inside box number two were a few twist ties and a pile of elastic bands. The card on the easel beside *it* read DIDO AND AENEAS.

Cube three was hanging from a thick iron chain. Yet inside it was a solitary lima bean. And a card read ECSTASY.

And that's when Dave looked up and saw Tish and Tish's boyfriend walking his way—surrounded by a group of people. One of the people was Yoko Ono.

"*So* important," one of them was saying.

"Seminal," said another.

And then everyone looked at Yoko, who had raised her hand to draw attention.

"There's no doubt that this work is mordantly percipient," she said with great gravity, "but the question is whether the work transcends or simply negates the ethos of modernity."

And then she looked at Dave.

"What do *you* think?" she said.

The world stopped.

Beads of sweat sprang from Dave's forehead.

"Yes," he blurted. Then, with his voice rising in panic, he said, "I mean, no." Then, almost yelling now, he said, "What was the question?"

Yoko Ono frowned.

The others turned away.

And Tish's boyfriend muttered under his breath, "If you don't like Tish's show, you could at least keep it to yourself."

It's not that Dave is *afraid* of art. Portraits, landscapes, and still lifes are all fine, but when the approach veers to the abstract, his heart starts to race.

What's the saying? Once beaten, twice shy? Set Dave down in a room full of esoteric pieces, and he begins to twitch.

Despite Dave's reluctance, Morley reserved a room at the little inn where they'd stayed the weekend they dropped Steph off at the beginning of her first year away. How many years ago was that?

They arrived in the afternoon and had lunch at a table by the water. The pond was so close you could almost touch it. The waterfall just out of sight.

"Same table," said Dave.

"I'm not sure," said Morley.

"Absolutely," said Dave, reaching for the ketchup.

And then he said, "So. What's been crushing him. *What,* do you think? The modern world? The media? The Maple Leafs?"

A few hours later they were standing in front of a blown-up, larger than life-sized photograph of a flattened snake, in a gallery full of close-up, poster-sized portraits of animals that had been run over by cars. Snakes crushed by cars. Frogs crushed by cars. A turtle crushed by a car.

"Crushed?" Dave is saying. "Crushed!"

He has said it several times.

With a question mark

An exclamation mark.

With bewilderment.

And now, with some distress.

"You're repeating yourself," said Morley.

"I actually thought, maybe, you know. Crushed on her. I was hoping not, but I was prepared for that. And everything that could mean.

"Doesn't this worry you? This is the man our daughter could be marrying."

Morley said, "No one has mentioned anything about marriage. Marriage is not on the table as far as I know."

Dave said, "They might as well be living together."

Morley said, "Actually. They are."

"Exactly," said Dave. "Our daughter is living with a man who takes pictures of roadkill. First off, that's not normal. Second off, I have no idea what they mean, or what I'm supposed to think of them. And third off, what do you mean they're living together? I thought he had his own place."

Before she could answer, Dave held up his hand.

"Don't look now," he said. "Wait a moment and then turn around slowly. Not yet. Wait. Okay—now. The woman in the corner, the one in the black beret. Is that Yoko Ono?"

"Dave," said Morley, "Yoko Ono is Japanese."

Before Dave knew it, he ended up exactly where he didn't want to end up—trapped in the corner—with Tommy's father and the mysterious woman in the beret.

He was desperate to have something to say if he was asked about the pictures—and he desperately wanted whatever it was to be both clever and congratulatory. But all he could think of, for some reason, was the moon landing. And in his imagination the lunar capsule had just splattered into the Sea of Tranquility. And the astronauts— Dear God, why was he thinking of lunar disasters?

The lady in the beret pointed at the large picture of the dead owl they were standing in front of and said, "The last act is always bloody. However pleasant the rest of the play."

Tommy's father said something Dave didn't catch, and then the moment he had been dreading arrived.

Tommy's father and the woman in the beret turned and looked at him, and Tommy's father waved his hand around the room and said, "So. What do you think of my son's photographs?"

From somewhere, somewhere just this side of panic, Dave said, "I admire his ... passion."

"Ah," said the woman in the beret, "one *always* admires what one doesn't understand."

Dave, overcome by desperation and the desperate need to escape, began to back away. "Can I get anyone more wine?" he asked, trying to sound calm, wondering, as he left, if he'd just been insulted or insulting.

He got more wine and then wandered around the room pretending he was a bumper car. His job was to avoid all the other cars and the conversations he didn't want to have about the show.

He kept his eye on his daughter and her boyfriend as he circled.

When the gallery owner stood on a chair by the front and tapped his glass, Dave joined the circle that formed around him and nodded along during his speech. The gallery owner talked about "existential ambiguity" and "adjacent polarity" and "didactic surrealism" and "referential reductionism."

Someone else, a professor from the university perhaps, stood up and proposed a toast. Dave raised his glass. When there was applause, he applauded. He tried his best to follow along, although nothing made much sense to him. He could see the woman in the beret out of the corner of his eye. She seemed to be staring at him.

When the speeches were over, Morley appeared at Dave's side.

"Come here," she said. "Have you seen this one?"

She steered Dave to a picture of a cedar waxwing—the photo enlarged so that it was almost as big as a child. The bird had been shot against a blue out-of-focus background, its eyes closed, its head bowed. It looked more like a monk issuing a call to prayer than a bird that had flown into a car.

Morley said, "It's beautiful."

Dave said, "But what does it mean?"

Then he said, "It makes me feel sad."

Then he said, "My father would have hated these."

Charlie.

Dave's father, Charlie, would pull his truck to the side of the road whenever he came across something that had been run over. Then he'd carry whatever it was into the bushes.

Charlie told Dave that they shouldn't let dead animals lie there in the road where they'd get run over again and again.

"There's no dignity in that," said Charlie.

Back then, it was embarrassing. Now, it seemed to make sense. Of course, it was easier to stop to administer to roadkill if you lived in the Narrows back in the day. Not so easy now. Not the way people drive these days.

When the show ended, they all went back to the inn to have dinner—Tommy and Stephanie, Tommy's parents, and Dave and Morley.

More fine things were said.

Tommy's mother said how proud she was.

Morley said how the pictures reminded her of her childhood.

"When I was a kid," said Morley, "we used to pick up dead things all the time."

Stephanie said her favourite was the waxwing that Morley had shown Dave.

No one said anything profound. It wasn't like the speeches at the gallery. Until Tommy's father stood up and proposed a toast, stealing liberally from the gallery owner's speech as he did it.

Which made Dave, who hadn't said anything, feel a bit better. Tommy's father, a university professor, clearly didn't have any more of a clue about his son's work than Dave did.

When dinner was over, everyone said their goodbyes. Tommy's parents were going back to the city. Dave and Morley were going upstairs.

But a half hour later, to his astonishment, Dave found himself in Tommy's car rather than in his hotel room. Alone with Tommy.

It had been Stephanie's idea.

"Just drive along the ridge," she'd said. "Just go out and back. Who knows, maybe you'll find something."

It was about a mile to the top of the ridge. The stars pinpricking the dark black sky. The road in front of them starless and blacker.

"Mostly, at night," said Tommy, "you find owls. They fly low. They get hit."

It was awkward. First, they'd never been alone in a car before. Second, there they were, alone in a car. Third, and worst of all, they were driving under the intimate cover of darkness. Under the intimidating influence of art.

Tommy had the radio on—but softly, country and western. You really couldn't hear it.

When they got to the top they came to a T junction, and Tommy turned left. Now the valley was below them, on their left, and the forest to their right.

They'd been going maybe twenty minutes along the ridge road, the forest gradually giving way to fields and woodlots, when Tommy braked.

There were no other cars around.

"What?" said Dave.

Tommy flicked on the high beams and backed up. Then he jockeyed around a bit, until the headlights caught the shadow.

"A raccoon?" said Dave, leaning forward. "Or is it a dog?"

"It's a fox," said Tommy.

"You're right," said Dave, who was reaching for the door.

Tommy said, "Wait."

Tommy said, "Before you get out you want to be sure there's nothing around. Coyotes or something."

Dave felt as if he were in a horror film—stopping the car in the middle of nowhere to check out a body.

As they walked toward the fox, he could feel his heart pounding.

In a weird way, it was exhilarating.

There was a light and a light stand in the trunk of the car.

Tommy went and got them. He set up the light and then crouched beside the fox. Dave leaned on the hood and watched him at work. Each time Tommy took a shot, the light flashed with a soft *woof*. Each time the light went off, the night seemed blacker.

When Tommy finished, they both stood by the car.

"I always wonder," said Tommy, looking around, "if there's a mate somewhere watching me. Or babies. I always wonder how it all went down."

Dave looked into the darkness surrounding them.

Tommy threw the light and the stand back into the trunk and closed it.

Tommy said, "I know some of the pictures are … beautiful in some weird way. And I like that. I have an appreciation of that. But mostly, I just feel sad when I see them. Mostly they don't feel beautiful to me."

Dave said, "That's how they made *me* feel."

Then Tommy said, "My grandfather died a few years ago."

"I remember," said Dave.

"That's when I started doing this," said Tommy.

Like poetry, you can find beauty in the most unexpected places: in a snowy wood and on the wings of a butterfly, yes, of course. But in sorrow as well as in happiness. In death as well as in life.

You buy a book in a second-hand bookstore and somewhere, halfway between the beginning and the end, waiting for you to turn the page, there's a flower pressed between the words. Sometimes poetry is hidden.

And sometimes it's lying on the side of the road in full view.

"I don't think it's poetic," said Tommy. "I don't think that at all."

Dave said, "All those people tonight thought so. All those people who bought prints and said all those things. That's got to mean something."

They were back in the car. They were on their way home.

Tommy said, "All that stuff tonight. All those things they said at the gallery. I didn't understand half that stuff."

Dave almost clapped his hands. He almost whooped. He almost said, "I didn't either."

But Tommy was staring intensely into the night. Tommy hadn't finished. So Dave didn't say anything.

"I'll tell you what I think," said Tommy. "I think it means that beauty trumps morality. That's the way it is, and that's the way it has always been. I don't think it should be like that. But that's the way it is. That's the way of the world."

Then he said, "Maybe it would be better if everyone came to my show and didn't like it and left."

Someone once said that you'll never find a better place in the world for a difficult conversation than in a dark car. You don't have to look at the other person. And you both know that when the trip ends, the conversation can too.

Dave closed his eyes and said, "You would have to be a special kind of person to see your show and not get it."

It wasn't a complete lie.

Dave said, "Here's what I think. I think there's a collision happening between civilization and the natural world. And I think you're the witness."

Tommy said, "I don't like it that animals are getting killed by cars."

And then he said, "Sometimes I'll find a little bird, like the waxwing. Did you see that one? He looked like he was praying, his head bowed and his eyes shut and that slash of red blood on his head. In some messed-up way that's one of the most beautiful pictures I've ever taken. But I don't have a clue why.

"That's the thing. I feel these big feelings and I don't understand why."

They were almost back at the inn.

As they turned between the stone gates, Dave felt that a weight had lifted off his shoulders.

There was no great big mystery—except for the great big mystery.

We live and then we die.

Someone once said that we all have exactly two and a half minutes to live. One for smiling, and one for sighing, and a half of one for love. For it's in the middle of that minute, the loving one, that we die.

"And what we want more than anything," said Dave, "between the living and the dying, is for someone to take notice.

"For someone to say it matters that we're here."

Tommy said, "You think that's what I'm doing? Saying it matters?"

"Maybe," said Dave.

"Mostly," said Tommy, "what I think I'm saying is that I wish people would drive slower. And also that my grandfather was still here. I miss him."

They were in the parking lot now. Dave hesitated for a moment before he opened his door.

"Thanks for taking me out," he said. "I loved seeing you at work. And I love your work."

It was true. He did.

When Dave came into their room Morley was still awake, sitting on the bed with a magazine in her hands. When he came in, she put it down, drew up her knees, and put her arms around them.

She said, "How'd it go?"

He said, "We found a fox. Tommy took pictures. And you know what he did when he was finished? He carried the fox to the side and covered it with some brush. Just like my father would have done. Do you believe that?"

He was about to reassure her that their daughter wasn't involved with an axe murderer. But he looked at her face and realized he didn't have to. She had already read Tommy's pictures the way they were intended. As usual, she was way ahead of him.

Instead of saying any of that, he shrugged, thinking—as he looked at his wife and thought of his daughter, and of his daughter's boyfriend, and of the night that had just passed, all of it—that he was a lucky man.

He could hear the clock. The clock was ticking. And he knew that he'd had his laugh, *and* his sigh, but that his thirty seconds of love was still not up.

YOGA

Stephanie's friend Becky broke up with her boyfriend at the end of the summer. She was still a mess at Thanksgiving. Still crying.

Stephanie said, "We're going away. You and I. One week."

Becky said, "Where are we going?"

Stephanie said, "I haven't decided."

She settled on a yoga retreat.

Stephanie said, "We're going for a seven-day cleanse."

Becky cheered up.

Then Becky and her boyfriend *made* up.

Becky said, "I'm sorry. He doesn't want me going anywhere without him."

Stephanie said, "But that's why you broke up."

Becky said, *"Sorrryyy."*

Stephanie called the yoga centre. She explained all about Becky and her stupid boyfriend. Stephanie was angling for a refund.

The man on the phone said, "They must often change, those who would be constant in happiness and wisdom."

Stephanie said, "Huh?"

The man on the phone said, "Sorry. No refunds."

Stephanie stewed for a week. Then she called her mother. Seven days with her mother at a yoga retreat wasn't exactly her idea of fun, but it wouldn't be completely awful. They didn't spend that much time together anymore. Stephanie said, "What do you think? You and me."

Morley said, "Sweetie, I would *love* to go with you. But we open a new production that week. I can't. I think you should take your father."

Stephanie said, "Are you out of your mind?"

Morley said, "He's right here. Let me put him on."

Stephanie and her father were in the car heading for the retreat.

Stephanie said, "This wasn't my idea."

Dave said, "Your mother thought we should spend time together."

Stephanie said, "She is stark raving mad."

Dave said, "It's not that bad."

Stephanie said, "Give your head a shake."

The retreat was in the country. Down a tree-lined driveway to an old Catholic monastery. On a hill, overlooking a lake.

They went to the main desk and registered.

There were three classes to choose from: gentle, inter-mediate, and vigorous.

Stephanie chose intermediate. Dave chose vigorous.

"I'm going to get as much as I can from this," he said.

The lady smiled at them.

The lady said, "You're here for the cleanse."

Dave looked at Stephanie.

Dave said, "Cleanse?"

The lady was nodding.

The lady said, "Bodi-dharma will search your bags."

Bodi-dharma opened Dave's suitcase and removed a pack of beef jerky and a bag of gummy worms.

There was a tour. A woman with flared pants, a cotton wrap, and a headband showed them around.

She left them at the Rejuvenation desk. "You can choose three treatments," she said. "It's part of the package."

Stephanie chose Pamper Yourself: a Swedish massage, a mineral mud bath, and a sea-salt pedicure.

Dave looked at the menu and relaxed.

The place wasn't as strict as it looked.

Dave chose Happy Hour:

Three honey-mint-refresh-colonic cocktails.

"What are you thinking?" said Stephanie.

"What I'm thinking," said Dave with a wink, "is when did I ever stop after one cocktail?"

Dave was first up in the morning.

"I'm going for coffee," he said. "Shall I bring you a cup?"

Stephanie said, "Um. I don't think there's going to be coffee."

"Don't be ridiculous," said Dave. "Of course there'll be coffee."

He came back holding two hand-thrown mugs.

"You're kidding," said Stephanie, sitting up.

"Matcha chai tea," said Dave.

"It's great," said Dave. "It's great. I like it. All good. I'll be fine."

His right eye was twitching.

There were already two women in the hall when Dave arrived at his first class. One was lying on a black rubber mat, her eyes closed, her arms stretched out, palms up. Corpse pose.

The other was busier—pulling an endless supply of stuff out of a cotton bag: four rubber bricks, two canvas straps, a round pillow, a purple-and-black blanket with an Aztec pattern, a water bottle, a mister, and three bananas. She was organizing everything with great precision. It seemed important to her that everything line up perfectly.

Dave took a mat off the wall and sat while the room filled.

For the longest time he was the only man in the room.

Then another guy came in. He was wearing knee-length yoga pants and a form-fitting black ribbed tank top. He had a red bandana around his shoulder-length hair, yoga beads around his wrist, and a tattoo of a lotus flower on his ankle.

He unfurled his mat in the middle of the room like a flag.

And then, while everyone else sat quietly, he let out a short, explosive exhalation.

Ha.

He stretched his hands above his head and leaned back. He bent forward at the waist as if to touch his toes. Except that he went beyond his toes. Way beyond. His palms landed on the floor. He rested there for a moment and then, impossibly, he kept going. Which is to say that, without any apparent effort, he went *right* over, like a mechanical toy. Over and then up, until he was upside down. In a handstand. Arms straight.

And then ... he started doing push-ups.

Upside down, handstand push-ups.

He did ten.

Then he rewound. Slowly. Until he was standing again with his palms pressed together in front of his chest. He looked as if he was praying, but he wasn't praying. He was looking around the room to see if anyone was watching.

After class, Handstand Guy came over to Dave and put his sweaty arm on his shoulders.

"Stick with it, bro," he said. "The poses don't begin until your mind forgives."

Then he said "Namaste" and walked away.

"Nama-stay?" said Dave.

Dave's first treatment was scheduled for just before dinner.

"Cocktail hour!" he said jauntily as he left the room.

He came back pale and sweaty.

"How was it?" asked Stephanie.

"A little different than I expected," said Dave. "But it was …
great."

Then he said, "Whoops. Excuse me." And he ran for the
bathroom. He didn't come out for twenty minutes.

He ached all over.

Not just his muscles.

His heart. His head. His *soul*.

He'd thought living without meat was going to be the
challenge. But it was coffee that he was missing. His head was
pounding.

After supper he said, "I'm going for a walk."

He prowled through the building. There had to be coffee
somewhere. In the basement, just past the laundry room,
outside the staff lounge, he spotted what he was looking for.
The warm glow of a vending machine. It was tucked into an
alcove. He couldn't see it, but he'd recognize that light
anywhere. His right hand slid into his pocket and fingered the
coins he'd brought for this moment. He began humming.
Unconsciously. James Brown, "I Feel Good."

He stopped humming when he came face to face with the
machine. It dispensed kombucha, coconut water, aloe vera,
and shots of wheat grass.

The next morning, class began with a sun salutation.

Tadasana.

Hands pressed in front of chest. Now drifting overhead,
back arching, bending forward, reaching for the floor.

Uttanasana.

Reaching.

He felt teacher's hand land softly on his back. He tried to reach farther.

But the backs of his knees were screaming.

"Soft knees," said teacher as she walked soundlessly away.

Dave opened his eyes and peeked around the room.

His arms were halfway down his shins. Everyone else had landed their palms on the floor. His hands were dangling in front of him like the end of an elephant's trunk. A geriatric elephant.

He felt clumsy and he felt awkward.

Surely there was someone worse than him. He caught the eyes of Handstand Guy. Handstand Guy winked at him. Through his ankles.

Dave pushed harder. It hurt. Lord, it hurt. It hurt. It hurt, it hurt, it hurt. Everything hurt. He hated this.

This went on for two painful hours. Between each posture, Handstand Guy jumped explosively. At the end of class he bust out a loud, explosive "OM."

And as Dave staggered out, there he was waiting for him in the hallway.

"Keep at it, bro," said Handstand Guy. "The pose doesn't begin until you want to leave it."

He started off, then he turned and came back and said, "It's not my business, bro, but I think you should have your chakras aligned. They look kind of funky to me."

The store was on the main floor by the reception desk. They sold books and tapes and candles and oils. Also clothes.

It hadn't taken long for Dave to realize that he was the only one in Bermuda shorts. He thought that if he got some official equipment he'd maybe do better.

He bought stretchy black pants, a grey cotton top, and a set of beads. He put the beads around his wrist like Handstand Guy.

When she handed him his credit card, the lady said, *"Namaste."*

"Nama-stay," said Dave right back.

Another classroom, another class.

Dave was lying on his back.

There was music playing softly.

"Bring your right knee to your chest," said teacher. "Hug it with your arms. Bring your head to your knees and exhale."

And right then, in the deep silence after teacher said "exhale," there was an explosion. Or more accurately, a series of rapid little explosions. Like a machine gun.

Dave winced.

Someone sniggered.

Teacher said, "Well. Now we all know why they call it the wind-releasing pose."

"Bro," said Handstand Guy on the way out, "when they say *Release the pose,* they just mean the pose."

The lotus position is not the most dramatic looking yoga posture—not by a long shot. At first glance, you'd think anyone could do it.

The Buddha did it, after all. And so did Gandhi.

"And neither of them," said Dave to Stephanie at dinner that night, "strike me as the most athletic looking dudes."

The pose is said to be the path to enlightenment.

"And all you have to do," said Dave, "is cross your legs and sit there."

Like a lotus flower. Open to the light.

Best of all, Handstand Guy couldn't do lotus.

"Aha," said Stephanie.

"It's not about that," said Dave. "Seriously. It is not about that."

The problem is that as simple as it looks, the lotus pose is essentially—impossible. Only a fool would try to pry himself into lotus pose without years of preparation.

But fools do rush in.

On day three, Dave woke early and slipped out of bed. He let himself into the studio at the far end of the building.

As the sun came up he stood by the window and studied the chart of postures.

He limbered up.

He sat down and placed his right foot on his left thigh.

Then he grabbed his left foot and tried to put *it* on his right thigh. There was no way.

But there had to be a way.

He leaned both elbows and all the weight of his upper body on his knee. There was a sudden snap, and a pop, and a flash of pain deep in his body.

Where exactly the pain was was hard to tell. Somewhere deep. It came and went like lightning. Hard and bright, there and then—gone.

That was odd, thought Dave.

He looked down at his legs.

His right foot was on his left thigh. His left foot crossed over and under, or maybe under and over, it was hard to tell—but it was resting on his right thigh—he was in lotus.

A profound sense of well-being washed over him, a sense of oneness with the world.

Until he realized that he couldn't move his legs.

He tried to *pull* them apart, and they wouldn't loosen.

His legs were knotted together, and the more he tried to free them, the tighter they got.

That's because he *wasn't* in lotus; he was in sheep shank.

It took him an hour to drag himself down the corridor back to the bedroom. He used his hands to pull himself along on his bottom.

Anywhere else in the world he would have been a disturbing sight.

Here, everyone just nodded as he passed.

It was exhausting work.

Halfway back to his room, he stopped and propped himself up against the wall.

He fell asleep.

When he woke there was an embroidered hat sitting on the floor next to him. It was full of change.

It took Stephanie forty minutes to untangle her father.

When she finished his legs were too wobbly to walk on.

Although he could put his feet behind his head.

"Look at this," he said.

That's what he was doing, sitting on the bed with one foot behind his head, when there was a knock on their door.

It was Bodi-dharma. He was holding a bucket.

He said, "It's cocktail hour."

That night Dave dreamed he was being chased through a dark kingdom. There were baboons and eels and in the distance a volcano that rumbled and groaned and kept erupting over and over and over again.

Maybe it was the next day. Maybe it was the day after. It must have been the next day. Day four. Right after morning class. They were given a longer than usual break—lunch and meditation.

Dave staggered back to the room. When Stephanie got there he'd changed from his yoga clothes into jeans and a green checked shirt. He was standing in front of the mirror combing his hair. He was humming "I Feel Good" again.

"Where are *you* going?" said Stephanie.

"To meditate over a burger," said Dave.

He didn't ask if she wanted to come.

He said, "I'll be back for lunch," placing air quotes around "lunch."

The nearest town was fifteen minutes away.

The hamburger joint was on the way. By a gas station. Dave had seen it on the day they arrived. A chain place. He considered going to the drive-through, but decided to forgo efficiency for the full experience.

He parked by a little grass island at the side and wandered in, breathing a deep, meditative sigh at the counter as he looked up at the neon menu. The healthiest choice was the deep-fried apple pie. He ordered a double bacon cheeseburger and an extra large coffee. A small consolation for the disastrous lotus, for all the indignities he had suffered.

He carried his tray over to a table by the window and sat down.

He inhaled the first half of the burger, and then made himself slow down. Hadn't he learned anything? It was important to eat mindfully. He put his burger down and looked around. There was a mother holding a child up to the condiment table so that he could help her pump ketchup onto a plate of fries. An older couple sharing a coffee in the corner. And a guy in a blue hoodie and sweatpants at the counter ordering.

There was something about the guy that seemed familiar.

Wait a minute.

Dave leaned forward and squinted.

Was it Handstand Guy?

It was hard to tell; he had his back to him.

It sure looked like Handstand Guy.

He was paying.

Soon he would turn around and walk to a table.

Got you, you phony, thought Dave.

Wait a minute.

The girl behind the counter was handing him a bag.

He was getting his order to go.

"Turn around," muttered Dave. "Turn around."

But the guy wasn't turning around. He was walking out with his grease-stained bag and a large Coke. Dave was sure it was him. But he couldn't be *completely* sure. It looked like him. It looked like him. Look at him. It was Handstand Guy. He was getting into a little— What was he getting into? What did Handstand Guy drive?

It all happened too fast. All that was left of him was the red glow of his tail lights pulling out of the lot.

Dave looked down at the uneaten half of his burger.

It *had* to be Handstand Guy.

All the good it did him. He couldn't tell anyone without admitting that *he* was in the burger joint himself.

He finished the burger and headed back to the retreat, more frustrated than ever, the hamburger doing an alarming dance in his gut.

He got there just as the afternoon session began.

Teacher said, "If you haven't done headstand, you should do tripod instead."

He had been defeated one too many times.

He was not going to be tripod guy in Handstand Guy's room.

Dave said, "I have done headstands."

He had.

He had done hundreds.

Not recently.

But as a boy.

It wasn't hard.

Teacher said, "Place your head on the floor in front of your knees. Now raise your legs slowly and gently."

That wasn't the way *he* remembered it.

The way he remembered it was to go up *quickly*. And with commitment.

To get to the top, you had to commit.

Everyone was lined up in front of the wall, their knees on their arms in a sort of tripod, squatty way.

Finally!

Something he could do better than everyone else.

While everyone else balanced, Dave counted to himself. *One for the money. Two for the show.* On *three to get ready,* he put his forehead on the ground. He looked over at Handstand Guy and kicked his feet up with all the force he could muster.

His heels hit the wall like some sort of medieval weapon—like two iron balls on the end of a heavy chain. They hit so hard he broke right through the drywall.

There was a thud.

An explosion of dust.

Everyone in the class dropped to the ground and stared.

Dave's arms had given out.

But he hadn't fallen.

He was hanging on the wall like a picture. Held in place by his planted heels.

He hung there, bits of broken drywall dribbling down his legs, thinking to himself, *What else could possibly go wrong?*

And that's when he heard a faraway rumble from his stomach—like the sound a volcano makes before it erupts.

The last thing he saw before he passed out was his classmates running for the door.

They checked out that afternoon.

Three days early.

They didn't charge him for the damage to the studio walls, but they weren't pleased.

"In light of circumstances," said the lady who checked them out, "you'll understand if we don't give you the third of your complimentary cocktails."

Dave nodded.

"Nama-stay," he said.

They spotted Handstand Guy sitting on a rock as they walked along the path to the parking lot.

"Leaving early?" he called after they'd walked by.

Dave stopped but didn't turn around.

Stephanie whispered, "What a jerk."

Dave just smiled.

"Bro," he called over his shoulder, "we're just going to town for a burger. Why don't you join us. You like burgers, don't you?"

Handstand Guy started to get up, then he sat down again. He started to say something but nothing came out.

Dave just smiled and put his arm around Steph and they bumped their way toward the car.

"Well I do declare," said Dave as they wandered through the trees. "I've been trying for that all week. And I do believe I just got it."

"What's that?" said Steph.

"Humbling pose," said Dave. "You can't force it. It takes great patience, good timing, and a little luck, of course. But then all good things do."

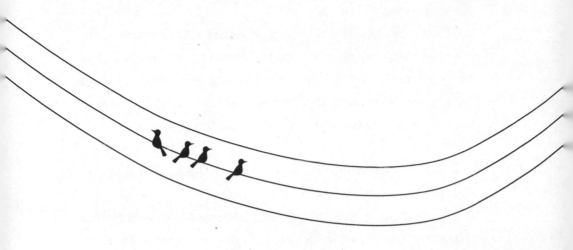

TOWN HALL

Everyone in town heard the lightning hit. It was well after midnight and most everyone was asleep, but they all heard it.

The next morning at the Maple Leaf Café, the group sitting in their regular spots at the back table were replaying the moment, and Smith Gardner said, "I heard it even woke Gordie Wilson."

Smith got a good laugh for that one.

They buried Gordie last summer.

But it was loud. The lightning hit town like a cracking big whip. And if anyone *did* manage to sleep through it, the thunder got them.

"Like the end of the world," said Alf MacDonald.

"Like the old days," said George MacDonnell—meaning the days when things used to happen at the mine. Though those were more bumps than bangs—muffled and deep. Those days were long gone. The last shaft closed fifty years ago.

Dave's cousin Brenda was the first in town to know what got hit.

Brenda was sitting in her taxi, right under the portico, her engine running, the Halifax radio playing along to the slap of her windshield wipers. Brenda was thinking she might as well pack it in, go home and play some online bridge. When … BAM!

It was so close that Brenda ducked, smacking her head on the steering wheel. It had been pure reflex.

The *next* thing she did was reach for her radio. That was reflex, too. Brenda called it in before she even saw the flames.

She knew right away it had hit the bell, which is ironic when you consider all the work that went into saving that bell, and getting it up there.

The fire department couldn't have got there any faster. Ten minutes at the most, although it seemed far longer to Brenda. It occurred to her that she should go in and save something. She had a key. Half the people in town had a key. But what was she going to save? The coffee machine? And then sparks started landing on the hood of her cab, and that settled that. Brenda threw it into reverse, backed out from under the portico, and started calling people instead.

Dave was her third call.

The firemen didn't even have the hoses out when, some two thousand kilometres away, the phone on Dave's bedside table rang and he lurched up with a gasp.

He did that thing everyone does when the phone wakes them in the middle of the night—he pretended it hadn't.

"Hi!" he chirped, as if he'd been sitting around, waiting for the call.

Brenda, who wasn't fooled and didn't care, said, "The hall's on fire."

The Big Narrows Community Hall.

Dave made some indistinguishable worried sound, and Morley, who'd also been woken by the ring, sat up abruptly.

Her mother is old. Their daughter has moved out.

"What?" she said.

So it was a relief, for Morley anyway, when Dave covered the mouthpiece and whispered, "The hall is on fire."

Brenda said, "I've posted a picture. I'll put up a video. It's not over."

But almost the moment she said that, the flames burst through the roof and started crawling down the walls.

Brenda said, "I got to go."

Next thing you knew, Dave's cell phone was beeping.

It was a text message from his boyhood pal Billy Mitchell.

"You awake? The hall is on fire."

Now that would be a thing—to get two calls in the middle of the night about a fire in your hometown—even if Billy still lived in the Narrows. But Billy is in Afghanistan.

"What kind of crazy world *is* this?" said Dave.

Morley and Dave were wide awake now. Morley had fetched her laptop and had it perched on a pile of pillows between them. They were staring at the videos Brenda was posting, at the people in the crowd as much as the fire.

"There's my mother," said Dave. "Is she in her nightgown?"

And then Morley said, "Okay. If we're staying up, I'm making tea."

While she was doing that the phone rang *again*.

It was either the kettle or the phone that woke Sam.

"Is something wrong?" he said. "Did someone die?"

"Sort of," said Dave.

And so the three of them sat on the bed staring at the computer and Dave told them the story of the hall that was burning right in front of their eyes.

It was the summer he was twelve.

Someone had the idea to tear down the old schoolhouse and build a community hall in its place.

The honest-to-God one-room schoolhouse, where Dave's dad had gone to school.

Dave had heard so many stories that he sometimes wondered if he hadn't gone there himself. Sometimes it felt as if *he* was the one who'd grown up on the farm, a concession to the north, and had walked two-three miles every day, there and back. Except, of course, in the winter, when you could ride a toboggan the first seven hundred yards if the snow was good—then stick it in the snowbank by the south fence and pick it up on the way home.

But it was his dad, Charlie, not him, who'd done all that.

In the spring, if no one was using the tractor, the little grey Ford, Charlie was sometimes allowed to drive it to school—once he was in grade four, that is.

By the time Dave came along, a school had been built in town and the Women's Institute had taken over the little one-room schoolhouse. So Dave never got to experience what it was like—all those kids and just the one teacher.

"Mostly," Margaret had told him, "you learned from the older kids. The older kids would check your work while the teacher was busy with others."

Most teachers only lasted a year. Two at the most.

Anyway, they'd closed the school before Dave got his chance, and the Women's Institute ran it for a couple of years—euchre nights and Friday suppers and whatever else it was they did.

And then it sat empty.

A deserted schoolhouse.

In those days if you had an idea to build something like a community hall, you could just go ahead and do it.

"I think they got a little money from the town," said Dave. "They used it to hire an architect from Glace Bay. But I don't think they followed his plans. Mostly they just did it themselves."

They were miners, and fishermen, and farmers, and they knew how to do things with their hands. There was no question of fixing up the old schoolhouse. The schoolhouse was done. They decided to take it down. But first they had to save the bell.

The whole town gathered to watch. They used a lift from Harrison's hayloft and jerry-rigged a pulley like you might use to run a man up the mast of a schooner.

As for the building, they had four tractors, with chains attached to each of the four walls. The moment they started pulling, the roof smacked down. A big cloud of dust rose up and suddenly there was an empty lot where the school had been.

It was every schoolkid's dream. All the *kids* thought it was fantastic. Everyone, however, who had *gone* to the school watched with tears in their eyes. The kids were cheering and the old folks were crying.

Isn't *that* the way of the world.

Of course, the older generation wasn't so broken up about the loss to ignore the practical advantages of the school's demolition. Everyone went through the building before it came down and carted away what they could. The windows, the wood stove, the heavy wood door, and all the hinges and hardware.

Dave's dad, Charlie, grabbed a big pile of the hardwood floor. It was good one-inch maple, and he had the idea to redo the living room with it. He ripped up the lino and nailed the boards down. Then he got a sander from the Co-op and set to smoothing it.

The moment he started the sander, great clouds of foul-smelling dust filled the air. Before long, the whole house smelled like a horse stable. All those kids, all those years, tramping out of the barn and into the schoolhouse. The planks had been marinated in manure.

Charlie had to rip up all the boards and get *new* lino for the living room.

"Like father," said Morley. "Like son."

Once the schoolhouse had come down and the wood and rubble was carted away, they set to building the new hall.

Sam said, "Did you help?"

"Of course," said Dave. "*Everyone* pitched in."

The kids would come home from school, the adults would come home from work, and they would gather at the hall—start in the late afternoon and work until ten at night. Five nights a week, then all day Saturday. People would bring supper. And they'd sit around the picnic table out back and eat together.

Mostly the kids did things like clean up—sweeping up nails and dead bits of wood and burning them out back.

"I hammered in the subfloor," said Dave.

His little sister, Annie, hammered in the window frame at the back of the kitchen, the one to the right of the sink. If you examined it, you could see the dents around each nail, as if they'd blindfolded her before they gave her the hammer.

"How old was she?" said Sam.

"Probably three," said Dave.

She was seven.

Dave reached for the phone.

"We should call her," he said.

It was Annie who reminded him about the basement.

"Your grandfather had a thing about concrete," said Dave.

Every time he poured concrete, Charlie got Dave and Annie to put their prints in it.

So the night they poured the slab for the community hall, Charlie waited until everyone had left and then snuck them back in.

"I will never forget it," said Dave.

They had to use flashlights. They crawled along a plank so that they were out in the middle. There's a picture somewhere: two sets of little hands and feet in the concrete floor of the Big Narrows Community Hall.

"I just can't believe it's burning," said Dave.

It's not often you get to hear your parents talking like this, and certainly not in the quiet, confessional middle of the night. Sam was lying at the foot of their bed, praying they wouldn't send him back to his. He was sleepy enough to go, but he didn't want the moment to end.

He needn't have worried. His father was staring at the videos of the burning hall and reeling off one story after another.

Sometime early that summer, the men had arranged to have a skid of lumber delivered. That evening, when they got to the site, the lumber, which they'd been told had arrived in the morning, was nowhere to be seen. Whoever took it—and they had a pretty good idea who that was—had dragged the skid away, so it was easy enough to follow the trail down the dirt concession roads.

Charlie and Fred were deputized to go after it.

"I went with them," said Dave.

Just as everyone expected, the skid marks led from the half-built hall directly to Digger Flowers's farm.

Now, the Flowers family had always been different. You hardly ever saw them in town, or even when you drove by their place. Maybe a shadowy figure going from the house to the barn, but no more than that.

The Flowers had been like that for generations. The grandfather, long dead, used to steal chickens and then try to sell them back to the farm where he'd stolen them.

Charlie, Fred, and Dave were standing by the road staring at the tracks that clearly turned down the Flowers's driveway.

"What did you do?" said Sam. "Did you call the police?"

"Nope," said Dave. "We drove in."

They found the skid, just as they expected, behind the barn. And not a Flowers in sight.

Dave said, "They were there. You could feel them. But we pretended no one was home. And they accommodated that."

"What happened?" said Sam.

"We hooked up the skid of lumber to Fred's truck and we de-stole it," said Dave.

Morley said, "Didn't they steal an outhouse or something?"

Dave glanced at the clock on the bedside table.

It was three in the morning.

Sam caught that glance and said, "Tell about the outhouse."

"The outhouse," said Dave, immediately forgetting the time. "That wasn't Digger Flowers. That was a fellow from the city."

When he said "the city" he meant Sydney, or maybe Glace Bay.

What happened was someone had donated an old outhouse, and they'd set it up at the back of the hall to use while they worked. Then one day, just like the skid of new lumber, the outhouse had disappeared.

They didn't find it for months, though they knew they would eventually. And when they did, it was this city fellow who had a camp along the creek at the base of Macaulay's Mountain.

"He was a hunter," said Dave. "He would drive up on Friday nights and sleep in a trailer."

By the time they located the outhouse, they had a new one and didn't need the old one back. Everyone figured that if this guy needed an outhouse so badly that he was prepared to steal one, they'd let him keep it.

Of course, a group did go out and serve the guy a dose of small-town justice.

"What did they do?" said Sam.

"Well," said Dave, "they picked that outhouse up, and they moved it three feet back from where the guy had it placed."

"I don't get it," said Sam.

"Think about it," said Dave.

"Tell me more," said Sam.

His father seemed to have forgotten about the time.

"Well," said Dave, "there was the Moonlight Ball."

The hall was about half built. They had the subfloor down and the studs were up, but the walls weren't *covered* or anything and the roof wasn't in place. They'd done a lot, but there was a lot still to be done and people were starting to run out of steam.

"They needed to build morale," said Dave. "They needed to do something."

So they held the Moonlight Ball.

The whole town came. Everyone brought something for the dinner—salads and pies, and they had the barbecue going. When dinner was done, they set up a record player on the pile of trusses in the corner. And everyone danced on the rough subfloor.

While the adults danced, the teens hung out in the parking lot and the kids played tag on the hay bales in the field next door.

"Which pretty much established the ground rules for every dance we ever had after that," said Dave.

That was the night they invented the world-famous Big Narrows Lobster Race.

It was late, and everyone was feeling festive, and there were these barrels around and about. Someone got the idea to tie rope handles on a couple of barrels, two handles a side. The way it worked, you had four guys carrying each barrel. They were called the claws. And then you had someone sitting on it, who was called the fisherman. They had to run fifty yards down and back. They ran heats. The Lobster Race became a local tradition: Big Narrows has run them every July 1st ever since. There's a lobster trap in the hall that's got all the winners' names on little plaques.

Or there used to be.

"I hope they got it out," said Dave. "Your grandfather won it three years in a row. I was the fisherman for the first year, but then they started using Annie because she was lighter."

"And she didn't fall off," said Morley.

There were so many stories from that summer. In one way or another, everyone chipped in.

Even Earl and Merle Declute. They were sworn bachelors who lived on what was left of the old Declute farmhouse on the Salt Cove Road. Earl and Merle had sold most of the shoreline in one-acre lots to people from the city. Mostly Earl and Merle sat on their porch, drinking beer and arguing about hockey.

Earl and Merle were twins. And best known because of their beards. One of them would grow out his beard and the other would shave. They started this the year they turned twenty-five. The idea was that it would help people keep track of who was who. The trouble was that they kept switching it up.

"It was easy enough for me," said Dave. "I just called them both Mr. Declute."

Anyway, one of them used to show up at the site every Friday night with something the other had cooked, a pie or something. And whatever it was, it was always burned beyond use, and often beyond recognition. But it was offered in earnestness, and was received the same way.

Earl and Merle always drove, but they never drove sober. In deference to the Mounties, however, they drove on the farm lanes and through the fields rather than on the concession roads.

One lunchtime that summer, Merle was crossing the concession by the hall, and the laneway jumped or something, and he ended up in the ditch.

There happened to be a young Mountie there, a new recruit from Saskatchewan.

Well, you could smell the alcohol from a hundred yards. The Mountie wandered over and asked Merle how much he'd had to drink.

It was only eleven in the morning, and Merle seemed genuinely confused by the question.

It happened that Charlie walked out of the hall at this moment.

Merle spotted him.

"Charlie," he called from the side of his car, "how much do you think I've had by this time of day?"

He wasn't trying to be smart. He was looking for clarification. He wanted to give the young Mountie an honest answer.

They finished the town hall in the early fall, although it's hard to pinpoint when, exactly—it had been the social centre of town all summer long, ever since that morning in April when everyone had gathered to watch the old schoolhouse come down, and through the afternoon in June when they found the skid of wood hidden behind Digger Flowers's farm, and the night in July when they held the Moonlight Ball and danced under the stars on the subfloor before the roof was on. Through all that and everything else. And it just sort of continued.

After they'd gotten the bell out of the old schoolhouse, they sent it to Boston for refurbishing. When it came back, they hauled the lift out of the Harrisons' hayloft again and spent the whole of one weekend installing it into a bell tower they'd added to the hall. The tower looked just like the one on top of the old schoolhouse. In the years to come they would ring the bell for any occasion that remotely called for a bell—not only weddings and wakes, but just about any event you could imagine.

"If someone wanted to get a ball game going on a Sunday afternoon," said Dave, "they would ring it. You didn't need social media or anything like that. If you heard the bell ringing you knew what it meant, and you'd get on your bike and head down."

They had an opening ceremony, of course. Moose MacIsaac was the mayor at the time, and instead of cutting a ribbon, someone suggested that Moose mark the moment by sliding down the metal slide that was still in the yard from when the hall was a school. Moose, who was a robust man, was always happy to oblige a constituent's request, and he struggled up the ladder but got wedged halfway down the slide. It took all the men there a good hour and a half to pull him out.

When Moose passed, they had his wake at the hall. Everyone had their wake there. And there was a lot of talk of getting him out of the casket and running him down the slide one last time, but out of respect for the widow MacIsaac they didn't do that. Although there are folks who will tell you they were there, or knew someone who was there, late that night, and that Moose did have a final moment of glory.

"Is that true?" said Sam sleepily.

"I don't know," said Dave. "I was too young for that sort of stuff. I've heard people swear it's true, but I've never found anyone who'll swear to have been there when it happened."

The phone hadn't rung for an hour. They had shut down the computer. There was more and more silence between Dave's stories. Morley was drifting in and out of sleep.

Not long after that, Sam got up and went back to his bed.

"Goodnight," he said.

Dave was left there lying on his back, with his hands behind his head, staring up at the ceiling.

A few minutes after Sam left, he said, "It makes me sad that he hasn't had a time like that."

He thought Morley was already asleep and was surprised when she answered.

Morley said, "He has his own times."

Dave said, "Yup. You're right."

And then he said, "Maybe what I was trying to say is that those were my times. And I am thankful for them."

We all have our own times.

In Dave's time monumental things have happened. We have flown to the moon and back. And by moonlight, we have seen the downtrodden both rise up and bow down.

But the times are *always* monumental. And the things we remember are never the monumental things. When the phone rings in the middle of the night, it's always about the things we hold in the small of our hearts.

They will rebuild the hall in Big Narrows this summer. Dave will go down for the ceremony the weekend it opens. The hall will look much the same, for they will do their best to recreate it. But Dave will no longer know the secret place where the floorboards creak, or the spot where you mustn't dance if you don't want to get the DJ's records skipping.

Before the night is over, Dave will go outside and get down on his knees by the front door, and because he knows exactly where to look, he will find a few small letters carved into the side of the old concrete steps that are all that will be left of *his* hall. SK *heart* ML 4EVER. It will make him happy to see them. Stephen and Megan still sitting in a tree. *Maybe not forever,* he will think, as he stands and brushes the dirt off his knees, *but maybe long enough.*

He will do one last thing before he leaves the hall. He will stand on the top of those stairs by the door for a brief moment. And he will slip his keys out of his pocket and try his key to the old hall in the lock of the new door. It won't fit.

It will make him strangely happy. He had his times. But life moves on. He will leave the key on his ring, however.

And every now and then when he notices it, it will unlock these memories. For it is no longer a key to a hall he seldom visits. Forged by fire, it has become a key to a small corner of his heart.